Leo Kessler is a familiar name to readers of war fiction. In addition to his numerous super-selling war series he is the author of several non-fiction works and of the screenplay *Breakthrough*. He lives in Germany between energetic bouts of travelling.

Also by Leo Kessler

In the *SS Assault Regiment Wotan* Series:
SS PANZER BATTALION
DEATH'S HEAD
CLAWS OF STEEL
GUNS AT CASSINO
THE DEVIL'S SHIELD
HAMMER OF THE GODS
FORCED MARCH
BLOOD AND ICE
THE SAND PANTHERS
COUNTER-ATTACK
PANZER HUNT
SLAUGHTER GROUND
HELLFIRE
FLASHPOINT
CAULDRON OF BLOOD
SCHIRMER'S HEADHUNTERS

In the *Stormtroop* Series:
STORMTROOP
BLOOD MOUNTAIN
VALLEY OF THE ASSASSINS
RED ASSAULT
HIMMLER'S GOLD

In the *Rommel* Series:
GHOST DIVISION
MASSACRE

In the *Otto Stahl* Series:
OTTO STAHL 1: OTTO'S PHONEY WAR
OTTO STAHL 2: OTTO'S BLITZKRIEG!
OTTO STAHL 3: OTTO AND THE REDS

Also:
THE SEA WOLVES 1: SINK THE SCHARNHORST!
BREAKTHROUGH

Leo Kessler

The Sea Wolves 2
Death to the Deutschland

Futura
Macdonald & Co
London & Sydney

A Futura Book

First published in Great Britain in 1982
by Futura Publications, a Division of
Macdonald & Co (Publishers) Ltd

ISBN 0 7088 2204 5

Filmset, printed and bound in Great Britain by
Hazell Watson & Viney Ltd, Aylesbury, Bucks

Macdonald & Co
London & Sydney
Maxwell House
74 Worship Street
London EC2A 2EN

DEATH TO THE DEUTSCHLAND

'War is not an adventure. It is a disease. It is like typhus.

Antoine de Saint Exupery, 1943.

Author's Note

'Savage by name . . . savage by nature!'

Back in the summer of 1943, when his young life was terminated so cruelly, those words could well have served as a suitable epitaph to the short, brutish career of Lt Commander Rodney Savage RN. Nearly forty years later perhaps we can be more charitable and see Savage as a product of his time. Perhaps we can even excuse him a little.

In those days there were many young men like Savage. They had no past and no future. They had fallen in love with the high drama and savage beauty of the war. With monomaniacal energy, they devoted their whole being to that one year, one month, perhaps even just one week of their lives in which the war embraced them in its fiery, all-consuming passion.

For some people, these young men, German and British, were heroes. For many, they were frightening creatures, whose motives could not be understood, for they lived an intense, fierce, mad life beyond the comfortable norms of the average individual. For a few, they were cold-hearted, single-minded, sadistic brutes. Today, perhaps, we can be a little more tolerant and understanding, and see that they were simply victims: victims of their times, their culture, their upbringing, their patriotism, that sad word that once meant so much to the young, savage men of World War Two.

This, then, is the story of a year in the life of one young Englishman who died violently before he had even begun to live. It is not a pleasant story. But then in those years there were no pleasant stories, were there?

L.K.
Hamburg Reinbek
Christmas, 1981

ONE: ESCAPE TO BATTLE

ONE

'*Ready, Number One?*' hissed the dispatcher.

Sub-Lieutenant Edwardes, in his shabby homemade blanket coat and German cap, face pale and glazed with sweat as if greased with Vaseline, nodded his head. He grabbed his sack and moved closer to the door. The rest of his waiting stick tensed.

The dispatcher nodded to the doorman. '*Now!*'

The doorman thrust the skeleton key, made from a sardine-can opener, into the lock. He grunted. In the crowded, yellow-lit room, no one dared breathe. Pegleg Pettersen, the SBO,[1] gripped his pipe hard till his knuckles whitened. The tension was electric.

Click! The muscles in the doorman's big right shoulder relaxed. He turned and nodded to the dispatcher. 'Spot on,' he whispered, his voice suddenly husky, as if his throat were parched. The dispatcher looked at Edwardes. There was no mistaking the fear written all over his sweating, pale young face. But there was no turning back now. Months of hard work and planning had gone into this op. The point of no return had been reached.

'*Ready?*' he barked.

Edwardes nodded. He couldn't speak.

The dispatcher's hand poised at the light switch. '*Now!*' he hissed and clicked off the lights. '*OPEN!*'

The doorman swung open the door. It opened noiselessly; they had been greasing the hinges with oil from sardine-cans for the last three days. Icy-cold air flooded into the warm fug of the hut. Outside the black-out was

[1] Senior British Officer.

perfect. The only light was the faint white glow given off by the snow which lay thick across the courtyard.

The SBO's heavy hand came down hard on Edwardes' shoulder. 'Good luck, Bob,' he whispered. 'Don't forget to send a postcard to my missus when you get back.'

'*Go!*' the dispatcher commanded harshly.

Edwardes stumbled forward through the door. The rest of the waiting stick caught a glimpse of his dark, crouched shape silhouetted starkly against the snow and then the door was closed noiselessly once more and the only sound the tense men could hear was that soft crunch of his flying feet over the hard surface of the frozen snow-mass. No sudden challenge, curse, dry, hard crack of a rifle. Nothing.

'Lights!' the dispatcher commanded, and turned the switch.

Blinking in the sudden light, the rest of the stick automatically cocked their heads to one side in order to hear better. But no sound came. Just the faint hiss of the wind in the branches of the skeletal oaks which surrounded the remote camp. Edwardes was making it.

Hastily Pegleg Pettersen began the countdown, eyes glued on the glowing second dial of his wrist-watch, while Number Two of the first stick stared at the old seadog as if almost hypnotized.

'. . . *Fifty-seven . . . Fifty-eight . . . Fifty-nine* . . .' He counted off the seconds, his lips dry and parched, voice a little cracked, and ended, '*Zero!*'

Absolute silence. Every man in that long, drab hut tensed. The air suddenly felt heavy with the stench of cheap black German tobacco, sweat, urine from the piss-buckets, and human misery. But from outside all was silent save for the hiss of the wind. Edwardes had made it to the thunderboxes.

Pegleg Pettersen moved, his artificial leg creaking alarmingly. The man in front of Savage started violently. Savage frowned, his long, dark, sardonic face a mixture of distaste and worry. The men of this stick were much too jumpy – even windy. Could he really trust people like that?

The dispatcher took over again, and once more the routine was repeated. Number Two, Petit, the Belgian captured at Ostend, slipped out. Aussie, who had gone into the bag at Crete, followed. Brylcreem, the Fleet Air Arm pilot shot down over Wilhelmshaven, was next. One by one the first stick disappeared into the night, while further down the long room, Number Two stick started to grab their bundles of concentrated food and the rest of their escape gear and began to form up.

Pegleg looked at Savage, the last man in the first stick. As always Lieutenant Rodney Savage RN's face showed no emotion save bold impatience. His thin lips were set in a hard line and his stern jaw with its pugnacious cleft chin was firm and unyielding. His dark eyes revealed nothing but one hundred percent determination.

The Captain frowned and wondered once more if Savage had been the right choice to command the first stick. He was a loner, a glory-hunter, impatient of other men's weaknesses; on the other hand, he had been in the bag since Dunkirk and knew all the tricks of the escaping game. Already he had been outside the wire three times and spent months in solitary in the cooler for his pains. He dismissed his doubts.

'Savage,' he whispered hoarsely, 'get ready.'

Rodney Savage threw a last look at the squalor of the hut which had been his home these last two years. His face wrinkled in disgust at the unshaven, scruffy officers, many with beards, lying on the two-tier bunks, or crouching over the smoking, spluttering candles, frying spam in herring-tin frying pans held over the flickering flame. Thank God, he was saying goodbye to them at last, with their dirty, raw, sullen faces. They had made their separate peace with the German enemy. Food, correspondence courses, smutty stories and the occasional furtive gropings in the smelly shadows of the thunder-boxes made up the sum total of their miserable existence now. His resolve steeled. The Hun would never catch him this time; he'd rather die.

The dispatcher threw him a hard glance. '*Ready, Number Six!*' he commanded. He nodded to the doorman. '*Now!*'

The doorman gripped the door handle.

The dispatcher flicked the lights off.

'Look after 'em, Savage,' Pegleg urged. '*Please . . .*'

'*OPEN!*'

Obediently the doorman thrust open the door to the barracks. Again the icy winter air flooded in. To the right a searchlight from the nearest German flak position parted the clouds with a finger of silver white. The dispatcher hesitated only a fraction of a second, then ordered '*Go!*'

Savage needed no urging. He sprang forward, knapsack grasped in his left hand, homemade knife in his right. The door closed behind him. For a moment he crouched there, blinking a little in the darkness, until he could make out the high wire, dominated by the stark silhouettes of the stork-legged towers. Each was manned by German machine-gunners, but being the naive sentimentalists they were, they would never expect anyone to try and escape on Christmas Eve, the most sacred of their holy days. Savage grinned in the darkness, but there was no warmth in his smile; only contemptuous amusement at human frailty. Then he was off, darting swiftly over the frozen snow, his heart pounding, a nerve at the side of his lean face ticking with excitement.

The stench of the eighty-seat latrine hit him in the face with an almost physical blow. He gasped. In two years of imprisonment he had never been able to get used to the stink of human shit, and he suspected that even most hardened 'kriegie'[1] never did. But now there was no time to concern himself with the nauseating odour of human waste. Time was of the essence.

[1] Name that WWII prisoners of war gave themselves, taken from the German word for POW: *Kriegsgefangene*.

He hastened down the narrow corridor between the tightly packed stalls. Here, every morning between eight and ten o'clock, shifts of eighty men went in to squat and strain urgently – for they were only allowed three minutes to carry out their natural functions before the guards herded in the next batch. Finally he reached number sixty-nine – 'My lucky number!' Pegleg Pettersen had chortled with a wink when he had picked that particular thunderbox. Quickly he dropped his bundle, raised the seat and lifted the stinking enamel bucket which rested inside the wooden box. Below, the concrete floor was sprinkled with lime. Hastily Savage bent down and swept it away with the side of his hand. There were the finger-holes. He stuck his outstretched fingers into them like a bowler might into a bowling ball, and grunted. The slab of concrete came away easily – as so it should; the 'concrete' was no more than a thin piece of wood which had been covered with a film of concrete three months before, when they had first embarked on the great escape.

Savage seized his bundle and dropped it into the dark hole below. Next instant he followed, replacing the 'concrete' slab above him. In the morning the first bunch of kriegies in the thunderbox queue would replace the bucket.

He crouched at the bottom of the pit while his eyes became accustomed to the gloom, his nostrils again full of that old tunnel smell – damp clay and earth, rats and mice, mildewed clothes and foul air. The odour was a hazard in itself. To the end of his days, he told himself as he entered the tunnel for the last time, it would never leave him; he would never forget how he had braved the claustrophobic nightmare of those underground workings.

Swiftly, on hands and knees, dragging his bundle behind him by means of a rope attached to his belt, he crawled forward through the pitch-black hole. For the first fifty yards it ran slightly downwards until it reached the edge of the thunderboxes above. Soon he should hit the angle to the right and the light. He hurried forward, scraping his shoulders and neck on the rough projections overhead. Now he saw the first flickering glow of the candle. He wasn't far off. He swung round the bend – and stopped dead.

A great grey rat faced him in the sputtering yellow light of the candle, its whiskers twitching, its wickedly sharp teeth displayed hideously, staring at him in beady-eyed menace. Instinctively he ducked his head into the damp soil. The loathsome creatures were utterly unafraid of human beings; they swarmed everywhere in the barracks. It was no use attempting to frighten it off.

He waited, fighting the wave of revulsion that swept through his tense body. The rat slithered over his head. He could feel its damp claws at the back of his neck. He fought back the scream of terror just in time. Then it crawled the length of his body and was gone, leaving him lying there, gasping as if he had just run a great race, sweating and nauseated at the repulsive contact.

But there was no time to lose. With a hand that trembled violently, he seized the candle that the others had placed there for him and pushed on, cursing hard as he crawled to frighten off any other of the loathsome rodents which might be lurking there. Then finally he was through, and the others of his stick were pulling him into the escape chamber, where they crouched tightly together, knees right up under their chins, bundles stacked in the middle of the dirt floor, their faces glazed with sweat.

'Christ, cobber, can't you curse for a Pommy!' Aussie said cheerfully, though his eyes were as wild with excitement and fear as the rest. 'You do better than a lot o' them bushwhackers out there in the outback—'

'Quiet!' Savage interrupted harshly. 'Don't you realize the Huns are only a matter of feet away?'

Aussie lowered his gaze before the Englishman's burning dark eyes. 'Sorry, cobber,' he muttered.

Savage turned to the rest. 'All right, a quick re-cap,' he snapped, already fumbling for his knife. 'If our guess is correct, we'll come out on the starboard side of the compound, facing the Moselle. Right?'

The others nodded their heads in agreement. Including Petit, whose English was limited.

'So with the Moselle to our *left* –' he emphasized the word as if he were speaking to a group of backward schoolboys – 'get it? *Left* – we should be heading in the right direction for Trier. Now at this time of year the vineyards that fringe the Moselle will be empty, especially seeing it's Christmas Eve. So we follow the wine-growers' path just below the ridge line. We don't want to give ourselves away by using the road that runs along the river or by walking along the ridge itself – we'd make too good a silhouette. Is that clear?'

Again they nodded. Edwardes flushed, a little angry at being lectured like this.

Savage ignored him. 'You all know the exit drill. I go out first and the rest of the stick follows at thirty-second intervals, crawling to left and right towards the woods. We assemble there and head for the river, single file, and woe betide anyone who puts his feet down carelessly. I'll have the guts off him for gaiters. Any questions?'

Brylcreem coughed, an elegant Fleet Air Arm pilot who managed to look smart even in dyed naval battledress and a gore-blimey cap made of a stolen cushion cover. 'When do we stop for our Christmas dinner, Savage?'

The others tittered, but Savage was in no mood for puerile jokes at this stage of the escape; he had been waiting two long years for this night. He turned and reaching up, started to hack away at the soil above his head with his homemade knife, face twisted to one side to avoid the wet earth already dripping down.

Five minutes went by. Another five. Suddenly Savage felt cool air on the hand which wielded the knife.

'Stand by,' he hissed. 'Here we go.'

There was a sudden slither of soil. Icy air came streaming in. A ragged patch of light appeared above their heads.

'We're through!' Edwardes gasped.

'Happy Christmas!' Aussie breathed.

'Keep it down to a dull roar,' Savage commanded through gritted teeth, 'or we'll be back inside with black bread and corned beef fritters for Christmas dinner. Come on, give me a leg up!'

Clasping the knife between his teeth, he stared upwards as Aussie and Edwardes grasped his legs and heaved him out. For a moment he paused there. There was no sound save the faint hiss of the wind and from far, far away, the high hysterical barking of a farm dog. From the German guards' barracks came a smell of rich cooking; the Huns would already have settled down to their midnight feast of goose and red cabbage. Savage nodded to himself, satisfied; everything was going well. He straightened up – and froze abruptly.

To his left there was the soft chink of metal, followed an instant later by an unmistakable *pad-pad* sound on the frozen snow. Someone – or something – was coming straight towards him!

Savage contained his hectic breathing. He crouched, knife clasped firmly in a hand that was suddenly wet with sweat.

The strange *pad-pad*, accompanied by the rustle of wire, came slowly closer. Savage felt the hot sweat trickle unpleasantly down the small of his back. From below came a frightened query. But the crouched man ignored it. A dark, squat shape had detached itself from the night and stood there.

Savage recognized it immediately. It was one of the half-wild German shepherd dogs the goons often used on night patrols. The escape committee had chosen Christmas Eve in the belief that even the dog-handlers would be staying indoors to celebrate on such a festive occasion. But the Huns had been smarter than they had anticipated. They had attached the dog's chain to the wire which ran around the last fence; the cold air did the rest, by keeping the freezing animal on the move all the while. Now one of the beasts was only a matter of feet away.

Savage swallowed hard. The dog came closer. It stopped again. Savage's heart missed a beat. Perhaps it hadn't spotted him after all? The hound raised his ugly snout and sniffed the icy air. Savage's hopes vanished as soon as they had come. The animal had seen him all right.

It came a few paces closer, still attached to the thin chicken wire by its chain. He could see its snout quite clearly now. It was filled with vicious, yellow teeth. Saliva dripped from between them sickeningly.

Savage's mind raced. The beast had only to open its mouth and bark and the whole damned camp would be alerted, Christmas Eve or no Christmas Eve. Slowly, very, very slowly, he began to bring up his knife.

The animal bared its evil, dripping teeth. Its upper lip curled back. Both ears sloped back against its long, vulpine skull. A low growl started up from deep down inside it. Savage knew the signs. He had only a matter of moments. Suddenly his hand shot out. In the same instant he whipped the chain around the dog's throat to stifle the bark and his knife flashed silver and slid deep into the startled beast's stomach.

The dog reared up as best it could on its haunches. One of its claws came up and raked Savage's cheek painfully. He gave a suppressed yelp of agony and felt hot blood jetting from the wound. Blood splattered the snow all round. But Savage did not relinquish his hold, while with his right hand he ripped ever deeper into the writhing animals's guts, feeling his knife-hand flooded with blood and gore. Desperately the dog tried to free itself from that killing grip. To no avail. Savage held on for all he was worth.

Abruptly it was all over. The dying dog gave a last sad little whimper, the kind of sound made by a harmless puppy rather than by an eighty-pound half-wild brute. Finally it slumped forward. Cautiously Savage relaxed his pressure on the chain. But there was no further need for caution. The animal was dead.

Five minutes later the rest of the stick were all out of the hole, staring numbly at the dead beast sprawled in a violent posture in the snow, while Savage gave them their last instructions.

'All right; into the woods over there. Single file, but at the double. I'll stay behind and bury this brute. Can't leave it here. Might give the second stick away. All right, on your way. I'll catch up with you on this side of Wehlen. And remember, keep due south and parallel to the Moselle. *Due south!*'

Savage watched them go, making no attempt to bury the dog sprawled at his feet. The brute had come in handy; it had given him exactly the opportunity he had been hoping for all along. As the last man, the little Belgie, Petit, disappeared into the snow-heavy pines, Savage turned and set off hurriedly. Due north.

Lieutenant Rodney Savage RN was on his way back to the war . . .

TWO

For Savage, the injustice and misery of it all had started back in May 1940, when he had received that fateful signal from his flotilla commander, Captain MacIntyre, just as his ship, His Majesty's Destroyer *Hercules*, had been about to return from yet another fruitless sweep in the Channel.

As always the bluff Ulsterman had neglected all standard signal procedure. The flotilla commander's Aldis-lamp man had sent the whole message in clear.

'Then read, Bunts,' Savage had snapped as the deck of *Hercules* heaved beneath his feet, wallowing in the green troughs.

Savage's signaller, an old-time three-striper to whom signal regulations were Holy Writ, had sighed and commenced taking down the meaning of the blinking white light a quarter of a mile away, reading it aloud to his young skipper as he did so.

'*Balloon gone up in France at last . . . BEF*[1] *retiring to Channel ports . . . Jocks of the Fifty-First Highlander in position in and around St Valéry . . . Include General Fortune, GOC*[2] *. . . have a look-see, Rodney . . . But keep half a mile at least off shore . . . On no account enter the harbour . . . and if the Luftwaffe appears, run like hell . . . Winnie can't afford to lose another destroyer this week. Is that clear? Mike . . .*'

The white light stopped blinking. Savage's mind raced at the prospect of action at last.

'Bunts, signal: "Message received and understood" –

[1] British Expeditionary Force.
[2] General Officer Commanding.

and, oh yes,' he added, with uncharacteristic exuberance for him, his black eyes flashing as he stared at the dull smudge of the French coast, where now the first faint, silent flashes indicated that battle had already commenced, 'signal "*Tally Ho!*" '

'Ay, ay, sir,' Bunts had called. 'But what about—'

But Lieutenant Savage was already running for the bridge, barking out urgent orders to left and right, galvanizing the hands into hectic action as he did so.

Five minutes later they were under way, a white bone of foam at their bow as the *Hercules* cleaved the waves at thirty knots, the thunder of the guns growing ever louder and pyres of smoke now rising along the whole length of the French coast as they neared the scene of the battle.

After ten years in the Royal Navy with his only taste of action a minor skirmish with junk pirates off the China coast, Rodney Savage was about to experience that violent tumult and desperate glory he had sought so fervently ever since he had been a sixteen-year-old midshipman. He was going into battle at last!

Dawn. Above St Valéry the sky was tinged with a sullen grey colour. Fog was beginning to drift away in slow, reluctant wisps. Beyond, ominous pillars of black smoke rose stiffly to the heavens.

Everywhere the sailors, tired as they were, crowded the rails to view the port. On the bridge Savage and his Jimmy-the-One[1] focussed their glasses. The tall white buildings that lined the sides of the harbour sprang into the centre of the calibrated glass. Men in khaki seemed to be milling about aimlessly everywhere. Most were without their helmets, many without weapons, and even at this distance the two naval officers could see that the soldiers of the 51st Highland Division were at the end of their tether. A group of them could be seen squatting by

[1] First Officer.

the roadside, heads sunk in their hands in the classic position of absolute, utter defeat.

Jenkins, a tall blond young man, sucked his teeth. 'Don't look too hot to me, skipper. Those brown jobs over there have had it, I reckon. Look over there at ten o'clock. They're beginning to smash up the engines of those lorries with sledge-hammers.'

Savage didn't reply. A small boat had left the harbour and was heading straight towards them, a figure in khaki balancing precariously on the bows, waving his hands frantically.

'It looks, as if we're going to get a visitor, Number One.'

Jenkins nodded and gave a mirthless laugh. 'And the chap's wearing a kilt of all things! Just like the ruddy Army. Thank God for the Navy.'

'Exactly,' Savage snapped and rang the bridge telegraph. 'Slow ahead!' he commanded and then, catching Jenkins' worried look, said, 'Don't worry, Number One. The ack-ack people are standing by their guns. There are air lookouts on port and starboard.'

'But what if the Jerry dive-bombers . . .' Jenkins left the rest of his protest unsaid. By now he knew Savage. Although he was very young for a Destroyer captain, he was ruthless, set in his ways like a much older skipper, brooking no objections to his orders. 'I'll go and see what the brown job in the skirt wants, sir,' he said and clattered down the steel steps to the deck.

Five minutes later he ushered on to the bridge a soaked Major bearing the 'HD' sign of the 51st on his shoulder, and with the red hackle at the side of his bonnet drooping miserably.

'Major Ferguson, sir,' he announced, 'of the divisional staff.'

Hastily Savage and the Major with the trim black moustache of a regular officer shook hands, while over in the port the first shrill tones of the air-raid sirens began to sound.

'I won't waste time, Captain,' the Major said with unusual haste for a professional officer. 'Our situation in St Valéry is decidedly sticky. Our outposts are being attacked by a whole Hun armoured division. Soon they'll hit our perimeter, and there isn't a hope in hell of our holding on for more than a few hours against Jerry tanks . . .' He shrugged a little helplessly, his voice trailing away, as if he preferred to leave the rest of his sentence unspoken.

Savage did not attempt to help. 'So?' he rasped brutally. In the background the first guns could be heard beginning to thunder on the heights beyond St Valéry. Brown puffballs of smoke started to dot the grey sky.

The Major looked down at his soaked tartan kilt. 'So I'm afraid the Div will have to surrender. There's no way of evacuating them, and the rest of the Army has got too much on its plate to worry about the Fifty-First.'

'What's this got to do with us?' Savage asked, face hard, eyes searching the horizon for the first sign of German planes.

'Well, Captain,' the Major answered unhappily, 'at div HQ we've decided we can't let General Fortune – that's our divisional commander – and his senior officers fall into German hands. My God, their propaganda wallahs would have a field day with a real English – excuse Scots – general in their hands! So while most of the staff will stay behind with the division till the – er – bitter end, we want the General and the senior staff officers to be evacuated now, while there's still time, and—'

'—You want *me* to do the evacuating?' Savage broke in.

Next to him Jenkins gasped. 'But we can't do that, Major,' he objected. 'We have no orders to carry out an operation of that kind. Besides, we have a specific order from our flotilla commander not to risk the *Hercules* under any circumstances. The Navy's lost too many destroyers as it . . .' His voice trailed away under Savage's blazing black-eyed glare.

'Have you finished, Number One?' he asked, and there was iron in his voice.

'Sorry, sir. Yes, sir,' Jenkins said lamely. 'But I just—'

'Don't. I do the thinking on this ship, Number One.' Savage turned back to the pale-faced Major. 'Where is your General located now, Major?'

'In that big three-storey *pension* at two o'clock next to the fish jetty.'

Savage swung his glasses onto the building hastily, noting that it was directly above the berths used by the fishing trawlers in pre-war days. He bit his lip and did some quick thinking. The berth might have sufficient draught to take the *Hercules*. He thought of MacIntyre's warning, but dismissed it almost immediately. Suddenly the newspaper headlines flashed before his mind's eye. '*Young seadog rescues General Fortune of the Highlanders! . . . Hercules Wins a Fortune! . . . Savage to the Rescue . . .*' He swallowed hard. It would mean a gong, an audience at Buckingham Palace, promotion to a bigger and better ship. Winnie dearly loved a winner.[1]

But before he committed himself altogether, there were questions to settle. 'Couldn't you get your General out in a small boat, that one you came in?'

The Major shook his head. 'No juice, I'm afraid, Captain. We're down to our last litre of diesel as it is. Hardly enough to get us back.'

As he spoke, the air was suddenly rent by a tremendous roar. Overhead, the gull-winged Stukas started to fall out of the grey sky above St Valéry, tearing down at 400mph, sirens shrieking, a myriad evil little black eggs dropping from their obscene blue bellies.

'There's only one way to get General Fortune and his chaps out, Captain, and that's for you to come in personally and pick him up!' he bellowed above the bedlam.

Savage made his decision. 'All right, Major, you're on!

[1] At this time 'Winnie', Winston Churchill, was the First Lord of the Admiralty.

Alert your General. We're coming in as soon as the dive-bombers leave. Off you go, at the double now. I want General Fortune on board as soon as we come in, alongside that fish jetty. It's in and out like greased lightning.'

The Major beamed with relief. Hastily he pressed Savage's hands, and then he was running back across the deck to his waiting craft, his kilt riding high to reveal a glimpse of white thigh, followed by the wolf whistles of the delighted matelots.

Cautiously, at half speed, HMS *Hercules* nosed its way through the débris of war, nudged back and forth by the troughs at the entrance to the port. Every man was at his station, tense and alert, eyes fixed on the smoke-filled sky above the town. On the bridge, watched by a gloomy, subdued Jenkins, Savage paced back and forth, ready to order the waiting gun crews into action at the first sight of a German plane. In five minutes' time they would be within the sea defences of the little port, and then it would be too late; they would be sitting ducks, a choice target for any ambitious Stuka pilot out to win a Knight's Cross by sinking a British destroyer. But for the time being the sky above St Valéry was empty of German planes. Perhaps they had gone back to their forward fields to refuel, or perhaps their own troops were too close now to permit further bombing. Yes – that would be it, Savage told himself, stopping his pacing and turning to face a gloomy, disapproving Jenkins.

'Smile. Give your face a treat, Number One,' he said with unaccustomed levity. 'We'll pull it off, I'm confident. We'll be in and out and on our way back to Dover within the hour. With a bit of luck, Number One, this op might mean you'll have your own command before this—'

'*Enemy craft to port, sir!*' An urgent voice broke into his confident prediction. '*E-boats, sir!*' It was the port look-out, his face suddenly ashen.

Instantly the two officers swung round and brought up their binoculars. Jenkins gasped, as the first rakish white shape swept into the circle of gleaming glass, its bow high out of the water, boiling white waves dashing to left and right. There was no mistaking that stark black and blood-red flag with its hated crooked cross streaming out stiffly behind. It was German all right. But there were more. Hastily he started to count. A mile away just under the towering white cliffs which had hidden their approach so far, the E-boats were starting to form up into battle-formation, two hurtling V's of five boats apiece.

'Ten of 'em sir. All armed with two 21-inch torpedo tubes and two 20mm Oerlikon.'

'I bloody well know!' Savage snapped angrily, and ran to the telegraph. All thought of rescuing General Fortune had vanished in an instant. 'Port, twenty-five!' he cried urgently. 'Full ahead together!'

The helmsman wrenched at his wheel, not waiting for orders. At his side, Jenkins cupped his hands. 'Sound action stations, CPO!'[1]

Almost at once the alarm bells started to shrill. Men in heavy sea-boots clattered across the metal decks. Down in the gun turrets, the gun-layers flung themselves behind their sights. Up above, the pom-pom gunners strapped in behind their rows of massed machine-guns, 'the Chicago pianos', frantically brought them down to deck level; they would no longer be needed for air defence. After a few seconds' confusion, everything was controlled. The *Hercules* swung round, its screws churning the water into frantic white lather, ready to meet the unexpected challenge.

Savage caught hold of the bridge with his free hand as the Destroyer completed the half-turn and surged forward suddenly. The chief engineer gave the craft the full benefit of her 30,000 horses. The whole ship vibrated like a wild thing as she surged forward to do battle.

[1] Chief Petty Officer.

'Stand by for surface action!' Savage bellowed into the tube. 'Local control.'

'Local control it is, sir!' his gunnery officer yelled back, as the men in the green gloom of the forward turret crouched expectantly behind their gleaming great guns.

Now the *Hercules* was heading on a collision course, striking each new wave like a brick wall at thirty knots, shuddering violently with each impact. The gunners were forced to hang on for dear life, each man's nerves jingling electrically waiting for the action to come, while on the bridge, Savage, suddenly very calm, watched the approach of the enemy through his binoculars.

Meanwhile the gunnery officer snapped out his orders. '*A-Turret . . . enemy craft, red . . . eight . . . oh . . . B-Turret . . . red, eight, oh, two . . .!*'

Madly the gun-layers whirled their brass wheels and dials, the sweat streaming down their tense, flushed young faces, eyes glued to their telescopes, as the roaring white shapes, razor-sharp prows high out of the water, hurtled towards them. At the other side of the breeches, other ratings, heads and chests clothed in white anti-flash helmets, poised cradling great gleaming yellow shells in their brawny arms.

The gunnery officer took one last look at the E-boats. Now the distance between the *Hercules* and the German craft was a mere seven hundred and fifty yards. Already the dark shapes of German sailors were frantically running around the heaving decks preparing their deadly tin fish. To the right, one of the E-boats had opened up with its 20mm cannon. Flak shells were streaming towards the *Hercules* in a lethal white rain.

Savage could wait no longer. He took a deep breath and yelled, '*Open fire!*'

The twin 4·5's of A-Turret erupted in frightening unison. The deck trembled. Scarlet flame stabbed from the gleaming muzzles. Thick, yellow smoke flooded the turret.

Up on the bridge, Savage flung up his binoculars.

'*One . . . two . . .*' He started to count off the seconds aloud. '*Three . . .*'

Two great whirling white spouts of water rushed skywards to the right of the nearest E-boat. For a moment it was obscured by the eruptions. Savage cursed angrily. They had missed. But as the E-boat slid through the cascading water-spout, he could see that her bow had fallen dramatically and that her whole side was buckled and steaming, with smoke pouring from her aft.

'We've hit her,' he yelled excitedly above the roar of B-Turret opening up. '*We've hit her!*'

'*Torpedoes starboard . . .*'

Savage acted immediately, not listening for the look-out's heading. There would be no time. The enemy was too close. 'Hard to starboard!' he yelled.

The helmsman swung the wheel round frantically. Savage ran to the edge of the bridge. A trail of bright water, erupting tiny bubbles to its rear, was running straight towards them. He held his breath. Would they do it? The *Hercules*'s every plate moaned and groaned in metallic protest at the strain. And then they were round, and the torpedo was running harmlessly by, to explode moments later in the shingle off-shore.

An E-boat heeled to one side dramatically, its superstructure nearly touching the heaving green swell. Men tumbled overboard. A mast came reeling down, dragging wires and aerials with it. It started to sink immediately.

'Zig-zag, helmsman!' Savage cried, carried away by the blood-lust and excitement of battle. '*For Chrissake, zig-zag!*'

'Ay, ay, sir!' the young sailor cried back. Dark blood was trickling down the side of his ashen face where he had been hit by shrapnel. He thrust the *Hercules* from side to side, as 20mm shells hissed flatly over the water directly at the Destroyer.

Everywhere men were falling. The air was full of the stench of exploding shells. A gunner flew over the side, still clutching a belt of ammunition, to be churned to a blood-red pulp by the *Hercules*'s whirling screws.

The 4·5's thundered once more. An E-boat stopped dead in the water, as if it had just run into an invisible wall. The whole razor-sharp prow disappeared. Thick white smoke poured from her stricken engine-room. An ammunition locker exploded in a ball of vicious red flame, sending white and coloured tracer shells zig-zagging crazily into the air.

Eyes gleaming with almost deranged excitement, Savage swung round. 'Three down, Number One, seven to—' He stopped short.

Jenkins lay sprawled over the compass housing. At his feet, still complete with cap set at a suitably jaunty angle, lay his head, neatly severed.

Green bile filled Savage's throat, hot and bitter. Next instant he vomited the full length of the bridge, groping for a stanchion to support himself. Just as he did so, the first pair of E-boats which had swung towards the sea as if attempting to escape, came racing in at forty knots an hour.

The gunners manning the 'Chicago pianos' swung their multiple machine-guns round desperately and took up the challenge as a solid wall of white 20mm tracer shells streamed towards the *Hercules*. The whole side of the ship erupted. In an instant, a smoking screen of choking fumes rose upwards, momentarily obscuring the E-boats, gleaming yellow cartridges rattling to the metal decks by the thousand.

'Bring her round! *Round! ROUND!*' Savage screamed, and jerked the wheel out of the helmsman's nerveless fingers. The man slid to the bloody deck – dead. The veins standing out at his temples, the sweat dripping thickly into his eyebrows like grey pearls, Savage wrenched at the wheel in a paroxysm of frenzied fear. He knew what was coming. Enemy torpedoes at broadside on.

Too late!

HMS *Hercules* reeled alarmingly. There was the reverberating echo of metal striking metal. An instant later a second hollow boom. As he struggled frantically with the wheel, which had suddenly gone thick and slow as if the fittings were packed in glue, Savage recognized the sound instinctively. *Hercules* had been struck below the waterline.

He tensed. For a long moment nothing happened. Then, from deep down inside the ship, there was a muffled explosion, so low in intensity that it seemed almost harmless. But an instant later it was followed by the terrifying ear-piercing shriek of high-pressure steam escaping.

Flame spurted a hundred feet into the grey sky, illuminating all around it with the startling, frightening clarity of a photographer's flash.

Savage reeled back against the back of the bridgehouse as HMS *Hercules* came to a slow stop, already sinking at the stern, his horrified gaze filled with a scene that would haunt him to the end of his young life: the claw-like, charred hands of the crazed sailors beating at the flames which consumed them; barefoot men hopping over the searingly hot paint of the deck, which boiled and bubbled at their naked feet; dead men everywhere, spines arched in final agony; men throwing themselves overboard, flames flaring up their bodies, into water which was itself ablaze. Death, violent death, on all sides. And then as the third E-boat came skipping and zooming over the waves for the kill, the twin torpedoes shooting from each side of its high prow, the deck vanished from beneath his feet and he sensed the searing shock of ice-cold water striking his guts. Red and silver stars exploded before his eyes. His head whirled madly. Black mist engulfed him, and the last sounds he heard on that fateful day of May, 1940 were words in a tongue that he did not understand.

'*Hier ist noch einer. Ein Offizier, Herr Oberleutnant . . .*'

THREE

Savage warmed his hands over the candles, while above his head the plaster cherub holding his mess-tin of corned beef stew became wreathed in steam as it finally came to the boil. Again Savage had cause to be grateful for the Catholic custom of lighting candles for their dead ones on important feast days such as Christmas. More than once in his previous attempts to get out of the bag he had used cemetery candles to warm himself and heat his food; the peasants never ventured into the cemeteries at night. They were much too superstitious.

Savage looked to the east. The night sky was slowly beginning to break up. In another hour it would be dawn on Christmas Day, 1942. He sniffed and, reaching up for his mess-tin, pulled out his spoon and began to ladle the hot rich soup down his throat. 'This one's got to be Christmas dinner, pud and mince-pies all rolled into one,' he whispered, speaking to himself in the fashion of all lonely men. 'Happy bloody Christmas!'

For a few moments as he crouched there eating his stew on the black marble tomb, surrounded by the snow-laden graves and mournful, dripping birch trees, he thought of home.

Back in England, the kids would already be awake, excitedly rummaging through their pillow-cases and stockings, gasping with gleeful surprise at each new treasure found there, while in the next bedroom their parents, still heavy-headed from the previous night's drinking at the local, would bury their faces deeper into the bed clothes, trying in vain to blot out the racket. In an hour or two, mothers everywhere would be busy in their steam-filled kitchens, preparing the chicken for roasting, lining the sides of the roasting-pan with potatoes, cleaning the sprouts, checking the steeping-peas, and performing all the other little tasks of a traditional English Christmas. 'And here I am,' he told himself, 'all on my Jack Jones in the middle of nowhere, with every man's hand against me.'

For an instant he felt a fleeting sense of self-pity. Then, almost as soon as it had come, it vanished.

'You've got no time for that kind of ruddy self-indulgence, Savage,' he muttered, draining the last precious drops of hot soup and then digging the mess-tin into the snow to clean it. 'Not if you want to get back to the war. Concentrate on the task at hand.'

For the last four hours he had been walking along the Moselle ridge-line, heading due north, reasoning that once the balloon went up at the morning roll-call, the Germans would immediately start their search for the fugitives to the south, especially as one of the escapers was Petit, who would obviously be heading for the nearby border with his own country. The Germans would assume that the escaped men would attempt to link up with one of the resistance movements in Belgium and France, so that they could be passed along the underground railway to the safety and freedom of Unoccupied France. The hunters would never suspect that one of them would try to do it the hard way – cross the whole length of Germany to one of the Baltic ports and stow away on a ship bound for neutral Sweden. That was exactly why he had been forced to ditch the others and take the northern route. Besides, a man on his own travels further and faster.

Thrusting the mess-tin into his home-made rucksack, he stared down at the dull-silver blur of the Moselle down below in the valley and the dark shapes of barges tied up along the nearest bank.

'Right on target,' he said, shouldering the rucksack and dusting the snow from his knees. 'That's Mullheim – and with a bit of luck, those barges are taking metal scrap up the Moselle, along the Rhine and then into the Ruhr for the war factories.' He gave the grave-stone that had served as his kitchen a mock salute. 'Bye-bye, *Herr Oberlehrer Schmitz, AD*,[1] Hope I won't get a wigging for abusing your hospitality on Christmas Day . . . And please, don't bother to get up and see me off the premises!'

Grinning happily, he set off at a jaunty pace, marching down from the hill-top cemetery with its flickering red candles on every grave, through the dank, forlorn vine-yards towards the village below.

A quarter of an hour later he was working his way cautiously through the shadows that lined the side of the narrow cobbled *Hauptstrasse*. The only sound was that of his boots on the frozen snow and the occasional snore wafted from the bedroom of one of the medieval half-timbered houses. Gratefully he noted that the whole village still slept. The Germans celebrated their Christmas on Christmas Eve, and this morning even the farmers would sleep in late, leaving their animals untended until later. He paused at the corner, praying that the same went for the bargees – for he knew nothing of those gypsies of the waterways, who plied their trade along the great rivers and canals of Northern Europe, passing more or less unchecked from one country to another. Perhaps, he told himself as he edged his way round the corner and halted again in the shadows to view the barges lined up in front of him – perhaps he might find a Dutch or French barge working for the Germans. That would be safer . . . But no – he dismissed the idea. 'Do it on your Jack Jones, Savage,' he whispered to himself. 'Trust no one. That's the safest way of going about it.'

Swiftly he drew on a spare pair of socks which he had kept by specially for this moment, so that he could approach the barges noiselessly. Cautiously he moved forward, trying to make out the home port of each barge in the half-gloom. Most of them came from Thionville in Northern France; presumably they would be carrying

[1] Literally, 'Mr Senior Teacher Schmitz, retired.'

coal from the Lorraine mines. But not to the Ruhr. The Ruhr had enough coal. The Thionville barges would probably be heading to Holland. Besides, it looked as though most of them would be staying at Mullheim right over Christmas. That was no good to him. He wanted to be away before the hue-and-cry really started. Because soon the goons would capture the main party and discover that he, Savage, wasn't with them.

Finally he spotted what he sought. A barge with its home port given as Saarbrucken. Unfortunately, the barge was German but it was only lightly moored to a buoy, as if as soon as it was light enough to navigate the Moselle it would get underway.

Savage darted forward. He lowered himself carefully onto the first barge, keeping well away from the wheel-house and cabins aft. Bargees usually slept on their craft, and he didn't want to risk waking them. On tiptoe he crossed the barge at the bows, and taking a quick breath, sprang onto the next one. Swiftly and silently he passed along the line of barges from Thionville, until finally he was alongside the German boat from Saarbrucken.

For a moment he crouched in the shadow cast by a hoist, his nostrils full of the pungent, biting smell of garlic and *Gaulloises* which came wafting up from the French barge. The German craft looked very shabby and sloppy; its paintwork was chipped and scratched all over and even the swastika flag drooped aft, ragged and torn. '*Very un-German*,' he muttered to himself. But that was all to the good. A sloppy ship meant a sloppy crew – and a sloppy crew meant less chance of finding Rodney Horatio Savage . . .

Cautiously he slipped across from the French barge to the one from Saarbrucken. Hardly daring to breathe, he tiptoed along the deck towards the aft wheel-house. It was empty, but the sound of heavy snoring from behind a dirty floral curtain indicated that someone was sleeping – very heavily – in the boxlike bedroom beyond. And now he could see why. A half-empty bottle of *Korn*, with two glasses upturned in a pool of the fiery spirit, stood on a little table, which served to hold the barge's charts and food, it seemed.

Looking around, Savage's eyes fell on a pair of black stockings and a suspender belt of pink elastic crumpled carelessly on the floor, as if pulled off in drunken haste. So there were two of them – a male and a female. Perhaps one of the husband-and-wife teams who often crewed these barges.

Stealthily he crept back the way he had come. Already it was beginning to grow light, and over in the barns of the village the cocks were beginning to crow, heralding the dawn. He had to get undercover soon. He halted at the big hatch and frowned. The catches were rusty, like everything else on board. They might well make a racket when he pulled them back, but it was a chance he had to take. Besides, the crew would still be too fast asleep to hear.

Gritting his teeth, he seized the first catch and raised it gingerly. It rasped harshly, setting his teeth on edge and his heart pounding. In spite of the freezing dawn cold, he felt sweat break out all over his body. He halted. Nothing – not a sound, save for the faint *lap-lap* of the water against the barge's keel. He pushed on, and finally with a rusty groan, the hatch-cover moved and he could peer down into the gloomy interior of the hold.

Immediately below him was the pile of rusting scrap he had been hoping for, wreckage from some engineering factory or other – the kind of stuff Germany's booming war industry desperately needed in order to keep the weapons flowing to the Eastern Front. Then his gaze fell on a pile of small cardboard boxes almost hidden in the far end of the hold. Taking a chance, he clicked on the zippo firelighter he had traded from Yank for two tins of corned beef. Blue flame spurted, and by its light, carefully shielded from above by his cupped hand, he saw that the cardboard box bore the legend '*Bastos – Tabac Pur*'.

Savage chuckled softly and let the lighter go out. So

that was it! The bargees were smuggling in cigarettes or tobacco, wartime Germany's only solid currency, to sell on the black market. Petty crooks! Savage smiled and crawled into the hold, drawing the cover closed above him. At least with crooks, he told himself as he clambered over the scrap, trying to find the best place to settle down for the trip to the Ruhr, you always knew where you were; if you didn't screw them first, they'd screw you. It was as simple as that.

'For you the war is over' *Kapitänleutnant* Hans-Helmut Brandt barked, rising from his desk, as the guards pushed a weary, half-starved, unshaven Savage into the Camp Commandant's Office at Offlag 16B that first day of June, 1940. 'You do understand, don't you, Savage?'

He had remained numb. He had heard the hackneyed phrase over and over again ever since the E-boat men had fished him out of the Channel a week before. But not one of his captors had said the stilted words with the same dogmatic conviction of this big, bearded sailor with his bright blue, confident eyes and the Knight's Cross of the Iron Cross hanging around his throat. The Camp Commandant of *Offlag 16B* was obviously not to be treated lightly.

Brandt thrust out his left hand. 'May I welcome you to my camp?' he said in his excellent American-English. 'Please forgive me tendering the left hand. I'm afraid your chaps of the *Exeter* did this to me last year, off South America.' He held up his right hand, which until then he had kept concealed behind his back. A dark grey officer's dress glove covered what was obviously an artificial hand.

The gesture caught Savage by surprise. 'You were on the *Graf Spee*[1]?' he gasped. 'But how come you're here and not—'

'—Interned in Uruguay?' an amused Brandt finished

[1] The British cruiser *Exeter* was engaged in the Battle of the River Plate against the German pocket battleship *Graf Spee*, which finally scuttled itself.

the sentence for him. 'Because unlike my more complacent comrades, who are now probably fathering a lot of little blond babies on the local senoritas, I wanted to continue the battle.'

His face hardened, and Savage could see from the way the German's chin jutted that he was a bold and determined man. Suddenly he realized he liked Brandt; they were two of a kind.

'As soon as the flipper was healed up fairly well, I was off into the jungle, waving an unfond farewell. It took me three months to get back to the Reich, but I did. I got this bauble for my pains.' He touched the Knight's Cross at his throat. '*Grossadmiral* Raeder awarded it to me personally, but they refused to give me another seagoing command. Instead, my dear Savage, I got this camp – and you. You see, we know all the tricks here. We know that you people will attempt to escape, and I'm here to show you right from the start that you don't have a chance. You understand that?' He leaned forward aggressively across the desk, his gaze challenging.

Savage found himself hoping *all* German naval officers weren't like Brandt. If they were, England wouldn't have a dog's chance of winning the war. Naturally, he didn't let the Camp Commandant in on his thoughts. Instead, he said as firmly and as coldly as he could, 'Sir, it is my duty as an officer to escape. Therefore I shall escape.'

Brandt opened his mouth and then seemed to change his mind. His face relaxed. 'So be it, Savage. But remember, as you say in English, there is many a slip between the cup and the lip.' He tapped the side of his finely chiselled nose in the Continental manner. 'Or as we say in Germany, wooden eye, watch out! Well, Savage, my particular wooden eye is on you. Good day to you.' Raising his voice, he beckoned to the guards. '*Posten*,' he barked, '*bringen Sie den Offizier 'raus!*'

That had been Savage's introduction to the POW Camp and *Kapitänleutnant* Brandt. Now, as he dozed in the hold of the barge, his blanket spread out over him to keep out the freezing cold, he smiled to himself dreamily as he tried to imagine the look on Brandt's face when he was told that his old opponent Savage had finally made a successful escape.

'*Nomen es omen*,' the big blond German officer had said sadly more than once, when he had been forced to throw Savage into the cooler after yet another of his escape attempts. 'Savage by name and savage by nature. Why in God's name don't you give up this absurd business and let both of us have a bit of peace? Why can't you be like most of your fellow officers and take up sport, or start studying? You could even try making that illicit potato whisky that I know you're all distilling at night in the washrooms.'

For two long years he and the Commandant had fought a duel of wits, although both of them lived in different worlds: the Commandant in the order and cleanliness of the mess, with its choice Moselle wines and good food; Savage in the dirt and squalor of the half-starved camp, with its stinking cabbage, ersatz acorn coffee and lice. Three times he had been over the wire, only to be caught within twenty-four hours.

'*Himmel, Arsch und Wolkenbruch!*' Brandt had cursed, the last time the guards had flung Savage to the floor of his office, smeared in blood from the routine beating he had been given after re-capture, worn and wan, his clothes ripped and covered in mud. 'Why do you go on doing it, Savage? Why? It can't just be duty.' He slapped the side of his head with his good hand in the Continental gesture of impatience. 'No one can be that dutiful, man. It must be something else!'

Savage had looked up at him through half-closed, red-rimmed eyes, his cheeks sunken and discoloured with bruises. 'No,' he had hissed back, 'it isn't just duty. It's ambition. I've been in the bag nearly two years now. I want to get back into action before it's too late. Officers who were far junior to me are lieutenant-commanders now and I'm still a lieutenant.' His voice cracked, as if he had been stung anew by the realization that promotion and glory were passing him by. 'I'm a *career* officer . . . I don't want to end the war an over-age lieutenant, when other people are full commanders, perhaps even captains.' He had let his head drop in defeat. '*I . . . I . . . must get back to the war . . .*'

Brandt laughed softly, but there was compassion in his laughter as he stared down at the ragged, beaten man on the floor of his office. 'Yes, yes, I understand,' he said slowly. 'I understand all too well, Savage.' He sucked his teeth reflectively, looking down at Savage's bent head almost sadly now. 'We're two of a kind, you and I,' he said slowly, selecting his words with care. 'In a way, I'm just as much in a cage as you.' He glanced at his gloved hand. 'The war is passing me by as well, old friend, in this damned arsehole of a place. All right, guards, off to the cooler with him.'

Shaking his head sadly, he watched as the guards half-dragged Savage out to the cell-block for another month of bread-and-water as punishment, then bent over his paper-strewn desk once again, eyes full of longing . . .

Now as the rusty anchor-chain of '*Saarbrucken-Metall Eins*' rattled into the locker and the barge's ancient engines started to throb, Rodney Savage turned luxuriously on the steel floor and smiled, feeling himself drift slowly off into a deep, contented sleep. He was out of the camp at last. He would never see *Kapitänleutenant* Hans-Helmut Brandt again! Slowly the barge began to chug its way ponderously into mid-channel. They were on their way northwards . . .

FOUR

'*Heaven, arse and cloudburst!*' Brandt exploded, as he stood in his cabin, completely naked, before the embarrassed young signaller who had brought the message. '*What* did you say, man?'

The young petty officer held up the flimsy yellow piece of signal paper and read out the news which had just shocked the big blond officer out of a drunken sleep.

'. . . Military District Five, Trier reports that eighteen prisoners of war have escaped from Offlag 16B. Border Police at Perl further report two Englishmen, a Belgian and an Australian taken into custody at zero nine hundred hours, as they attempted to cross the border into France.' He looked up. 'That's it, sir.'

With a finger that trembled violently, Brandt pointed at the champagne bucket, now full of melted ice and with two empty bottles perched inside it. 'Get rid of those dead soldiers,' he commanded, 'and let me have the full benefit of that ice water.'

'But sir,' the petty officer protested.

'Don't "but sir" me,' Brandt growled. 'I've got the father and mother of a hangover. What a shitting thing to happen on Christmas morning. *Los, Mensch . . . Hier mit dem Wasser . . . dalli!*'

The sailor hesitated no longer. While outside the bosun's whistles sounded the first orders of the day on the *Deutschland*, followed by the clatter of nailed sea-boots on the deck, he flung the contents of the ice-bucket straight in the face of the waiting officer.

White with shock, Brandt rubbed his good hand up and down his face, trying to dispel the effects of last night's drinking orgy with his old 'crew', who had invited him to spend his Christmas leave at Wilhelmshaven on the *Deutschland*.[1]

'Fine, fine,' he spluttered, while the sailor handed him a towel. 'That did the trick. Mind you, it still feels as if there's a little swine armed with a sledge-hammer trying to knock in the back of my skull. All right, whip up top to the signal shed and send this. "Confirm receipt of message. Returning next train. Report most immediate whether prisoner Lieutenant Savage –" he paused to spell out the name for the signaller "– involved in escape. If yes, is he one of those recaptured? Brandt." '

The signaller went. Swiftly strapping on his artificial arm, Brandt began to dress, but his movements were still awkward. As he fumbled with his stiff trouser buttons, he swore – not for the first time – that he would never get used to the damn wooden flipper. 'In three devils' name,' he urged the stiff metal fly-buttons, 'come on, come on! I've not got all the time in the world!'

Succeeding at last, he flung on his cap at its usual jaunty angle and hurried out of the cabin to inhale the deep draughts of the icy December air.

In spite of the shock news from the camp, Brandt had time to feel a twinge of envy for those of his old academy crew who sailed on this fine ship. How sleek and powerful the *Deutschland* looked, with her beautiful streamlined shape! And those guns! Why, they could blow any British ship – save perhaps their latest *Prince of Wales* class – right out of the water! At ten thousand tons displacement, the *Deutschland* could sink ships twice her weight, and with her tremendously thick armour survive anything, with the possible exception of a direct hit in her main powder locker . . .

As Brandt stared glumly at the shabby waterfront with its sailors' dives and brothels, he wished again that

[1] 'Crew' is the German equivalent of the British naval 'term', ie, it designates the members of the same year at naval college.

he was at sea and in action, even in the most humble capacity. At last, however, his thoughts turned back to the problem of the escape, and while he waited for the signaller to return with the answer to his query, he tried to visualize what the Tommy escapers would attempt to do.

The greenhorns, naturally, would head for Belgium and France, full of the belief inspired by British propaganda that the Frogs and Belgies were waiting to receive them with open arms – which of course they weren't. For the most part, the Frogs and Belgies were doing far too nicely out of the war to risk their skins.

The more experienced ones would have a crack at getting into neutral Switzerland. The Swiss, as always in their long history, were backing every horse in the race, favouring Germany when she was winning, favouring the Allies when it was their turn. The veteran escapers knew the Swiss wouldn't turn them over to the German police, unlike Belgium and France, where an escaper always ran that risk.

But what about Savage? If he were with the group, as Brandt suspected he was, would he do either one of those two things? The damned young Englishman with his dark, bold face and hard eyes had been outside the wire often enough; he knew the dangers. What would *he* do?

Brandt stared out at the stores piled up under snow-covered canvas tarpaulins all along the jetty. It wouldn't be long before the *Deutschland* sailed again. His comrades of the crew had not to reveal the pocket battleship's destination, but last night in their cups they had made pointed remarks about 'fur-lined boots' and 'hot-blooded Eskimo maidens just waiting in their igloos for a good length of hard German sausage.' You didn't need to be a mind-reader to know what they meant: the *Deutschland* was heading for northern waters, perhaps to act as a raider among the Tommy convoys sailing from their north-eastern British ports to carry supplies to the Ivans at Murmansk. Brandt clenched his jaw. God in Heaven, he'd give his other arm for just this one cruise with the *Deutschland*!

'*Herr Kapitänleutnant! Herr Kapitänleutnant!*' It was the excited voice of the young signals petty officer, running down the *Deutschland*'s immaculate deck, forgetting all naval protocol.

Brandt swung round, the future cruise of the *Deutschland* forgotten. 'Where's the fire, man?' he barked. 'What is it?'

'They've got them, sir! *Got the lot of them!*' the signaller gasped. 'It's the latest from Trier.' The excited young man gasped for breath, then added: 'All of them save one, that is, sir.'

Brandt nodded significantly. 'All save one – *named Savage*, I'll wager.'

'Yessir. This Englishman, Sa-va-ge –' he drew out the unfamiliar syllables – 'he is still at large.'

'*Gottverdammt!*' Brandt cursed.

The signaller, meanwhile, waited impatiently for further orders; but when they came they made him gape with shock.

'Contact the River Police for me – and Petty Officer, I know it's Christmas Day, but do you think you could get in touch with one of the local pavement-pounders? One who caters for you horny sailors? I'd like to ask her a couple of questions.' He beamed at the astonished sailor. 'Yes, you heard correctly, Petty Officer, I want to talk to a nice, fat, juicy, experienced waterfront whore – *at the double!*'

The shrill shriek of the siren, muted a little by the walls of the hold, alerted Savage to the fact that all was not going as planned. He shook his head to wake himself up and, cocking his head to one side, listened intently. The *throb-throb* of powerful engines grew closer, and a harsh, metalically distorted voice cried, '*Achtung . . . Achtung! Wasserschutz-polizei! Achtung . . . Achtung!*'

Savage's heart missed a beat. *The river police!*

Hurriedly he squirmed from his burrow beyond the pile of scrap and clambered up towards the hatch-cover. Gingerly, very gingerly, he eased it open, as the beat of the river police launch died and the scraping of metal against metal told him that the craft had come alongside. Cautiously he raised his head above the hatch-cover and peeped out.

A flat slattern of a woman in men's boots with a reefer-cap on the back of her head was standing aft next to the cabin, staring down at someone below. Savage guessed it was the police launch, and by the look on the woman's bloated face, he could tell that the police weren't exactly welcome. He knew why. The contraband bound for the Ruhr's black market.

Savage bit his bottom lip, his face set in a worried frown, as heavy sea-boots started to clamber up the aft ladder. Whatever the purpose of the river police's surprise visit this Christmas Day, one thing was certain; they couldn't help but discover him if they searched the barge – there was only the hold in which to hide. While there was still time, he had to abandon *Saarbrucken-Metall Eins* – and quick.

He cast a swift look across the river. The far bank was bordered by thick, snow-heavy firs. They would provide an excellent hiding place. But even though he was a powerful swimmer the police in the unseen boat would be sure to spot him before he was halfway across. There was the current to consider too.

No. It had to be the nearest bank. But there was still the little runt in the wheel-house. He would see him go over the side and warn the police. No doubt he would be only too happy to do so, and thus avert the risk of the tobacco being discovered. Somehow or other he *had* to create a diversion and then do a bunk over the side.

Then he had it.

He dropped hurriedly back into the hold. Grabbing his pack and slinging it over his shoulder, he picked up two of the cardboard cartons of tobacco.

He reached the hatch-cover again just as a big red-faced policeman with a white cap on his head breasted the side of the barge, pistol held at the ready in his free hand. Savage immediately knew why. They were looking for *him*. He hesitated no longer. Taking a deep breath, he slung the two packages, one after another, at the fat woman. Shrieking with alarm, she hastily bent down and tried to gather them up to her ample bosom before the cop saw them. His eyes fell on the woman, his attention momentarily distracted. Savage waited no longer. Just as the cop yelled a harsh command and the woman cried something back in protest, Savage went over the side in a shallow dive.

He gasped with shock as he struck the icy water. For a moment he panicked as the breath fled from him, then he was swimming for all he was worth, striking out for the bank, blind to everything but the fact that he was fighting for his life.

The bank loomed up in front of him: a stretch of frozen mud with beyond the cobbled towpath, a cluster of half-timbered houses grouped around an onion-towered Baroque church.

'*Halt!*' a harsh voice cried from the barge. '*Stehenbleiben oder ich schiesse!*' There was the angry throb of powerful engines.

Savage ignored the command. He pulled himself up the bank, dripping water. A shot rang out. A slug howled off the cobbles in a shower of blue sparks twenty yards away. The cop was rattled. Savage started to pelt down the cobbled path away from the village, the roar of the police launch getting ever louder. A woman pushing a child in a basket-like pram loomed ahead of him. She screamed. Savage pushed her. The baby sailed from the upturned pram and lay yelling in the snow. He ran on.

Suddenly he skidded to a halt. A man was standing in the field to his right. He looked like a farmer in his heavy grey Loden coat and Federhut – and he was armed with a shot-gun. For one long instant the two men faced each other and Savage saw a kaleidoscope of emotions – shock, fear, determination – race across the farmer's ruddy, healthy face. He raised the shotgun and pressed both triggers just as Savage sprang off the path, back into the Moselle.

The shotgun erupted in a blast of scarlet flame. Scores of vicious little pellets whizzed through the air at close range. Savage yelped with pain as he felt his back peppered with tiny slugs. Next instant he was back in the icy water, swimming for his life, while the farmer began to yell and the police launch surged forward again, an angry metallic voice crying through a loudhailer, '*Bleiben Sie stehen, Mensch! Halt . . . sofort!*'

But now Savage was beyond caring. They could kill him, but he was never going into the bag again. He *had* to escape!

Then he saw an opening: a dark stone chamber in the side of the bank, the flags worn by time and covered with slippery green moss. He dived just as a burst of machine-gun fire whipped the surface of the water into a whirling white fury. His hands struck stone. Next moment he was clambering inside and running frantically on, deeper and deeper into the darkness, heavy with the stench of centuries.

The first burst of sub-machine-gun fire crashed into the sewer. Flame erupted like a blossoming scarlet flower. Savage whipped round a bend, his progress illuminated momentarily by the glowing light.

'He's down there!' he heard an angry voice call.

'Shut up!' someone else exclaimed. 'We'll never hear the son-of-a-whore if you shout like that!'

Savage ran on wildly, not knowing where he was or

where he was going, aware only that he had to put as much distance as possible between himself and his pursuers.

On and on he blundered, with all around him in the glowing gloom a confusion of pipes and tubes, covered with an ugly white fungus, and all dripping with the noxious slime of generations. Behind him he could hear the clatter of heavy nailed sea-boots, magnified tenfold by the hollow tunnel. They were after him all right. Twisting and turning desperately, in and out of high-roofed, dripping corridors, the slimy-green walls rushing by in a crazed, wild phantasmagoria, he sought desperately to throw them off. In vain! The clatter of their boots came ever closer.

Suddenly his feet went from beneath him. He was in space. Screaming in absolute panic now, he found himself falling . . . falling . . . falling . . .

With a hellish splash, he hit the pit filled with water far below. He went under, fighting desperately for breath, and came up to find his nostrils assailed by the stench of stagnant water. He had landed in the drainage pool.

With an effort of sheer, absolute willpower, he forced himself to be calm and not cry out for help. His arms struck out blindly, and just when he thought there were no sides to the pit his nails rasped against a rough stone surface. With the last of his strength, he held on, in the same moment as the heavy nailed boots came level with him, high above.

Savage took a deep breath and ducked his head beneath the green scum, which parted and closed above him almost immediately. The boots stopped. There was a distorted mumble of voices. A torchbeam flashed down the pit and across the surface of the green scum. He could see it faintly through the glowing surface. Someone rapped out an order. He held his breath, one hand anchoring him to the side of the pit, body rigid and motionless. A second later the beam flashed away, leaving him in the darkness. The boots were running off down the corridor. He forced himself to count to ten and then raised his dripping head above the surface, gasping violently for air, his lungs threatening to burst at any moment; but there was triumph on his face. For the time being he had thrown them off. The Huns still hadn't got him!

FIVE

Every step was an agony. The snow came down in solid white sheets, blinding the lone figure staggering across the fields, up to his ankles in new snow. The wind raged, whipping the flakes against his livid, frozen face. Shivering uncontrollably, Savage struggled grimly on. At first the snowstorm which had descended on Southern Germany so suddenly this second day of Christmas had come as a blessing. It had stopped the police chase dead. Only a fool or a fugitive would venture out in weather like this. But now it had turned into a nightmare. With every passing moment he had to fight the almost overwhelming craving for sleep and warmth. More than once he was tempted just to fling himself down into the snow and sleep.

But always he caught himself just in time, muttering through gritted teeth, 'I *can't* die now . . . I *can't* . . . It's not fair to let the Huns win over me now . . . *I must keep going!*' And he did, slogging over that snow-engulfed plain hour after hour, fighting the pitiless icy wind and the raging, blinding storm of snow. He would never know how he managed to keep going, but he did.

At two o'clock on that terrible afternoon of December 26th, 1942, with the sky as black as night, he took shelter as best he could in a small fir wood and attempted to take stock of his position.

His camp-made compass shaped from a razor-blade, some stolen brass and cardboard from a Swiss Red Cross parcel, was functioning perfectly. He was exactly on course, heading north, with the Rhine between him and the lonely rural area of Hesse, through which he would march till he struck the River Elbe, the last water barrier before Lubeck on the Baltic.

His first objective, though, was to get to the Rhine. He looked down ruefully at his dyed battledress suit, which was soaked and stained from the snow and the sewage tunnel. In that outfit he would stand out immediately. Then there was the pong . . . 'No, Savage old fellow,' he told himself, 'your first priority is to get out of this damned snow, warm up and beg, borrow or steal a new set of clothes.'

He narrowed his eyes to slits against the whirling white glare and stared to his front. At the moment he was somewhere between Rheinbach and Remagen on the Rhine. If he remembered the map correctly, there were a few hamlets located between the two towns. The question was, dare he approach anyone to ask for food and warmth and possibly clothing? He had Marks, collected one way or another over the last six months in preparation for this escape. But what good was money when dealing with Germans? The whole bunch of them would be fervent Nazis or patriots at least – or even just plain scared of the Gestapo. Who could blame them if they turned him in immediately? He bit his bottom lip. There was only one way out. Grimly he took out his knife and slid it – opened – into his pocket. Nothing must stop him now.

One hour later, Savage spotted the yellow gleam of an oil lamp shining through a few scraggy trees a hundred yards or so to his right. He paused wearily and wiped the wet snowflakes from his frozen features. A rough stone cottage typical of the Rhine plain lay there, yellowed tobacco leaves hanging under the eaves, a great pile of logs set near the door and of course, as always in that area, a heap of manure just underneath the kitchen window.

For nearly thirty minutes Savage watched the cottage from the cover of the trees, trying to assess how many people were in it and failing to come to any conclusion, save that there were animals in the barn to the right of the place and that the fortunate occupants had a damn good fire going; smoke was pouring from the chimney in thick grey clouds. Then he made his decision. He had to find shelter soon; night was approaching quickly. He just had to take a chance that he could deal with whoever lived in the place.

He crept forward, knife gripped in his right hand, face set in grim determination. The storm howling about him deadened the sound of his approach – but not altogether. Suddenly, somewhere to his right, came a hoarse growl and the rattle of a chain. There was a hound tied up behind the barn. Savage threw caution to the winds. In a moment the animal would start barking and alert the whole place. Grabbing the door handle he wrenched it open violently, knife held clenched to his right side, ready for the plunge.

A woman shot up from the old armchair next to the green tiled stove that reached right up to the beamed ceiling. Her hands flew to her long scraggy neck – obviously she was terrified.

But Savage was taking no chances. There might well be others close by. As she shrank back in her chair, he grabbed her by her dank grey hair, sending needles and wool tumbling to the floor.

'Listen, old woman,' he cried in German, 'one word out of you and I'll cut your skinny throat!' He slashed the air with his knife to make his meaning quite clear, and the woman's eyes bulged with abject terror, saliva trickling down the side of her skinny chin out of a toothless mouth.

'*Now*,' Savage said in a softer tone, realizing that the woman was frightened out of her wits and that he would get nothing more out of her with threats. '*Alles in Ordnung, Oma* . . . It's all right, Granny. I'm not going to hurt you.' He did his best to inject a soothing note, but his nerves were jingling with electric tension as much as the old woman's. 'Are there any other people in the house?'

He had to repeat his question twice more before finally she shook her head. Savage breathed out a sigh of relief and placed the knife deliberately back into his belt, watched by the old woman's rheumy, petrified gaze. Slowly and carefully he placed his hands on the warmth of the green tiled stove and smiled at her. 'Food,' he said. 'Get me some food, Grandma . . . *Bitte*.'

She rose with an audible creak. Still terrified out of her wits by this ragged, mud-splattered intruder who had appeared from nowhere, she backed along the wall to the door, while Savage continued to smile winningly at her. With an audible gasp of relief she slipped through – with surprising speed for such an old woman – and was gone.

Savage gave her a minute, still smiling inanely. Then his smile vanished as if washed from his face by an invisible hand, and he sped after her to peer through the half-open door.

What he saw there made his shoulders slump with relief. The old woman hadn't vanished to alert someone else in the house, or run away. No – she was standing there in a large, bare kitchen, obediently slicing one of the wheel-like brown loaves of bread typical of that area, while next to her lay a side of salt bacon with which she was preparing sandwiches.

Noïselessly, Savage tiptoed back to the blessed warmth of the stove. 'Thank God for Hitler,' he whispered happily to himself. 'He certainly taught his womenfolk to obey their lords and masters. *Kinder, Küche und Kochen.*[1] Maybe there's something to be said for him after all . . .'

Savage waited till the old crone had finished packing the last of her food – a week's ration of hard, salted German bacon, a chunk of black bread and six hard-boiled eggs – into a briefcase he had found in her bedroom, together with the shabby suit he now wore, and then as dramatically as he could, he stood up and looked down at her.

[1] Children, kitchen and cooking – a Nazi slogan for the housewife.

She cringed against the wall as he towered above her; yet there was still a look of defiance in her faded eyes.

Savage took his time. For the last hour he had been considering what to do with her while he had devoured the rest of her larder. At first he had told himself he should kill her. Once he had left, she would be bound to talk. All the same, he simply couldn't bring himself to kill her in cold blood, even though he knew it was really the only solution to his problem. To hell with the consequences – the Huns were never going to take *him* alive again . . .

In the end he decided to try and frighten her into at least temporary silence. With a bold sweep of his right hand, he knocked all the pots off the little kitchen table. They clattered and broke on the stone floor. Behind the house, the grey dog started to bark hysterically. The old crone's face blanched with fear. Savage reached out and grabbed her by the skinny throat. He squeezed it, and she gasped in horror.

'Listen, you old witch,' he breathed, bringing his own face close to her leathery wrinkled one, 'I'm going now. I *should* kill you . . .'

She gasped again.

'. . . But I've decided – after some consideration – not to.'

'*Danke, danke!*' she croaked, as slowly, very slowly, Savage released his hold on her scraggy neck. '*Danke, Herr.*'

'Remember, though,' Savage held up his finger in warning, 'if you tell anyone I was here, I shall come back . . .' He clasped his hands together as if he were squeezing the life out of someone; the woman cowered back. 'And I'll kill you. Do you understand that, eh?'

Unable to speak, the old crone nodded her head urgently.

'Good,' Savage said, slowly and menacingly. He picked up his cheap cardboard briefcase and the peaked, sailor-type working men's cap which had belonged to her only son, killed the year before near Moscow. He gave her one last, hard look. 'Remember, old woman,' he hissed. Then he crossed the kitchen towards the door. Outside, the dog still yelped.

Suddenly the woman's wrinkled old face flushed with animation, fear giving way to defiance. 'You are a bad one, Englishman,' she croaked hoarsely, 'to do this to a poor old woman . . .' In a burst of anger, she shook her finger at him, as he paused at the door to pull out the key. 'You will never have luck in this world . . . You are . . . *accursed*, Englishman!'

Savage felt a frisson of fear sweep down his spine. The short hairs at the back of his cropped skull stood erect. He had no idea why, but there was something eerie, uncanny about the old woman as she stood there, eyes blazing, trembling finger outstretched like some medieval witch in one of those old German fairy tales . . .

Hurriedly he slammed the door behind him and locked it with a hand that trembled violently. Ignoring the hysterical barking of the chained dog, he hastened down the path, flinging the key away into the snow, feeling her eyes burning into his back. Then, for some reason he couldn't explain even to himself, he began to run . . .

'One of the Baltic ports, *Herr Oberkommissar*,' Brandt said confidently. 'He's a sailor and he'll head for the sea – that's my guess. And it's got to be up here on the Baltic, where he can find a ship heading for Sweden. I *know* I'm right. He's been out three days now.'

Oberkommissar Harsch, a fat, heavy-set man, moved the stub of the 10-Pfennig cigar from one side of his loose, thick-lipped mouth to the other, and said in his slow, lazy way, 'You could be right, *Herr Kapitänleutnant* – and you could be wrong.' He smiled slowly, but his green eyes did not light up; they remained wary and suspicious. He nodded at the window of the police HQ, where snowflakes struck the glass like white tracer. 'Can't see anybody hoofing it far in this kind of weather. Not fit for dogs.'

Brandt laughed, showing his excellent white teeth. 'But definitely fit for Englishmen. They're all crazy, you know. Besides, if what I've learned here is true, he wouldn't find it too difficult to find a warm bed for the night if he goes about it the right way. I've been talking to one of the ladies of the night.'

'Whores?'

'Exactly. And they tell me that when a sailor overstays his leave or doesn't want to sail with a particular ship, they'll help him out for a – er – small consideration.'

The big Gestapo man made as if to count money with his thumb and fat forefinger.

Brandt nodded. 'Yes – pay them right, it seems, and you could hide out for eternity. The whole shitting fleet could lie low if they felt like it!'

Harsch nodded slowly, as if every movement was an effort for his big frame; in spite of the warmth of his office, he was clothed in an ankle-length leather coat. 'The registered pavement-pounders are easy enough to check, of course; but it's these amateur whores who've flocked into the ports since the war started that cause all the trouble. While their menfolk are at the front, they're up here spreading 'em for business – and for pleasure.' He frowned, as if at some unpleasant thought or other. 'But you have a point, *Herr Kapitänleutnant*. If he's heading for Lubeck or Wismar, he might well try and find himself a pavement-pounder to hide out with until he finds a ship bound for Sweden. I'll send out a call to the local whore-mothers to keep a lookout for him. I'll pass it on to the block wardens, too. They can watch those of their lady tenants who entertain sailorboys and the like. They'll report anything suspicious. The men on the beat as well.'

The handsome blond naval officer looked suitably impressed.

'*Kolossal!*' he exclaimed. 'You're certainly turning this

into a large-scale operation. I'm surprised and of course pleased as well. But it seems a lot of fuss for one naughty escaping Englishman . . .'

Harsch sniffed, rolled his unlit cigar from one side of his mouth to the other again, and gave Brandt a gold-flecked, cold smile. 'We've got orders to do so – from above.'

'From above?'

Harsch nodded his head in the direction of a large portrait of a shaven-skulled man with the cleft chin of a sadist, dressed in the uniform of a full general of police. 'My boss,' he explained. 'General Mueller . . . Gestapo Mueller, they call him.'

'Yes, yes, I've heard of him, naturally. But why should he concern himself with an English prisoner-of-war?' Brandt asked, puzzled, a suspicion dawning that events were moving beyond his control.

'Mueller ordered this morning from Berlin that when your Englishman is found . . .' Harsh hesitated, as if trying to select the appropriate word '. . . he should meet with a little accident.'

'*Accident?*'

'Yes, *Nacht und Nebel*[1], *Herr Kapitänleutnant*,' Harsch answered, fixing the blond officer with an unwinking gaze, as if he could see things in Brandt's face unknown to Brandt himself.

Brandt stared at the middle-aged cop, aghast. 'But why? Why, *Herr Kommissar?* It is not a criminal offence for an officer who is a prisoner of war to escape. I did so once myself – that is why the Führer cured my throatache for me.' He fingered the Knight's Cross hanging around his neck.

'Agreed, *Herr Kapitänleutnant*,' Harsch agreed easily. 'But there have been too many of these damned Tommies escaping of late and rousing the whole countryside. Mueller – and naturally the Führer, too – have had

[1] Literally 'night and fog', the Gestapo expression for people who are to disappear without trace.

enough of it. I have been ordered to make an example of this naughty boy of yours – what's his name?' He flashed a glance at his blotter. 'Oh yes, Savage. Once we catch him – and we will, never fear – he will simply disappear.' Harsch sucked at the end of his cigar, rolling it between his lips reflectively. 'But the word will get out, of course. Eventually the news will spread from camp to camp, until the whole damned lot of them behind Swedish curtains[1] will know that there is no future in the business of escaping, save,' he smiled at a horrified Brandt, 'a nine-millimetre slug in the back of the turnip . . .'

[1] I.e. prison.

SIX

Carefully, Savage followed the tramlines, past the *Holstenturm*, deeper into the heart of the seaport. It was an old ploy for getting to the middle of a town in the early morning without asking questions. All around him, workers were streaming into the centre and the docks, all of them shabbily dressed and looking exactly the same as himself, carrying similar shabby briefcases containing their sandwiches and flasks of cold tea.

He paused at a corner, blowing his frozen hands and stamping his feet in the dirty snow, face wreathed in his own misty breath, like a workman perhaps waiting for his mate to appear. In reality, he was surveying the road to his front, looking out for the familiar black-lacquer shako and grey-green overcoat of a policeman who might bar his progress on the next leg of his escape.

For the last three days he had made his way steadily northwards, walking, hitch-hiking, using local buses and trams and keeping his journeys short so as to avoid having his papers checked by the police. He had soon come to realize that a massive search had been launched for him. On the main roads there had been police and troops everywhere. Twice he had spotted the roadblocks just in time. In spite of the terrible weather and the continued snowfall, he had nearly been discovered by low-flying *Storch* reconnaissance planes more than once.

Putting two and two together, he had concluded that the Huns had somehow guessed he was heading north for the Baltic ports. As a consequence, he could expect a very strong guard on all shipping leaving for neutral Sweden. For nearly a day he had mulled the problem over as he battled through a snowstorm towards the bridge across the River Elbe at Lauenburg, just south of Lubeck. Finally he had come to the conclusion that, with luck, he could turn the increased vigilance at ports such as Lubeck and Wismar to his advantage. For while the Hun concentrated his efforts there, he would continue north into Schleswig-Holstein, cross the border into Denmark at Flensburg, and press on through Denmark to where the peninsula almost touched Sweden. The journey would be much longer, but he would be in a friendly country, and the local resistance could help him across the narrow straits to freedom.

There was only one catch. Both his boots and his strength were beginning to give out. He doubted if he could go on like this for another week. He needed wheels. A rail ticket to Flensburg – for he reasoned that there would be many sailors of the *Kriegsmarine*[1] travelling between the two naval bases of Lubeck and Flensburg.

Ahead of him he could see the two stout, middle-aged policemen stamping their booted feet outside the entrance of the *Hauptbahnhof*, below a banner proclaiming '*Wheels Roll for Victory*'; occasionally they would crook their fingers at one of the workers streaming towards the trains and check his papers. Obviously the time wasn't ripe to enter the station just yet.

He frowned and sucked his bottom teeth. Rush hour would be over in thirty minutes or so. What would the fat *Schupos*[2] do then? Would they stay at their post? Or would they go over to one of the bars and cafés which surrounded the square for a coffee and a warm-up before returning to the entrance to the main station for the next rush of travellers?

Letting his shoulders slump in the manner of a badly nourished worker who has been forced out of bed too early on a chilly morning, Savage followed the rest of the shabby crowd towards the station, shuffling through the

[1] Wartime German Navy.
[2] Police.

slush and dirty snow, his nostrils heavy with the smell of the Hun: black, coarse tobacco, sweat and human misery. He stopped to let a party of sailors march past, faces reddened with sea duty and the ribbons of their black caps fluttering in the wind; behind them they were pulling a car on which rested crates clearly marked *SS Deutschland.*

'*Schlachtschiff Deutschland*,' Savage muttered to himself. The pocket battleship. *That* should be of some interest to naval intelligence when he got back to the UK! He pushed on towards the two boards attached to the wall of the station announcing *Ankünft* and *Abfahrt*[1].

Doing his best to ignore the pig-like *Schupo* who stood only yards away from him, his small red eyes filled with suspicion, Savage ran his finger down the list of departures. Then he saw it: a notice in red, indicating that a fast express would be leaving Lubeck for Flensburg at fourteen hundred hours. It was just the job! An hour or so after the midday rush hour. If the cops weren't on duty then, he could walk in unnoticed. But everything depended on his being able to slip into the station when it was unguarded.

Shoulders still bent, Savage shuffled back across the square, head drooping as if in defeat, but gaze keen as he sought a spot from which to observe the station's main entrance.

It was the sort of run-down part of town Savage remembered from a dozen ports all around the world: the place matelots waiting for a train, a ship, a transfer, would seek out to kill a few hours' boredom before they continued the next stage of their long journey. There were the same old dingy bars and cafés, reeking of stale beer and smoke; the same hard, raucous laughter from the whores and loud, brassy music from the blaring radios. Occasionally a drunk would stagger out and vomit in the dirty snow, cheered on by his shipmates from within. Here and there, aged pros with dyed-blonde hair and too-short skirts stood in doorways, smoking with the

[1] Arrivals and departures.

bored, brooding, greedy-eyed single-mindedness of their kind. Sudden fake animation would light up their raddled, heavily-powdered faces whenever they saw a potential customer; their animation changing to pouting anger as soon as he turned them down.

Savage wrinkled his nose in contempt. Before the war he had occasionally been forced to resort to such places in China or in the Med, but he had never liked them and had always been grateful to hurry back to the cleaner air of the ship. Yet at the same time he knew he could be safe here, as long as he had money to pay for his drinks. The trick was to find the right place – a spot that was busy enough for a stranger not to be noticed, yet at the same time not so noisy as to attract the attention of a shore patrol and their demands for identification.

Now he was almost approaching the end of the street and the two fat cops at the entrance to the *Hauptbahnhof* were almost disappearing from view. He *had* to find a place, or it would be too late.

'*Eine kleine Spende, Mein Herr . . . Winterhilfe . . . für unsere Soldaten in Russland . . .*'

Savage turned round, startled. A little blond boy in the short pants and black jacket of the Hitler Youth stared up at him cheekily, rattling his collecting box. Hastily, Savage dug in his pocket and brought out a 50-Pfennig piece. 'Here you are for *our* soldiers in Russia.' He couldn't quite conceal the contempt in his voice.

The blond boy with his frozen knees and chapped face seemed not to notice. Instead, he winked knowingly and whispered *sotto voce*, 'You want a little fun?'

'Did you say *fun*?'

'That's right. You ain't got tin ears have you, mister?' The boy winked and made an obscene gesture with the thumb and middle fingers of his free hand. 'I could show you a nice time.'

Savage stared down at the boy aghast. 'Do you mean . . . that you're . . . a pimp?' he stuttered in amazement.

The boy shook his head. 'No, *mein Herr*. Just helping the war effort – you know; our brave boys at sea, fighting the cruel English enemy . . .' He lowered his voice conspiratorially. 'Fräulein Hoffman lives up there.' He indicated a window two storeys above his head, and placed his cold hand in Savage's. 'This way, *mein Herr*. I can promise you a good time. Fräulein Hoffmann is generally regarded as quite a talent on the mattress.'

Hardly aware of what was happening, Savage let himself be led into the house and up the stairs.

'Comrades,' Brandt said, putting down his glass of rum and black tea. 'May I have your attention, please?'

The members of his old academy crew – Roof-Hare, known for his daring in the top-rigging; Pox, who had gained his nickname from an unfortunate happening during their 1936 training cruise to Rio; Hairless, the *Deutschland*'s completely bald gunnery officer, and all the rest of them he had assembled (with the captain's permission) in the wardroom – looked up at his worried face.

'Come on, Master-Jailer,' Pox said, lowering his steaming glass, 'it's about time you told us what the game is. I've got an appointment with a little beaut at midday down in town. You've never seen a girl with so much wood before her door!' He made a great curving gesture in the air as if outlining two large balloons.

Roof-Hare grinned. 'I thought yours dropped off years ago, Pox.' He ducked hastily as his old friend threw one of the wardroom's leather cushions at him.

But this morning, *Kapitänleutnant* Brandt was amused neither at their use of his nickname nor their high spirits; he was still too worried at what he had learnt from Harsch.

'Comrades,' he said urgently, 'I know we're all honourable men who value the traditions and reputation of the *Kriegsmarine*. I think we can all say that we've fought a clean war so far and that all of us here intend to keep it that way.'

Roof-Hare opened his mouth as if to ask something, then he seemed to change his mind and closed it again; his face registered puzzlement. Even Pox's usual high spirits had vanished.

'Now, you know the kind of rotten job I'm being forced to do because of my wooden flipper. Well, the whole stinking business has become even messier, because one of my Tommies has gone and escaped.'

'You should have remembered to close the door,' Pox said.

Brandt ignored him. 'Now, it's not the first time some of my – er – charges have escaped. In itself, an escape is no problem; the police usually round up the Tommy after he's had a couple of days on the outside, so that I can send him off to the cooler for a week or two on bread and water. Unfortunately, this time—' Brandt cast a quick look at the door and the nearest port-hole to check if anyone was listening: a gesture not unnoticed by the others. It was a familiar one in Germany in 1942, and each man present knew what it meant: Brandt was on the look-out for spies or stool-pigeons. 'This time the gentlemen of the Gestapo have decided to take a hand in the matter.' He paused and let the full impact of his words sink in.

'How do you mean?' Roof-Hare asked.

'They've been ordered to make an example of this Englishman when he's captured – which he undoubtedly will be, sooner or later.'

'*Example?*'

By way of an answer, Brandt crooked the finger of his good hand, as if pulling the trigger of a pistol. '*Nacht und Nebel,*' he said, his voice low; 'to convince the others that there's no point in escaping.'

Pox whistled through his front teeth; Roof-Hare groaned, and Hairless, stroking his bald pate, whispered in that peculiar hoarse voice of his, 'But even the Gestapo wouldn't *dare* to do that, Jailer?'

'Oh yes, they would,' Brandt answered resolutely, 'especially when the order comes from the very top. And the man they want to do away with isn't just some ordinary stubble-hopper of an infantryman – he's a naval officer the same as us.'

Brandt's remarks were greeted by a long silence, broken only by the steady tread of the sentry on duty on the quarter-deck above and the rattle of the steam winches further off as more and more stores were loaded on board ready for the *Deutschland*'s departure. In the end Roof-Hare said a little hopelessly, 'But what's this got to do with us, Jailer?'

Brandt licked his lips. 'Remember *Obermaat* Matiessen? *You* know – he was in charge of the crew back on the South American cruise of the *Schleswig-Holstein*?'[1]

Pox nodded. 'Don't I just! He had a sharp tongue on him, old Matiessen – and an even sharper toe to his boot if you weren't quick enough carrying out an order. My arse is still tender.'

The others laughed softly. Brandt said, 'Well, our old *Obermaat* was badly wounded and blinded at Narvik in Spring 1940 when the Tommy destroyers attacked up the fiord. Of course, he was invalided out of the service. He swears he wouldn't have been alive today if the Tommies hadn't fished him out of the water before he froze and delivered him to the Norwegians. They gave him to our people after the Tommies were driven—'

'—But Jailer. What's all this with poor Matiessen and your Tommy got to do with the problem in hand – *and with us*?'

'This.' Brandt knew it was time to take the plunge; his old comrades of pre-war training days wouldn't betray him, he knew. 'Our old *Obermaat* went to a rehabilitation centre after he was released from hospital and trained to be a telephonist.' He waited and delivered his punchline.

[1] A training ship of the pre-war days.

'Do you know where he works today?' He answered his own question with a thin smile of triumph. 'Main Gestapo Headquarters here in Lubeck – and all confidential messages go through his hands. In short, our old task-master of Rio days knows what's going on in Lubeck before his masters do . . .'

SEVEN

A whistle shrilled, and the clatter of heavy boots was heard on the frozen cobbles down below.

'*Aufmachen! Polizei!*' a harsh voice cried. There was the sound of rifle-butts slamming against a door.

'*Razzia!*' a woman's voice screamed fearfully.

'Shut up, you dumb bitch!' an angry male voice yelled in answer, 'and put yer damned drawers on – *quick*!'

The clatter of breaking glass was followed by boots running swiftly down the alley behind the brothel.

'*Halt! Halt!*' an urgent voice cried, '*Stehenbleiben oder ich schiesse!*'

Fräulein Hoffman, a big blonde woman with a battered, good-humoured face and an impressive bosom which seemed continually to be attempting to escape from her too-tight, artificial silk blouse, put down her cup and stared across at Savage and the boy. 'The chain-dogs,' she exclaimed. 'They're pulling one of their dawn raids, looking for deserters.' She cast an experienced eye over Savage. 'You're young enough to be in the services. You're a bit on the skinny side, though.' She chuckled in a throaty drinker's manner. 'But they always say a good cock doesn't get fat, don't they. You're a foreigner, of course, so perhaps you don't have to join up.' She lowered her voice and looked significantly at her visitor. 'Mind you, whether you're a German or a painted-arsed Hottentot, they'll still want to see your *papers*.'

Savage made up his mind. He felt he could trust the big, blousy whore and her smart little pimp. Besides, he had no choice. Already he could hear the military police stamping around on the first floor below, flinging open doors and making harsh demands for '*Ausweis*' and '*Papiere*'.

'Listen,' he said urgently. 'I'm an escaped British prisoner-of-war. Help me, and I'll give you this.' He place the 50-Mark note he had been holding in his hand the whole time on the table in front of the whore.

She didn't even look at it. Instead, her faded, red-rimmed eyes were fixed on his face with a look of compassion. 'You poor devil. On the run at this time of the year!' Her face hardened again. 'You – three-cheeses-high. Get the *Herr Engländer* out of here – *quick*!'

'But I'm in the Hitler Youth,' the boy-pimp protested without enthusiasm. 'What would the Führer say?'

The whore stuck up her fat middle finger. 'The Führer can sit on that!' she snorted. 'You and the Führer. You'd sell him and the whole Nazi pack of them to Schurchill if the price was high enough. Now off you go.' She pushed the 50 Marks back to an astonished Savage. 'Here – and give me a kiss.'

For an instant Savage felt as if he were sinking into a sofa-full of soft cushions as she clutched him to her impressive bosom. Then the boy seized him by the hand and was dragging him out of the whore's overheated room and up the stairs, with the clatter of heavy policemen's boots only yards away below.

Together they pushed through a door at the head of the dingy landing, cold air striking them almost like a blow in the face. They appeared to be in some kind of loft, with lines of frozen washing strung back and forth between the beams. '*Los!*' the little pimp urged, his collecting box rattling and jingling as the two of them ran the length of the room, Savage ducking every now and again to avoid the roof timbers. From below they could hear the hysterical cries of a woman and a man protesting over and over again in a hollow, broken voice, 'But I just wanted a few days away from the sea, Sergeant. *Only a few shitting days!*'

They swung through another door at the end of the

dark loft. Savage stopped dead. He was high above the street. Below, helmeted military policemen could be seen grouped around a covered truck, while others, carbines in hands, patrolled the cobbled lane. On the far side, away from the truck, civilians gawped upwards, talking animatedly to one another, obviously enjoying the little show on this dreary grey December morning.

Hastily the little pimp dragged him down below the cover of the balustrade. 'Listen, Englishman, this is as far as I can take you. Understand?' He spoke slowly and very clearly, as if he had suddenly discovered that Savage was an idiot. In spite of the danger of his position, Savage smiled. The boy-pimp would go far. 'Now, you follow the cover of the balustrade to the rear of the house. You'll see another roof below you. If you can jump the gap and make it, all you've got to cover is the roof below. From there there's a fire-ladder running into the yard that backs on to the station. Understand?'

'I understand, *Junge* – and many thanks.'

The boy-pimp looked up at him, no fear in his winning, knowing blue eyes. 'Can't buy much with thanks, Englishman,' he said. 'What about that 50 Marks you were going to give Fräulein Hoffman?'

Savage shook his head in mock-wonder. 'Here you are.' He thrust the note into the boy's waiting palm.

'Say Hello to Mister Schurchill,' the little fellow called after him, then Savage was scurrying away the length of the roof, the cries and the curses, the pleas and the protests dying away behind him.

He came to a halt. There was a gap of some three feet to the next slate roof, which was half-covered with frozen, dirty snow and lay some two foot below. Savage bit his bottom lip. He had never been afraid of heights; he had soon overcome all fears on that score at Dartmouth. But the prospect before him wasn't too inviting. He would have to jump out and land on a slippery roof which sloped at a near forty-five-degree angle. And if he slipped . . . He decided not to think that particular thought to an end. Instead, he took another look at the roof opposite. Here and there he could see iron fire-hooks protruding from the slates. On the Continent, slaters used them for fixing their ladders on repair jobs. If he could manage to grab onto one of those, it would give him the halt he needed . . .

Savage took a deep breath. Time was running out rapidly. The police would soon be searching the loft he had just left. The boy-pimp wouldn't be able to hold them up indefinitely. It was now or never.

'One . . . twoo . . . *th-r-ee!*'

He sprang out into the air and started falling immediately. He struck the roof hard. Desperately he grabbed for a hook. He felt himself sliding . . . sliding. A slate came tumbling down . . . and another, rattling over the eave and crashing to the snow far below. His hand connected. He yelped with pain as its point gashed his hand. He was still falling, his heels flailing the snow, trying to dig in – and failing. His hand caught a hook. He felt the point stick deep into his palm. Instinctively his hand closed around it. The strain was almost unbearable. His whole arm trembled. Red-hot pain surged up and down the muscles with electric intensity. He bit his bottom lip till his mouth flooded with copper-tasting, warm blood. And then slowly, very slowly, he began to draw himself up the slippery tiles, reaching from hook to hook, his blood staining the dirty snow a bright scarlet, gasping for breath, his nails torn, bleeding and agonized.

A few moments later he was sliding down the other side, smashing into the eaves, which acted as a brake, his breath coming in great gasps. He looked down. Below him lay a solitary steam-engine, chuffing along behind a line of freight-cars. For a few moments he lay there in the snow, the sweat streaming down his face despite the icy cold. He grinned at the leaden grey sky. He had almost done it. He was right above the station's marshalling yards. He might not get the train to Flensburg now; it was too risky. But down below there were the 'wheels' he sought. Somehow or other he would leave Lubeck and from there he would get into Denmark; he was sure of that now.

He wiped the sweat from his face gingerly and then, trying to forget the burning pains in his torn hands, swung himself over the eaves onto the fire escape. Hastily but carefully, he began to tiptoe down it, past blank or opaque windows. Plainly he was moving down the back of the building; perhaps the windows were those of lavatories and bathrooms. Whatever they were, they concealed his departure from whoever might be inside.

Before him there was a low wall, begrimed with the dirt of decades. He looked to left and right. No one. He grinned. He had almost made it! A minute or two more and he would be in the marshalling yards and on his way again. He took a deep breath and sprang forward. He cleared the wall easily and dropped into the pile of dirty snow on the other side, grinning happily to himself, ears full of the magic noise of the chattering, shunting trains.

Next instant he heard an angry grunt just behind him. He half-spun round. But it was already too late. The heavy, brass-bound butt of a rifle came crashing down at the back of his head and the world was disappearing in a flurry of brilliant, exploding silver and crimson stars . . .

'*Die haben ihn, Herr Kapitänleutnant!*'

The blind man's voice came over the phone in an excited whisper, as if he were covering his mouth with his hand to prevent his voice from carrying.

'What did you say?' Brandt asked, and flashed a look at the waiting crew.

Their training CPO from the good old days of the pre-war South American cruise repeated his excited news. 'They've got him, sir, the—' his voice sank even lower '—the Tommy. Found him in a knocking shop just off the main station, as you guessed they would.'

Brandt tried to keep calm, posing his next question

precisely. '*Oberkommissar* Harsch – has he seen him yet, *Obermaat*?'

'No, sir,' the blinded CPO answered smartly, obviously happy at being addressed by his old rank. 'Some dum-dum of a hairy-arsed railway cop smashed up the back of his turnip. He's still knocked out cold. Besides, Harsch is busy with a group of red commies they've discovered down at the docks. Thinks they belong to the Red Orchestra.[1] Anyway he's telling everybody that, because if they are, it'll mean promotion for him.'

'Good.' Hastily Brandt interrupted the old sailor's flow of words. Telephone messages with Lubeck's main Gestapo HQ had to be kept as short as possible; anybody might be listening in. 'Thanks for the information. I'm very pleased the damned Englishman has been recaptured. Now he will be severely punished, as is just.' He lowered his voice hastily and added, 'Sailors' Home, twelve sharp. *Auf wiederhören*'. He slammed the phone down in the cradle and faced the others. 'Well, comrades, you still have time to back out.' His hard gaze swept round the circle of their serious, set faces. 'But remember we *are* concerned here with the honour of the German Navy.' He waited a second. 'Well, are you with me?'

'We're with you, Jailer,' they declared as one.

'*Grossartig, Kameraden!*' Brandt exclaimed, unable to conceal his relief. He flashed a look at his watch. 'All right. I'm to meet the *Obermaat* in the Sailors' Rest Home near the fish dock at midday. He'll give me all the necessary info. By the looks of it they won't start giving Savage a working-over till he recovers consciousness; and as you know, that kind of dirty work normally takes place at night. Fewer witnesses that way.'

The others nodded glumly, as if they had suddenly recalled the nature of the state they served, with its loud-mouthed, jackbooted, boastful brutality.

[1] A notorious communist spy ring within Germany, mostly rounded up by mid-1942.

'All right, so that gives us time to get ourselves organized. Pox, you're in charge of the motor transport.'

The young officer nodded. 'Fancy the Admiral's Mercedes, Jailer?' he quipped.

Brandt ignored the crack. 'You, Hairless, you're in charge of all necessary documents. We all know that warm brother of a purser is devoted to you. He'll do anything for you.'

Hairless swept his hand over his gleaming bald pate and simpered in a high falsetto, 'It's my locks, you know. All those warm brothers love a chap with beautiful hair like me.'

The others laughed, and Brandt continued. 'Roof-Hare, you're with me, as we agreed. The rest will stand by.' He flashed a look at his naval chronometer. 'All right, gentlemen, Operation Tommy has officially commenced. Can I ask you to—'

'—*Circumcise* your watches!' Pox beat him to it with the hoary old pun as the others adjusted their watches to Brandt's time, and then added, with a wry look on his face, 'Heaven, arse and cloudburst, if it ever comes out that a group of German naval officers helped to kidnap a Tommy in the middle of total war, the shit will really hit the fan – fast and furious!'

Brandt reached for his cap and nodded grimly. 'Of that you can be sure, comrades,' he said, his voice hard, eyes set and unyielding. 'It'll be the camps for each and every one of us, regardless of our past service to the Reich. But I, for one, would prefer that – or even worse – rather than let the honour of our service be besmirched. *Kameraden!*' He clicked to attention and touched his good hand to his rakishly tilted cap.

Eyeing each of their young, eager faces as they snapped to attention, Brandt reflected that they were the best the New Germany could produce. If these men lost their courage and their honour, then everything else was of no importance. Without men like these, honourable, principled men, Germany did not deserve to survive.

Moments later he was hurrying down the gangplank to the shrill of the bosun's whistle into the raging snowstorm that had suddenly – providentially – descended upon Lubeck. Operation Tommy was underway.

EIGHT

Soft-footed, they padded through a thick curtain of gently falling snow. A faint yellow light at the gate of the Central Prison illuminated the police sentries, heads dug deep into their collars, carbines slung over their shoulders, hands rammed into their pockets.

Brandt winked at Roof-Hare, who was directly behind him. They could expect no trouble from the middle-aged cops; on a cold December day like this, they would be far too busy trying to keep warm.

'All right, it must be a little further on – to the right,' Brandt commanded.

Obediently the little group of naval officers spread out to search for the coke-shute their old CPO had told them about. It was left unlocked – and it led directly into the prison's cellars. Moments later they had found it and were sliding, one by one, into the grey darkness of the cellars which housed the boilers, any noise they made muffled by the sudden wail of the air-raid sirens outside. Brandt smiled grimly. So far everything was going to plan. Hairless's idea of having the Central Lubeck air-raid sirens sound was excellent; it would get people thinking about other things.

Slowly and carefully they began to file through the cellars, ducking low under the whitewashed curved ceiling, with Pox, who was nearly two metres in height, cursing.

'Shit on the shingle, I feel like the damned Count of Monte Cristo!'

'If you're not quiet,' Brandt hissed back, 'you'll probably end up *being* him!'

Now Brandt could hear the muted sound of many voices and from somewhere to the right, the crackle of a radio. He guessed that they were under the great communal cell that the *Obermaat* had told him about, where they kept the riff-raff – deserters, minor crooks, black marketeers and the like. If that was the case, Savage's cell should be to the left. He turned in that direction, threading his way through the piles of coke and the tall old-fashioned boilers.

Five minutes later they had found the stairs and had emerged into a gloomy corridor, already blacked out for the night with a snatch of yellow light coming from under a door at the far end. That would be the duty-room of the cops on guard on this floor. Everything was just as the ex-CPO had described it.

With a wave he beckoned to the others to follow him down the corridor away from the duty-room. Like shadows, they glided towards the door at the far end. Cautiously, Brandt opened it and peered outside into the white whirling world of falling snow. The courtyard was empty, hemmed in on all sides by the high walls of the cell blocks. There was no sound save the dying wail of the sirens in the far suburbs of the seaport. He grinned momentarily. There'd be a devil of a row tomorrow when the air defence authorities tried to work out who had sounded the false alarm.

'All right—' he whispered – then stopped short.

A man had emerged, shoulders bent against the flying snow, carbine slung over his back.

'A *sentry*!' Brandt hissed.

The men behind him froze. The sentry couldn't fail to see them as he came closer and closer, his heavy boots making a soft, sucking sound in the ankle-deep snow. Brandt tensed. He was almost level now. Of course, he could nobble him, but . . . He tensed for the moment of discovery, the challenge, the cry of alarm which would alert the whole prison and bring their impossible mission to a swift end.

Nothing happened.

The sentry, head bent and tucked deep into his collar, passed by a matter of metres away without even seeing them. A moment later he mounted the steps at the far end of the courtyard. A yellow knife of light slid into the night. A door squeaked. The light disappeared and the sentry was gone.

Behind Brandt, Pox whispered, '*Himmel, Arsch und Wolkenbruch!* That was close, Jailer! I can feel the hot and wet stuff trickling down my right leg at this moment.'

'You're lucky. I've had all the piss dried up in me with shock. Come on. Let's get this job over and done with.'

Swiftly, like grey ghosts, they slipped around the corner and disappeared into the snow.

Savage moaned and stirred on his narrow bunk. The hinged circlet of steel clamped to his ankle rattled and he felt pain shoot through his right leg once again. But even the agony was muted this time, vague, as if felt at a distance like everything else. He tried to open his eyes. After the third attempt he managed it and the cell swung into focus, blurred at the edges, seen as if through a wavering screen. With another moan he closed his eyes once more.

Twice now the fat civilian, who he knew instinctively to be Gestapo, had tried to beat and bully him into some semblance of consciousness, but without success. The excruciating pain at the base of his skull still outweighed that of the blows which the fat civilian had aimed at his face. But even through the fog of pain that kept him on the fringe of unconsciousness most of the time, he knew he couldn't allow them to take him back to the camp once he had recovered sufficiently to be transported. He would never go back – *never*. He would rather die.

But how?

At first he had considered starving himself to death. The food was impossible anyway. So far it had been a can of swede soup, with white maggots floating on the yellow surface, and three slices of black bread, with what appeared to be straw hanging from them. But fasting would take too long. Besides, they would force-feed him in the end. No, it had to be the other way.

By a sheer effort of will, Savage raised himself up and the room immediately whirled around his head in a grey fog. The pain in his bandaged head was hellish, but he bit his lip and continued. He clawed his fingers around the lip of the enamel piss-bucket, the cell's only item of furniture apart from the bunk, and drew it to him, the metal-ring cutting into his swollen ankle as he stretched the chain to its fullest extent. He gasped and lay back almost exhausted, waiting for the fog to clear and the cell to come back into proper focus. Then he bent over the evil-smelling, lime-encrusted pail and commenced the task he had set himself this afternoon: breaking away a fine sliver of the enamel which lay beneath the lime. Suddenly he gave vent to a chuckle of mad, slobbering ecstasy at his own cunning. He would escape them yet!

Brandt positioned himself in the centre of the courtyard, directly below the cell which he knew was Savage's. The strange bell-shaped pistol which Hairless, the gunnery officer, had found for him was clasped firmly in his good hand. Behind him, the others crouched in the falling snow tensely, all save Roof-Hare, who had now changed his boots for rope-soled rubber shoes and was now pulling on fine black silk gloves.

'Ready?' Brandt whispered.

'Ready,' Roof-Hare whispered back.

'Here we go!' Brandt pressed the trigger. There was a soft whoosh, and the four-pronged grapnel at the end of the barrel flew upwards in a strange wobbling flight, dragging loop after loop of fine rope behind it. There was a sound of metal striking metal. All the watchers froze. Surely someone must have heard the sound? But all was silence. Brandt breathed out hard and then, handing the pistol to one of the others, hastily pulled the rope hard. It held. The grapnel had caught between the bars.

'All right, Roof-Hare, it's up to you now. But make it as quick as you can!'

'Ay, ay, Cap'n,' Roof-Hare answered, with more confidence than he felt. Grabbing the rope, he reached up, placed his feet against the sheer wall and walked upwards into the night almost effortlessly.

Roof-Hare came level with the barred window. The cell was already blacked out, so he couldn't see inside. But the Tommy was awake – and apparently not alarmed by the sound of something striking his window; for as Roof-Hare hung there by the thin rope, he could hear a strange scratching noise accompanied by chuckling and curses coming from within. He dismissed the sounds and got down to the job. Hastily he roped himself in a sitting position to the lower part of the barred grating, which was exactly as the CPO had described it: a ready-cast barred grating, anchored into the concrete of the wall by two iron brackets. Once those were disposed of, the whole grating would come away. He took out the bottle which he had carried up the wall in his trouser pocket and gingerly uncorked it. Choking fumes came from it, and he turned his head away hastily, biting his bottom lip to prevent himself from coughing. With his free hand, he poured half the contents of the bottle on the one bracket and the remainder on the other. The metal sizzled and hissed, and little clouds of smoke rose into the air. Roof-Hare, hanging there in the rope-sling, closed his eyes to stop himself from being blinded with tears, counting off the seconds the acid would need to eat through the metal as he did so.

'. . . *one hundred!*' He opened his eyes. The acid had ceased to bubble and hiss. His heart leapt. In both cases the brackets had been neatly eaten through. He seized the middle of the grating and heaved. Nothing happened. He exerted more strength. The grating gave. He pushed once more and the whole structure fell against the window.

'Ahoy down there!' he called softly, and then, grabbing the grating, tossed it to the snow below.

Two minutes later he had opened the catch of the window with his knife and was peering in. An emaciated man lay below, head swathed in bandages, muttering crazily to himself, bent over the piss-bucket and completely unaware of the stranger as he worked away at his self-imposed task.

'Savage – Lieutenant Savage,' Roof-Hare whispered softly. '*Lieutenant Savage, Royal Navy . . .*'

Slowly the man lying on the bunk raised his head out of the piss-bucket, blood dripping from his fingers where he had torn them on the sharp enamel, eyes bulging crazily out of his starved visage. 'Who are . . . are you?' he choked, staring up at the stranger at the window.

'Don't ask questions, Savage. All you need to know is that I'm here to help,' Roof-Hare said in his strange English. 'Can you get up, please?'

'Yes, but there is this.' Savage raised his leg and the chain rattled alarmingly.

'*Scheisse! Das auch noch!*' Roof-Hare cursed, seeing the steel ankle circlet for the first time. 'All right, no problems . . . I fix.'

He dropped lightly to the floor, flashing a quick look at the judas hole as he did so, but the peephole was closed. 'The guards – when do they come?' he asked, examining the mounting of the chain.

'Irregular,' Savage gasped, trying to make his eyes focus correctly on this stranger, who wavered back and forth like some creature seen at the bottom of the sea.

'Then warn me, if you hear a sound. Clear?'

'Clear.'

Now Roof-Hare, knowing that every minute was precious, began to scrape at the concrete around the mounting of the chain, the sweat pouring down his face as he did so. Below they would be wondering what in three devils' name was taking him so long. Soon, inevitably, someone would spot them out there in the yard. He had to free the Englishman within minutes, or all would be lost.

Five minutes passed. He had scraped a hole several millimetres deep around the anchorage of the chain. He dropped his knife and hissed. 'Savage, help.'

'Help?'

'Yes, help to pull. Now . . . one, two, *three*!' Assisted as best he could by the man lying on the bunk, Roof-Hare exerted all his strength, the veins standing out at his temples with the effort. Nothing happened. The chain remained firmly, stubbornly, embedded in the wall.

'*Ach, du grosser Gott!*' he swore fervently, and grabbed his knife again.

Five minutes went by. Ten. Now Roof-Hare was lathered in sweat. Twice in his nervous haste, he had slashed his hands, but in spite of the blood dripping from his knuckles, he laboured on furiously, knowing time was running out – and fast.

Yet another five minutes passed in frantic-fingered, furious haste. Now Roof-Hare's eyebrows glittered with pearls of sweat. With his every move he splattered gobs of blood everywhere. From far down the corridor there came the clatter of tins. Without ceasing his frenzied efforts to free the Englishman, he hissed, 'What's the noise?'

'It'll be the evening soup,' Savage answered weakly. 'They usually dish it out about now.'

'Do they open the door?'

'No, not normally. They push it through the trap in the bottom of the door.'

'But they do look in through the thing?'

'Yes, they check me.'

Roof-Hare dropped his knife. 'Come on, we've got to make it this time.' He seized the chain, with Savage aiding him as best he could in his weakened condition, and heaved furiously, cursing angrily to himself. Again nothing, save for a small trickle of concrete dust. Roof-Hare swore and then took the strain again, with his feet pressed hard against the wall on both sides of the socket, eyes bulging, red-hot pincers nipping at his shoulder muscles as he tugged and tugged.

There was a faint crumbling noise. He increased his effort. The rattle of the tins was drawing closer. He could hear the trusties talking to each other quite plainly and the command at each cell door given in a harsh official voice. '*Los . . . Essenfassen!*'

The crumbling noise grew louder. The chain-ring was starting to give. He pulled harder. The men with the soup were nextdoor now. He had seconds left. Roof-Hare gave one last mighty tug, flying backwards as the chain gave and falling against the concrete floor – hard. Then he was scrambling furiously under the bunk, while Savage attempted to arrange his blanket over the severed chain.

Lying there, crouched under the bunk, hardly daring to breathe, Roof-Hare heard the click of the judas-hole cover being slipped to one side, and the harsh grunt of the Gestapo guard spying through it. Next moment, the bottom flap of the door was open and his nostrils were assailed by the smell of pea soup. He lay absolutely still, knowing that this was it. If he were found *now*, it would be the camps for him and all the rest of them. But nothing happened. The tin was shoved across the floor with a long wooden spoon and one of the trusties said coarsely, in the thick German of the Waterfront, 'Mind you don't mix it up with the piss-bucket, Englishman. Not that it would make much difference.' His companion laughed and they passed on.

Roof-Hare gave a great sigh of relief and simply lay there for a moment, completely unable to move . . .

The thin blue light of the blacked-out car headlights swept round the corner of the quay and momentarily illuminated the great yellow and blue flag that adorned the freighter's side, together with the word '*Sweden*' painted in bold white letters. The driver braked, and at the gangplank the armed naval sentry snapped to attention as he saw a tall, erect figure in an admiral's uniform emerge from the car.

The Admiral acknowledged the sentry's salute with a casual, if curiously stiff gesture of his gloved hand. 'Nasty night to be on duty, sentry,' he said, tendering his papers, as the sentry switched on the little lamp attached to his greatcoat.

Behind him the driver and another officer were helping a civilian, muffled to the eyes in thick scarves, out of the car.

'We've come to see Captain Larsen, sentry,' the Admiral said, following the direction of the sailor's gaze. 'My driver has got the papers of Director Diersken. He doesn't feel at all well, as you can see, but Schnapps is Schnapps and duty is duty, as they say – and he has to sail for Sweden tonight, come what may.'

'Yessir,' the sentry answered automatically, a little awed by this visit from such a high-ranking naval man so late at night. 'The *Gripsholm* sails within the hour.'

'Yes, I know. And I expect you'll be glad to get inside out of this snow and pour a nice stiff hot grog down inside your collar, what?' the Admiral said heartily.

'Yessir,' the sentry said, making only a half-hearted examination of the Director's papers. He had never spoken to an admiral before; it was all rather overwhelming.

Captain Larsen, a middle-aged Swede with the thick-nosed, bloated look of a Swedish seaman addicted to alcohol, was waiting for the party in the shelter of the bulkhead.

Money changed hands rapidly, while the Admiral carefully kept his back to the sentry down below. 'When do you think you'll arrive at Bornholm, skipper?'

Larsen shrugged. 'Too soon for me, *Herr Admiral*. The

island's as dry as an old maid's you-know-what. Late tomorrow afternoon, I expect.'

The Admiral chuckled. 'Next time you're in Lubeck I'll buy you a bottle of *Korn*.' Then he was serious again. 'All right, see he's well looked after, and as soon as you reach the island, contact the British Consul there. He'll notify the appropriate authorities. They'll be waiting for you – and remember, Larsen—' there was iron in the Admiral's voice '—my people will know whether he's arrived in Sweden or not – so no chucking him overboard once you're at sea.'

The Swedish captain started to bluster, but the Admiral cut him short. 'You've nothing to be afraid of. His papers are perfectly in order. I signed them myself. If you *are* stopped by a German naval vessel, you will see that.'

'Naturally, naturally,' Larsen agreed. 'I know everything is perfectly in order, sir.' He looked at the civilian's ashen, pain-twisted face and bit his bottom lip. For the first time he realized that he had allowed himself to be bribed into a very tricky situation – and that it was too late to back out now.

'Leave us now, Larsen, please,' the Admiral snapped. 'I just want a few last words with *Herr Direktor* Krause before you sail.'

The Swedish skipper moved up to the bridge and they could hear him above them, greedily taking a large swallow of the last of his gin, while up on the bows the deckmen started to make preparations for casting off.

'Well, Savage,' Brandt said, keeping his voice very low, but speaking slowly so that the half-conscious fugitive could understand him. 'We've got you out and I think the rest should be fairly plain sailing.'

Savage stared up at the taller German through half-closed eyes. 'But why, *Herr Kommandant*? Why?' he whispered huskily.

Brandt gave him a soft smile. 'It's something you don't need to know, Savage. Let us say that it concerns the honour of the German Navy.'

Below, the engine telegraphs began to jingle and there could be heard the first throaty coughing and spluttering of the old tub's motors starting up.

Brandt touched his gloved hand to his cap in a last salute. 'Well, Savage, you're almost on your way. It's taken you two years, but you've finally managed it – with a little help of course.' He smiled faintly at the other man. 'I hope it's been all worth it?'

'It has . . . it certainly has.' Savage tried to reply with a trace of his old energy, but the effort was too much for him and only the quick action of the driver saved him from collapsing against the bulkhead.

The Swedish freighter's engines now thundered into life. Seamen were running up and down the deck, casting off lines. Out on the seamole, the green lights began to flash off and on – the signal that the harbour-master was opening the anti-submarine nets to let the *Gripsholm* out.

Brandt took a last look at his former prisoner and said softly, 'Well, I doubt we'll ever meet again. So I'll wish you all the best – and a long life. Goodbye.'

'Thank you, *Herr Kommandant*,' Savage said weakly, leaning against the vibrating steel plating. 'Goodbye . . . and a long life to you too, sir.'

But Brandt and his party were already clattering down the gangway to the snow-covered dock below, leaving Savage to stare dully at the broad back of his friend-foe, the man he would one day kill.

TWO: HELL BELOW ZERO

ONE

'*Here come the sods again!*' an excited voice yelled across the dock. '*Off the port bow . . . ten of 'em!*'

Everywhere, the off-duty ratings flung themselves behind the gantries and stores piled high on all sides, ripping off their caps and pulling on their helmets, while the gun-crews made a dash for their pom-poms and machine-guns. Across in the shattered smoking city, the sirens started to sound for the third time this Spring day, and alarm bells shrilled from ship to ship.

The German bombers were coming in in their usual formation, the slow-moving Heinkels high in the sky, attempting to attract most of the port's anti-aircraft fire, while out to the east the antiquated Stukas came lumbering in, an easy target for the flak; but behind them, fast Focke-Wulfs and Messerschmitt dive-bombers came racing in almost at ground-level, hoping to catch the fat, juicy merchantmen which crowded the port while the gunners concentrated on the easier targets.

The first Stuka hovered over the crowded estuary, packed with laden merchantmen. For one long moment he hung there like a sinister metal hawk. Then, with frightening suddenness, it flung itself out of the smoke-pocked sky, sirens screaming, engine howling, and came hurtling down, shells exploding in furious puffs of dark smoke on both sides of it. Just when it seemed it must smack right into the estuary, the pilot hit the air-brakes. It staggered visibly. A profusion of evil little black bombs tumbled from its ugly belly, and then it was screaming upwards again, pursued by an urgent white morse of tracer bullets. Below, the bombs exploded to left and right of a fat freighter, its decks laden with tanks, sending it reeling like a toy ship as the sheets of whirling white water raced hundreds of feet into the sky.

Now the whole weight of the Stuka attack descended upon the port. The morning was hideous with the howl of their sirens and air-brakes, the *thud-thud* of the flak, the hectic chatter of the machine-guns, the crump of the bombs. A stricken Stuka, its pilot blinded by escaping glycol, plummeted straight into the sea. Another, roaring in at 300mph, trailing thick smoke behind it, smacked into the side of a merchantman and exploded there in a blinding flash of angry red flame. The first freighter was struck. A supplementary oil tank on her crowded deck ignited under the impact. A gigantic torch of roaring flame a hundred foot long swept all before it on her deck, turning all on board into shrunken, charred pygmies within seconds. A final Stuka was hit. Great chunks of metal flew from the diving plane as the pilot pressed home his attack. Suddenly its right wing broke off and it fluttered slowly round and round down to the sea like a great black metal leaf. The Stuka, for its part, roared in low, slammed into the side of the sea-wall and crumpled there like a banana skin.

Now the Messerschmitts and the Focke-Wulfs, radial engines roaring, came racing in at mast-top height, machine-guns and cannons blazing, the tracer from below ripping into their sides as they pressed home their attack with reckless bravery. A blinding flash of scarlet light. A tanker had been hit. Almost immediately it was on fire from end to end, its panic-stricken crew flinging themselves into the boiling white water, the flames already leaping up their contorted bodies. A Focke-Wulf went down, flame streaming from its tail. Another was hit. The pilot baled out, but at that height, his parachute never had time to open. Like a black ball he hurtled through the air, turning round and round, to smack right into the side of a Destroyer and disintegrate like a pulpy, overripe scarlet fig.

In an instant the world went crazy, as the gunners fought back, pom-poms chattering furiously, machine-guns slamming tracer at two hundred rounds a minute at the evil black raiders, their engines howling madly as they twisted and contorted devilishly in a desperate bid to get at the merchantmen. Another fighter-bomber was hit. It staggered visibly in mid-air, then exploded in a great rending ball of fire. A long Norwegian freighter was hit. It started to sink, oil spreading from its holed tanks. Next instant the oil caught fire, racing after the swimming men with greedy fingers of fire and sending a huge column of smoke billowing into the sky. The freighter broke in half, its two gigantic parts rearing upwards into the air, scattering crewmen into the boiling water like pitiful insects. Next instant they both disappeared below the surface of the estuary, with huge, obscene bubbles of air exploding after them.

A minute later it was all over. High above, sinister black shapes, the Heinkels dropped their deadly load, out of range of the ack-ack, with the surviving fighter-bombers racing back towards the east, leaving the port to lick its wounds yet again.

Lieutenant-Commander Savage DSC breathed out hard, and trying to forget the nervous tic at the side of his lean, hard face – something that had plagued him ever since Lubeck – he replaced his helmet with his jaunty new white cap. All around him in the forecourt of Paragon Street Station, civilians and sailors were rising to their feet or hurrying up from the air-raid shelters in the public lavatories to stare awe-struck at the plumes of dark smoke now rising from the docks.

Already the first ambulances were racing by towards the port, bells jingling. A fire-engine rattled up, the men still pulling on their old-fashioned pre-war brass helmets, the furiously sweating driver still in his undershirt. Wardens rode by on their bikes, whirling their rattles, and on the traffic cop's dais opposite the station an elderly special constable cupped his hands to his mouth and shouted 'All clear . . . it's all clear . . . But you sailormen, don't go down George Street; there are unexploded bombs down there . . . All clear!'

After dusting himself down, Savage merged with the crowds of civilians and sailors leaving the station. In this Spring of 1943, England was in every bit as bad shape as Goebbels' propaganda back in Nazi Germany had made it out to be. In spite of the recent victories at El Alamein and Stalingrad, the island was still under siege, its population battered, grey and despondent. He stopped at the bus stop. But it was crowded with pale-faced sailors, kitbags slung over their shoulders, artificial silk scarves knotted around their open necks, caps pushed at non-regulation angles to the back of their heads. Obviously they were leavemen, returning to their ships and going the same way as he was.

'Going to naval HQ, sir?' a flat East Coast voice queried.

Savage swung round. It was an elderly man driving a battered 1936 Morris with 'Taxi' painted in white across the bonnet.

'We're going that way, mate!' a couple of sailors yelled from the bus queue, but the driver waved the disgruntled sailors away with a grunt. 'The officer saw me first.'

He winked as Savage entered the cramped rear, pushing his case in front of him. 'Lousy tippers, them matelots, when they've just come back off leave. Broke to the wide, most of them are. Don't blame them, though, when you think where they're going.'

Savage settled back in the cracked old leather upholstery as the driver engaged first gear and they moved slowly forward, nosing their way through the crowd that was still pouring out of the station from the London train.

'Where are they going, driver?' he asked without too much interest.

The driver winked at him in the mirror. 'Same place you are, I 'spect, sir. The Murmansk run.'

'Murmansk run?' Savage frowned. 'Is it that obvious? Security must be lousy here at Hull.'

'Not really, sir,' the driver answered, expertly driving round a sandbagged First Aid post into which stretcher-bearers were hurrying with their moaning, groaning bloody bundles of human misery. 'Ever since the Russkis came in, that's all we've been doing from Hull – running convoys of supplies to Murmansk. That's what all that shindig was about just now. The third bloody air-raid in one day.' He shook his grey head. 'Poor old Hull. It's taken some stick since 1941, ever since it became the main supply port for Russia. A lot of good Hull lads have gone for a Burton up there off Bear Island – ay, that they have!'

Savage forgot the driver and gazed out at the scenes of chaos and destruction. All around lay fresh piles of smoking débris and great brown holes that could have been the work of some gigantic mole, where sappers were already at work trying to get at the delayed action bombs that lay buried there, before they exploded and destroyed what was left of the ruined city centre.

For what it was worth, the King had received him very graciously at the Palace. Indeed, after the presentation of his medal, the poor, frail, stuttering monarch dressed in the uniform of Admiral of the Fleet had talked to him personally about his amazing escape from Germany. Apparently he was only the second naval officer in three years to succeed in pulling it off. The gentlemen of the Admiralty, however, hadn't been so gracious. In Room 39,[1] they had been very pleased with his information on the *Deutschland*, but Personnel had been hard and direct. They had laid it on the line, informing him in no uncertain manner that he would have been court-martialled for the events of St Valéry had it not been for his escape and his gong.

The medics hadn't been very helpful either. MacGregor, the chief surgeon, had passed him fit for sea-duty

[1] Room which housed naval intelligence at the Admiralty in WWII.

only after long consideration. Indeed, he had called him back to Whitehall to inform him personally that he was doing so only under duress and pressure from the Palace. 'The King has taken a shine to you, laddie,' he had said in his soft Scots burr, his keen eyes never leaving Savage's lean, dark face. 'But I dinna know whether their Lordships are doing the right thing by letting ye go back to sea.' He stroked his long chin thoughtfully. 'You've been through a lot, ye ken, and it's left its mark.' For a moment he eyed Savage's nervous tic and dark, haunted eyes. 'I'm not one to take much heed of those trick-cyclist fellers from Vienna, mon. But . . .'

With that, he had shaken his head and left the rest unsaid.

'We're there, sir,' the driver's voice broke into Savage's reverie, cutting short that parting phrase about the 'trick-cyclist fellers from Vienna', which still plagued him.

Looking out of the window, which was criss-crossed with brown sticky paper against the blast, he saw the sand-bagged eighteenth-century structure with smart, helmeted bluejackets outside, bayonets fixed – and felt a sudden sense of relief. After more than two years out of action, he was back. Before this day was over he would be feeling the roll of a ship's deck under his feet again and the salt breeze on his cheeks; he had his active command at last. The war wasn't nearly over yet. Glory and fame could still be his.

'That'll be one and a tanner, sir,' the cabbie said.

Suddenly, flushed and excited, Savage pulled out a brown ten shilling note and thrust it into the driver's hand.

'Here,' he said with new exuberance, 'keep the change.' And with that he was bounding up the stairs, two at a time, leaving the driver to stare down open-mouthed at the tremendous tip, before whispering to himself, in the manner of the canny East Coaster that he was, 'Puir feller – he must be barmy . . .!'

The Flag-Officer-in-Charge, Hull, stood with his back to the door, staring intently across the estuary and its burning ships, as the Wren officer ushered Savage in. The pretty Wren with the too-short skirt nodded and he clicked to attention.

'Savage, sir,' he barked, cap under his right arm as regulations prescribed. 'Lieutenant Commander Savage!'

Slowly the heavy-set Admiral at the window turned – and Savage caught himself from giving a gasp of shocked surprise just in time. It was his old flotilla-commander of 1940, MacIntyre, white at the temples now and with two deep lines of worry etched down the side of his mouth.

MacIntyre caught the look. 'Ay Rodney, you're not seeing ghosts – or perhaps ye are in a way. It's me all right.' He stuck out his hand. Dazed, Savage took it and shook it, but there was no warmth in their greeting; they had both been through too much in these last two terrible years for that kind of emotionalism. Friends died and you got hurt; it was better to stay just acquaintances. You saved a lot of heart-ache that way.

The Admiral gestured to Savage to sit down, though he remained standing. 'Well, Rodney, I asked for you to come up here to the arsehole of the world after most other people turned you down because of your record in 'forty.' He raised his hand. 'No – don't thank me. This might be the worst posting you've ever had. In fact, it might well be your last.'

He let the words sink in, while outside on the mole the survivors from the Norwegian freighter were carried to the waiting ambulances, most of them terribly burnt, with their skin hanging from their charred bodies in long, dripping scarlet threads. Over the Admiral's shoulder Savage could see a blinded man, his face horribly charred, being led down the gangplank by a nurse.

'I suppose you know what starts here, Rodney,' MacIntyre continued. 'Churchill's called it the "worst voyage in the world", and he's right. The lads have another name for it. Hell below zero! And they're right, too. If the

Jerries don't get them up there off Bear Island and in the Barents Sea, then ice and devilish cold do. I've survived it twice myself, laddie, just as an observer; but I swear to you—' there was real emotion in the old sailor's face now '—I won't do it again! The metal rips the flesh off a man's hand in seconds if he's daft enough to touch a bulkhead or gun without gloves on. If you're torpedoed, you ain't got a chance in those waters. You're frozen to death within minutes. Just standing lookout up there is an ordeal in itself. When you come off-duty, your face looks like underdone steak in that hellish wind.' He breathed out hard. 'So don't thank me for what I'm sending you to.'

'What's the assignment, sir?' Savage asked, trying to change the subject, eager to know at long last what they had given him.

'Well, you've got a ship, Savage, as you already know. But it's a damned old bucket. One of the surviving four-funnel jobs the Yanks gave Churchill back in 'forty in return for their bases in the Bermudas. Slow as hell and armour like tissue paper. But ships are expendable on the Murmansk run, so their Lordships don't want to waste their best craft supplying the Bolshies. Oh, and a word of warning at this point, Rodney. You've made some powerful enemies in Whitehall, due to what happened in 'forty and the way His Majesty has taken you up. So none of the Nelson blind-eye bit this time, eh? Obey orders implicitly, or otherwise you're out on your ear. Got it, Rodney?'

'Got it, sir.'

'Right. Now let me give you a quick briefing before you meet Jenkins, the Convoy Commodore.'

Savage's heart sank. 'Convoy work, sir?' he asked in a desperate voice. 'I thought their Lordships had assigned me to the Destroyer flotilla as an independent command?'

'Well, Rodney, you thought wrong. For the next couple of months you're going to act as a very tame sheepdog. As I said, you have powerful enemies and they're not going to give you the chance of getting another good gong like that one.' He indicated the bright new ribbon of the DSC on Savage's tunic. 'I ain't got *that* one myself, you know – and I'm an admiral.' He grinned at the younger man, but Savage didn't respond; after all, there was precious little glory to be won shepherding a lot of slow-moving freighters to Russia. 'You sail with Convoy PQ 18 this late afternoon on the tide. This time, in order to avoid losses, we're going to sail up the coast under the cover of our own air and rendezvous with some Yank freighters bringing tanks from Boston at Hvalfiord.'

'Iceland?'

'Yes, Iceland. It's a new trick the smart lads of Room 39 have worked out. Instead of running the gauntlet of Jerry air from the fields in Norway, we try to outsmart them by going to Iceland first and then making the run for Bear Island and the Barents.' He shrugged. 'Naval Intelligence say it'll work, but I have my doubts. Old Jerry'll be on to you soon enough, once you've left the air cover of our own island.'

'So there'll be action, sir?' Savage said, cheering up.

'Oh yes, there'll be more than enough action for you, laddie.' Rear-Admiral MacIntyre bit his bottom lip, a worried look on his face. 'You'll not only have the usual stuff to contend with – the German Fifth Air Fleet in Norway, Doenitz's subs[1] – there's also the *Deutschland*.'

'But I reported the *Deutschland* in Wilhelmshaven, sir,' Savage objected.

'I know, my boy, and a very useful piece of intelligence it was. As a result, the Brylcreem boys kept a constant recce patrol over the harbour all last month. One night, though, she just slipped anchor and off she went into the unknown. Coastal Command completely fell down on the job, as usual. They did a twenty-four hour search, but they missed her. So where could she be? Don't attempt to answer, Rodney.' He held up a hand. 'I'll tell you. It's vital for the Jerries to stop the Bolshies receiving war

[1] Doenitz was head of the German submarine service.

supplies from us and the Yanks. After all, it's in Russia that the land war is being decided. So why waste the *Deutschland* in the Atlantic, cruising around looking for targets? All she has to do is to make a quick dash into the North Atlantic, beat up the Murmansk convoy and then scuttle off back home before our Home Fleet can react.'

'So, she's somewhere in Norway then, sir?'

'Exactly Rodney. Narvik, or more probably Bergen, with her steam up, waiting like a greedy spider for the poor little flies to come crawling into her web.'

Savage forced a smile. 'Not a very inviting prospect, sir.'

Outside they had cleared away most of the casualties now, and a rating, cap at the back of his head, cigarette hanging out of the corner of his mouth, was hosing down the blood-stained jetty, as if it was all in a day's work. With his gum-booted right foot MacIntyre saw him kick what looked like a severed arm into the débris-littered water of the harbour. The Admiral looked away hastily.

'No, it isn't, Rodney. On this one the balloon is really going to go up. I can feel it in my bones. All right, I expect you'll want to see your new command.' He thrust out his big hand, gnarled with old rope cuts around the knuckles from his days as a cadet. 'Best of luck, my boy. Remember: obey orders this time and . . .' His voice softened and the hard, tense look vanished from his face for an instant. '. . . And don't take any chances.'

But even as he said the words, Rear-Admiral MacIntyre knew that the lean young man with the dark, restless, ambitious eyes wasn't listening to his warnings. He wouldn't see Rodney Savage again.

TWO

'*I've got spurs that jingle-jangle-jingle*,' sang the gunner at the 'hot potato cart' with monotonous regularity, as, in common with the rest of the crew, he watched the four-engined German reconnaissance plane make yet another turn about the convoy stretched over ten square miles of the North Sea.

Already Commodore Jenkins – something of a humorist, it appeared – had signalled to their shadow in German, 'Can't you fly round in a different direction, *please*? You're making us dizzy.' The German had signalled back '*Goetz von Berlichingen*', which had puzzled them all, until one of the German-speaking Norwegian captains had translated the phrase for them. It meant crudely, 'Kiss my arse!'

So the German circled them yet again, as the long, grey afternoon dragged on. So far, the 'hot potato cart' had only been used to shoot hot potatoes from one ship to another; but it was intended as a home-made anti-aircraft device, firing hand-grenades soldered inside a tin can at low-flying aircraft.

Savage lowered his glasses and, blowing on his frozen fingers, turned to Rogers, his Number One, a wartime volunteer for the 'wavy navy', as the Royal Naval Voluntary Reserve was called contemptuously by the regulars. It was said that the full extent of Rogers' sea-faring experience before joining up was some 'mucking about in boats' on the Solent before the war.

'Just going down to the ward-room for a cup of coffee, Number One.'

'Ay, ay, sir.' Rogers, a fair-haired, freckled-faced

youngster seemed confident enough, but his eyes showed otherwise.

Savage clattered down the steps, already beginning to go white and furry with hoar-frost. In spite of the fact that it was already April, the air was freezing and snow flurries were expected later in the day.

Savage's keen gaze took in his guns and their gunners, muffled up to the eyes in their heavy khaki duffle-coats and stamping their feet as they watched and waited. There were two 20*mm* Oerlikons on the bridge wings, twin Browning machine-guns behind them, and two batteries of PAC rockets which fired wires high into the air to entangle dive-bombers. 'All right on sodding sparrers,' his gunners usually quipped, when questioned about their efficiency; '– *weak 'uns.*' But the matelots manning them were alert enough, as were the gunners in the 5-inch gun turrets fore and aft.

He gave a thin smile as he entered the warmth of the ward-room and threw his cap on the battered leather sofa. Yes, the crew of HMS *Ypres* – 'Wipers', to the matelots – were as rough and ready as the old ex-American Destroyer herself; but they were keen and alert and experienced. He accepted the steaming cup of coffee from the steward Higgins, who wore his life-jacket even when he slept, and buried his frozen nose in its warmth to thaw it out. They'd need to be tough – all of them. For the journey in front of the convoy was long and arduous.

'. . . Once we reach Iceland, gentlemen,' Jenkins, the Convoy Commodore, had told the assembled captains in his own ward-room the day before, 'we'll follow the same tactics as previous convoys. The merchantmen, together with the minesweepers and trawlers, will sail up Iceland's west coast and turn north-east, where we'll be rejoined by you gentlemen of the destroyers, sailing up from Seydisfiord.' He nodded to the younger, slimmer destroyer captains, who sat in a group a little apart from the merchant skippers and those of the 'wavy navy'. 'Thereafter we commence the long haul past Bear Island into the Barents Sea.' Jenkins sucked his teeth, as if not quite sure how to phrase the next part of his briefing. 'A shadowing force of US and British cruisers from the Home Fleet will be aft of us there; but on no account will they sail further than Bear Island or the longitude of North Cape. From there, you destroyers will take over the main protection of the convoy again, plus any help the Russians might be inclined to give us.'

'If it's like the last Murmansk run I did,' one of the merchant skippers growled over his rum, 'it'll be "B" for Bugger All!'

They all laughed, until one of the destroyer captains asked, 'But why the shadowing force? What are *they* expecting?'

Jenkins had lowered his gaze, as if suddenly embarrassed, and had dodged the question, finishing with a gruff, 'Let's worry about getting to Iceland first.'

For a moment Savage sipped his coffee thoughtfully, unable to put his finger on it, yet knowing instinctively that something was going on. He had known it ever since Hull. It had something to do with the *Deutschland*, but what it was he didn't know . . .

He dismissed the worrying thoughts and concentrated on the task in hand. Within twelve hours they would be leaving the protection of the land-based planes. From then onwards until they reached Iceland, they would have to depend upon their own Sea-Hurricanes, fighters designed to be catapulted from the deck of a freighter, fight for five minutes or so and then crash-land into the sea, where, with a great deal of luck, another ship might winch them up before the freezing water claimed both the plane and pilot. As Commodore Jenkins had aptly said at the briefing, 'Let's worry about getting to Iceland first.'

Suddenly up above the alarm bells started to jingle furiously. Heavy, nail-studded sea-boots clattered down the companionways. Abruptly everything was noise, shouts, cries, orders.

Savage slammed down his cup. Across in the little galley, Higgins took out the false teeth he was so proud of, placed them inside the protection of his steel helmet, and thrust it on his bald head. 'Jerries!' he gasped, 'Here they come again, sir!'

Half a mile away, three V's of Junkers 88 dive-bombers were racing in in attack formation, spreading out to left and right as the flak opened up, looking for a quick, soft target. Weaving from side to side now, not more than a hundred feet above the water, they raced in, red-nosed and terrifying, at 300mph. Black eggs began to tumble from their yellow-painted, shark-like bellies. On all sides, great pillars of white, furious water erupted. In an instant the grey sky was peppered with black smoke, the air a crazy mess of exploding shells and streaking, zig-zagging tracer.

With an ear-splitting roar the bombers swept over the *Ypres*, her machine-guns and Oerlikons pounding away madly. The 'potato cart' boomed. A tin sailed upwards, whirling furiously. The grenade it contained exploded in a flash of scarlet. Right at the end of the flying V, one of the Junkers staggered. Small lumps of metal flew from its port engine. The prop feathered at once and almost unbelievably – at least to a staring, open-mouthed Savage – the Junkers 88 started to lose height, smoke streaming from her crippled engine as her companions zoomed high into the air and away for another round of tip-and-run.

With a tremendous crash the Junkers hit the water, its nose-turret splintering into a gleaming spider's web of shattered perspex. For a moment the plane rested there in the trough. A heavily-clad aircrew member clambered out of the wreck, hands raised above his head. A machine-gun chattered on the *Ypres*. The man screamed thinly, clawed at the air as if climbing the rungs of an invisible ladder. Slowly he sank to the deck of the plane and went down with it. There were no other survivors.

'*Hurrah! Hurrah!*' The shouts of triumph ran the whole length of the deck, as one by one the guns stopped firing and the gunners pushed back their helmets, faces gleaming with sweat in spite of the cold.

Savage swung round excitedly on Higgins, who had followed him out of the ward-room. 'We've got her, Stripey!' he yelled excitedly. 'The old Wipers has been blooded—'

He stopped short. Higgins hung by the handle of the ward-room door, bald head almost touching the deck, his life-jacket stained scarlet; the only sound he made was the steady *drip-drip* of his own blood to the dirty wood below, where his false teeth rested mockingly. HMS *Ypres* had had her first kill under the command of Lt Commander Rodney Savage. She had also suffered her first death.

It wouldn't be her last.

'That Yank's as pissed as a sodding newt!' Petty Officer Bolton said contemptuously, as the boarding party clambered up over the side of the stricken American Liberty ship.

'Be quiet, Bolton,' Rogers said, with more authority than he felt, as he fought his way up the sloping deck, which was littered with the débris of battle, bodies and the smashed American tanks that had once been the deck cargo.

It was their third day out of Hull, and this was the first casualty among their charges, the 10,000-ton *American Minuteman*, torpedoed by a hit-and-run Arado torpedo-bomber just after dawn. Now, while the rest of the cowed convoy sailed on into the Atlantic, HMS *Ypres* stood by while a decision was made about the fate of the US ship.

As Rogers advanced on the obviously drunken American captain, he couldn't see much hope for the Liberty ship. In addition, he knew Commander Savage was fuming at the delay caused by the torpedoed ship. That strange tic at the side of his dark face had become more noticeable now; in fact, his impatience bordered on—

Rogers cut short that particular thought. But there *was* something strange and very frightening about his new skipper.

Walking up to the American skipper, Rogers touched his hand to his cap in salute. 'My Captain's compliments, sir. He requests a brief statement of your situation.'

The bear-like, unshaven American touched the bottle of bourbon to his bare head by way of response. 'Shitty, sonny boy, decidedly shitty . . . Come and have a look-see.'

So saying, he grabbed the red-faced officer's arm and led him midships, the pair of them fighting their way as if up a hill, stepping over the débris and trying to avoid the lines where the panic-stricken crew had cast off the boats an hour or so ago.

They passed the galley. Floating in the confused mess of loaves of bread, great cans of strawberry jam and hamburger patties ready for frying, the cook bellied back and forth, held afloat by his life-belt, not a blemish on him, save that the whole of his bottom half had been separated from his trunk by the explosion and now hung, straddle-legged from the light fitting, like a monstrous salami sausage.

Rogers gasped, and the Captain laughed coarsely. 'Some cook. That guy could even burn S-on-S.'

'S-on-S?'

'Yes, shit on shingle. Chipped beef on toast to you.' Again he laughed and took a swig from the bottle he held clenched in his ham-like fist.

They struggled on, coming ever closer to the source of the huge cloud of smoke that rose hundreds of feet into the sky aft. They stopped at the edge of the nearest hold. It was open, with giant air bubbles gouting to the surface of the water which had poured in through the freighter's holed side.

The Lieutenant peered down in surprise and flashed his torch from one side of the moving green water to the other. Apart from the odd flotsam and jetsam to be found in any hold, it was empty. 'That's funny,' he exclaimed, forgetting his mission for a moment.

'What's funny, son?'

'Your hold is empty.'

'Yeah. They're all empty except for ballast.'

Rogers straightened up and stared at him in bewilderment. 'But why load your deck with all those tanks when you had all that space below decks?'

The drunken American shrugged easily. 'Search me, sonny. I just carry out orders. That was my manifest in Boston; the rest is the owner's problem and the Department of Defense's.'

Remembering Commander Savage's impatience, Rogers dismissed the strange business. 'Well, Captain, it looks bad, doesn't it?'

'It might look bad, but it ain't *that* bad,' the American answered surprisingly enough.

Rogers flushed again; it was something he was always doing when in the company of women, matelots and superior officers, and it always annoyed him. 'I don't follow you,' he said.

'Then I'll spell it out for you, sonny. Okay – we've been hit by a torpedo; but the hole is just *above* the waterline. If I could get that yellow-bellied crew of slobs back over here, we could work in a patch toot-sweet, pump her out with the pumps and then you could give us a tow to Iceland. Now,' he stared triumphantly at the young officer, eyes red with booze and strain, 'how do you like that, eh?'

'Well, Captain, I don't know.' Rogers hesitated. Over on the *Ypres*, which could be seen some way off, riding up and down on the green swell, the Aldis lamp was beginning to flash on and off. He turned to Bolton, who was a signaller. 'Read it please, Petty Officer,' he said, while the American leaned against a shattered bulkhead and took another tremendous swig out of his bottle.

' "*Don't keep me . . . waiting . . . any longer . . . Report situation . . .*" ' Bolton spelled out the signal in his East

End whine and then looked at Rogers expectantly. 'The Skipper's right to be impatient, sir. These here Liberty ships are only held together with Yank chewing gum and spit.' He shot a scared glance at the boat bobbing off the bow and then back at the black column of smoke billowing out of the Liberty ship. 'Looks like she could go down at any moment, sir.'

Rogers ignored him. He was frightened himself, but not *that* frightened; he could almost smell the other man's fear. 'All right, take this. "Ship seems in bad condition . . . badly holed . . . but skipper confident he can keep her afloat . . ." '

'You're damned right I am!' the American grinned.

' ". . . if we return crew . . . and give her a tow." All right, Petty Officer, send it.'

Bolton commenced wigging his flags, while the Captain took a few more swigs and the bubbles continued to explode with obscene regular gurgles below in the hold.

Bolton had hardly finished when the Aldis lamp started to flick off and on urgently. ' "*Tow impossible . . . Return to Ypres . . . at once . . . Bring merchant Captain with you . . .*" ' As he sang out the message, the relief was all too obvious on his runtish face.

Rogers turned to the American. 'Well, sir, you heard. My captain says you must come back with me. I'm sorry—'

He stopped dead.

A big blue-black old-fashioned Colt revolver had appeared in the American's big paw, as if by magic. 'Sonny,' he said slowly, as if selecting his words with great care, 'this vessel will be seaworthy with a little help from you. Now *I'm* not leaving her and you're not going to force me either. You get back over there and tell your skipper that, right?'

'But, Captain—'

Bolton tugged Rogers' sleeve urgently. 'Don't argue with him, sir. He's pissed. Come on – quick.'

The American jerked the muzzle of his revolver up

threateningly. It did the trick. The two Navy men stumbled back across the littered deck, followed by the mocking laughter of the American.

'All right. If that's the way he wants it,' Savage said calmly, after listening in silence to his First Officer's account of what had happened on the *American Minuteman*. 'He stepped over to the speaking tube and pulled out the plug. 'Get me the gunnery officer,' he rapped.

A minute later a faint, disembodied voice called, 'Guns here, sir.'

Almost carelessly, Savage said, 'Oh good, Guns. Would you mind putting a fish in her midships? And get the old digit out of the orifice. We're losing a lot of time.'

'But sir—' Rogers cried aghast, 'you *can't* do that. That skipper's still aboard! I mean, you ought at least to give him a—' The words died on his lips.

Commander Savage was staring at him. There was a thin smile on his narrow lips, but no emotion in his eyes. They were blank – completely, utterly blank. It was then that young Lieutenant Rogers began to realize that his skipper was at best a monster, at worst – a madman.

Fifteen minutes later they were on their way again, the bone in their teeth. Astern of them, the *American Minuteman* was sinking slowly, the black column of smoke reaching to the grey, ominous sky like a funeral pyre.

THREE

An hour later the fog came drifting in from the west. At first it was nothing more than a few grey wisps, curling themselves gently, softly, around the speeding Destroyer, almost unnoticed. But slowly it thickened and thickened, bringing with it a freezing, bone-chilling cold. On the exposed gun platforms, the matelots did physical jerks in their heavy clothing and their nailed sea-boots. A couple waltzed together in mock-solemnity. But as it grew steadily colder, their high spirits deserted them and they sank into a brooding, chilled lethargy.

The freezing fog thickened even more. Cursing to himself on the bridge, Savage was forced to order the engineers to slow down. Now lookouts were posted everywhere, ears straining for the slightest sound as they drifted through the wet, freezing greyness, eyes searching the murk for the lost convoy. Down below, the specialists crouched over their Asdic, faces glazed with sweat in the green, glowing light, headphones clutched to their ears, listening to the regular *ping . . . ping . . . ping*, waiting for a change in the rhythm which would indicate a submarine lurking there in wait for them. It was said that all Asdic ratings went mad in time.

Inwardly Savage raged as he paced the bridge, flinging burning glances to left and right periodically. He knew he must be at least four hours behind the main convoy by now. That meant that if the Germans intended to attack by sea-going vessels – which they might well do now that they had the cover of the fog

– he wouldn't have a chance in hell of taking part in the action. That bloody American freighter, taking so damned long to sink after it had been torpedoed! And no doubt the thick column of smoke from the stricken ship would have attracted all German surface craft for a hundred sea-miles around.

Rogers watched him anxiously, more afraid of the Captain than the dangers which lurked out there in the fog. The skipper was eaten up by impatience; he had never seen a man in whom the raging fires below were so obvious in his every move and gesture. Those long, long years in the bag had taken their toll, there was no denying that. Lt Commander Savage was a seriously disturbed man; the signs were all too clear.

The usually welcome cry of '*Rum-O!*', indicating that it was time for each man in the crew over the age of eighteen to receive half a tumbler of thick dark-brown issue rum brought no relief that day; they were all too tense and on edge. They had even begun to see non-existent shapes and forms in the billowing banks of grey. Twice, look-outs had given false sightings, only to be turned on by the skipper, his eyes blazing with fury.

Now there was no sound save the *throb-throb* of the engines and the steady, tense pacing of the lookouts as they strained to see through the gloom. Every crew member was aware of the danger they could be in. Many had had shipmates who had vanished without trace in these northern seas; and all of them knew that to spend more than a few minutes in that freezing green water that rolled sullenly back and forth as they passed meant certain death.

It was now three in the afternoon, but it could have been midnight for all Savage knew. They had been out of touch with the convoy for nearly half a day, and he was beginning to contemplate breaking radio silence in order to contact the Commodore. Of course the Germans wouldn't be able to crack the code he was using in time to intercept him – if they really *were* out there.

But they could still get a 'fix' on his radio. Besides, if they were after the convoy, as he suspected, Commodore Jenkins wouldn't give away his position by radioing a reply.

'We're really between the Devil and the deep blue sea, Number One,' he rasped. It was the first he had spoken in an hour. 'For all I know, the convoy might have changed course, and here we are, taking all sorts of risks trying to reach them and in reality not knowing where they could be.'

Rogers nodded, licking parched lips. 'Yes, it's a real short and curlies sit—'

His words of sympathy were disturbed by the whistle of the voice-pipe. Savage snatched it up.

'Bridge,' he rasped.

'Asdic, sir,' the operator's voice answered excitedly. 'I'm getting a signal!'

'It's not a shoal of fish?' Savage objected, knowing that only a real expert could distinguish between the varying echoes of the return signal.

'No, sir. I'm getting her loud and clear. It's a sub, sir. Very definite!'

Savage swung round on Rogers, eyes gleaming excitedly now. 'Do you hear that, Number One – *a sub*! If we could bag her, that would really make all this mess with the fog and the Yank worthwhile.'

But Rogers didn't share his enthusiasm. 'But sir,' he protested, 'I don't think we have much chance of bagging a sub in this fog. Besides, we don't know how close we might be to the convoy. I mean we could be involved in a collision if we started to run a depth-charge pattern . . .'

But Savage was no longer listening to anyone but those strange inner voices that had plagued him for months now . . .

'*There she is, sir!*' the lookout cried, as the thick, muffled crump of the final depth-charge died away and a great gout of boiling white water came tumbling down. '*Over there!*'

Savage strained his eyes, peering through the grey bank of fog.

'To port, sir!' Rogers snapped, hurriedly adjusting his glasses.

Savage swung his round. He gasped. There wallowing in the trough, still half-submerged, lay that familiar shape, hated by Allied seamen from half-a-dozen different countries: a German U-boat. There was no mistaking it.

Savage flung one last glance around the tense bridge and saw his men's faces set and hard in the glowing green light given off by the instruments. They were all at their stations, staring at him expectantly. He rapped out his orders. 'Port twenty . . . Full ahead together!'

The helmsman wrenched at his wheel. Rogers sprang forward and pushed home the telegraph. Down below, the engine-room responded immediately. The Destroyer, shuddering at every ancient seam, rushed forward, given full benefit of her thirty thousand horses.

Savage thrust his face over the wind-break. 'Guns!' he yelled above the thunderous racket, 'stand by for surface action! Local control!'

Now, as the Destroyer raced forward, lean prow cleaving the fog, the turrets swung round to take up the challenge. Meanwhile, on the submarine, forced to the surface by depth charges, men poured out on to the deck, stumbling and sliding along towards their own guns.

Down below now in the turrets the gunners tensed, waiting for orders; the gun-layers with their eyes glued to the rubber pad of the sights, sweating despite the cold. Behind them, the rammers stood ready with their charges and rods. Next to the breech the loaders waited, hundred-pound gleaming-yellow shells cradled in their brawny arms, ready to re-load in a flash, looking like medieval men-at-arms in their flat helmets and white anti-flash hoods, waiting for the contest to commence.

The Germans were first off the mark. Red lights flashed on the sub's turret. White zig-zagging lines streaked towards the racing Destroyer, growing in speed by the instant. Bullets ripped the whole length of the ship with a sound like a metal rod being run along a series of iron railings. Holes appeared everywhere. A seaman screamed and went down into a quivering heap, clutching his face with hands tightly pressed together, through which scarlet blood seeped. A gunner slumped dead over his pom-pom.

'*Fire . . . A!*' Guns cried. '*Fire B!*'

The twin five-inch guns of A-Turret roared into action, followed an instant later by B. Scarlet flame stabbed from their narrow, gleaming muzzles. There was a sound like that of a huge piece of canvas being ripped apart. Smoke flew upwards and the destroyer heeled under the impact, as if struck by a sudden wind.

One . . . two . . . three . . . four . . . The shells struck the water. Huge gouts of boiling water shot upwards. The U-boat reeled crazily and disappeared from view.

'We've hit her!' Rogers yelled madly, his fear and apprehension forgotten now in the excitement of the battle. But next instant the water came reeling down, to reveal that the U-boat was still there, her rigging ripped to shreds by flying shrapnel. The turret gunners reloaded frantically, pushing in their wads of explosive, ramming them home into the smoking breech and thrusting in new shells.

Meanwhile the German captain reacted, swinging his ship round so as to present the smallest possible target to the oncoming destroyer, while on deck his gunners prepared to fire their own cannon.

In spite of his tension, Savage could not help but admire the unknown U-boat skipper. The *Ypres* was now in no position to ram the sub – and her guns would have a hard time dealing with such a small target . . . 'Guns,' he yelled over the wind-break, 'aim for her turret! That's the best tar—'

The rest of his order was drowned by the howl of a German shell, as it ripped the air apart just over Savage's head. A star shell exploded a moment later, bathing the bridge in hard, silver light. Savage narrowed his eyes to slits against the glare. The U-boat captain was a tricky bastard. He was trying to pin them down while his torpedomen prepared. Savage realized the danger he was in just in time.

'*Hard to port!*' he screamed, in a frenzy of apprehension, as a second German shell exploded yards away, sending the Destroyer reeling under the impact.

The helmsman flung the wheel round. Savage grabbed for support. Rogers stumbled against a stanchion painfully, but just as he caught himself from falling, he caught a frightening glimpse of the trail of bubbles erupting from the sub's bows. 'Torpedoes! *Torpedoes!*' he cried frantically.

The violent action of the Destroyer threw the turret gunners wildly off mark. Their next salvo roared harmlessly into the sky. But it saved the *Ypres*. Two deadly steel fish hissed by her wildly heeling body with only yards to spare.

Savage, however, had no time to congratulate himself on his quick thinking – and luck. Another German star shell had exploded directly ahead of them, blinding the bridge party. Already the German gunner manning the twin Spandaus on the conning tower had got their range again and was hosing the deck of the *Ypres* with nine-millimetre slugs. Tracer was burning everywhere and the ricochets were howling off the plating on all sides. A radio mast came tumbling down, dragging a confused network of rigging and wires with it and entangling the dying man below it in its blue-flashing, fiery-sparked metallic spider's web.

'*We'll ram her!*' Savage yelled above the vicious snap-crackle of the German small arms fire. He cried out a heading. The helmsman, bleeding from a wound in his forehead, swung the ship round. She heeled madly. Twin Vs of white water whirled high to left and right of her stern. Her screws churned madly – and then, with a great white sweep, she was swinging round, curving inward to catch the submarine midships.

The German machine-gunners spun their Spandaus round to meet the fresh challenge, while the German skipper, clearly visible now, yelled orders through his tube – orders which Savage guessed would be to his engine-room, tongue-lashing the sweating, frantic engineers below to get the boat trimmed in order to submerge before it was too late.

Slugs raked the front of the bridge. The windscreen disappeared. The helmsman screamed shrilly and reeled back, gasping with shock, twin scarlet pits where his eyes had been. Rogers sprang forward, elbowing the crumpling, dying helmsman cruelly out of the way, and grabbed the wheel.

'Good show!' Savage yelled, peering through the shattered glass as Rogers heaved the *Ypres* back on course, the ship's plates screeching in protest at the violent manoeuvre. 'That's the stuff to give the troops, Number One.'

Now they were hurtling forward again, striking each fresh wave like a brick wall. The German gunners were scuttling back towards the conning tower. Alarm bells were shrilling. They were going to crash-dive. In minutes she would be gone. But Savage was determined not to be cheated of his victim. 'Give her every last bit, Chiefie!' he shrieked down the tube.

'The boilers, sir!' the E-9's plaintive Scots voice protested.

But Savage cut him off with a harsh, '*All!*'

On they surged. Now only the German captain remained on the conning tower, and another officer in black leather gear. White trickling waves licked the length of the sub's hull. Her screws churned the water furiously.

Still the *Ypres* was closing on her. Rogers turned the helm. They were heading straight for the U-boat's conning tower, the last part of her to disappear beneath the waves – and the most vital.

'*We'll do it, sir! We'll do it yet!*' Rogers screamed, twisting and turning with the wheel, his eyes blazing with excitement, carried away by the mad blood-lust of battle. 'She won't escape us now.'

'Sir! Sir!'

Savage swung round. It was Sparks, the radio operator, message tendered ready in his right hand, while he clung on for dear life with the other.

'Not now!' Savage bellowed at him above the roar of the engines and the thunder of the guns, which were now throwing up huge spouts of water to left and right of the escaping sub.

'But it's most urgent, sir – top priority,' the helpless Sparks yelled. 'From the Commodore. You must read it!'

'No time . . . no time!' Savage snarled.

Sparks knew he was taking his life into his hands, but he was more scared of Commodore Jenkins that he was of the new captain, who was still an unknown quantity. ' "To Captain HMS *Ypres*. Cease firing at once. We hear you well." ' Sparks' voice almost broke under the stress as he saw the sub grow ever larger, the waves already licking about the base of the conning tower. ' "*Cease action now!*" '

'*WHAT?*' Savage grabbed the message out of the radioman's trembling hand and stared at the flimsy in utter, uncomprehending disbelief. But there it was, in a neat signaller's screed. ' "*Imperative. Cease all action now. Acknowledge receipt and compliance this order.*" '

For one long moment, with the sub disappearing rapidly now only a few hundred yards away, Savage considered refusing. Then he remembered MacIntyre's warning. Kill or no kill, he knew he wouldn't get away with disobeying an order a second time. Wearily, all energy gone from him, he issued his commands, while the sub disappeared beneath the waves for good; then, like a blind man feeling his way, he moved back from the bridge. A few moments later he had disappeared into his cabin, leaving a very bewildered Rogers in command.

First the empty holds of the *American Minuteman*, then the strict order not to sink the German sub. Rogers stared out at the heaving green sea and the last wisps of the departing fog. *What the hell was going on*?

FOUR

'*Stillgestanden!*'

The harsh command echoed and re-echoed the length of the great shed. Seven hundred pairs of jackboots snapped to attention, and the air was suddenly wreathed in foggy breath as the blue-jacketed figures with their flat beribboned caps exhaled.

Kapitänleutnant Krueger, the officer in charge of the parade, swung round, right hand on his ceremonial dirk, and reported the parade 'all present and correct'.

Slowly the ancient *Grossadmiral* with the old-fashioned wing collar of the Imperial Navy acknowledged the salute. Before he started to speak he paused, letting his gaze range from one end of the shed to the other, as if attempting to memorize each one of the young sailors' healthy, hard faces. 'You may stand at ease,' he ordered in a gentle manner.

The sailors' right feet shot out, hands going behind their backs. They waited.

Again Great Admiral Raeder took his time. Watching him at the head of his paymaster section of the crew, Brandt was aware that hadn't much time left. Doenitz would soon replace him; the Admiral was too old, too slow, too set in the tradition of the old Imperial Navy. He wasn't ruthless enough for the Führer. His days were numbered.

'*Men of the Deutschland . . . Comrades!*' Raeder's weary voice boomed over the tannoy and echoed down into the far recesses of the cavernous Norwegian shed. Outside on the docks, where it was snowing again, the scavenging gulls rose shrieking into the air.

'I will not waste words, comrades. Soon you will sail to meet the English enemy, as did your beloved sister ship the *Graf Spee* in '39, on a do-or-die mission. So far, on the orders of the Führer, it has been our comrades of *Herr Admiral* Doenitz's Submarine Service who have borne the brunt of the fighting against the English in the North Atlantic. No doubt you are aware of this – the Lords[1] are not exactly shy of publicity.'

There was a murmur of resentment, intermingled with soft laughter from the assembled blue-jackets. Doenitz and his ruthless band of Lords, Hitler's most favoured branch of the Navy, had hogged the headlines ever since the war in the Atlantic had hotted up. Every day seemed to bring yet another newspaper picture of some cocky submarine hero with his beard and rakishly tilted cap being awarded the Knight's Cross by the Führer – while the men of the big ships were left out in the cold.

Brandt smiled, too. He guessed that Raeder, the spokesman for the big ships, resented Doenitz's success as much as the blue-jackets did. He badly needed a spectacular success by one of his fleet in order to restore his prestige as head of the *Kriegsmarine*. That was why the aged Admiral had flown all the way from Berlin to Bergen to address them personally on such a miserable, freezing cold day.

'Now we shall have a chance to aid our brave comrades of the Army fighting in Russia. Our target, as you have surely guessed, will be the Anglo-American convoys to Russia – in particular, to Murmansk. Yesterday, one of Admiral Doenitz's Lords successfully escaped a surface attack by an English Destroyer, surviving to inform Berlin that a large convoy of merchantmen is sailing towards Iceland. You all realize what that means.'

There was another excited murmur from the assembled crew, and Brandt beamed. In spite of the fact that his new assignment was the least glamorous a fighting sailor could imagine – managing a bunch of middle-aged sea-

[1] Slang name for Doenitz's submariners.

going clerks and pen-pushers – it did mean he would be with a ship going into action. All his string-pulling had at last paid off. He had said his last goodbye to the 'gentlemen behind wire', thank God.

Raeder continued. '. . . now when that convoy sails from Murmansk, the Tommies, if they stick to their normal procedures – and believe me, comrades, the English are creatures of habit – they will be accompanied by their heavy ships approximately as far as Bear Island. At that point they always turn back – the capital ships, that is – and leave the job of escorting the merchantmen to their Destroyers. In theory, the Ivans are supposed to provide airborne protection from their bases in the Arctic Circle, but they never do. So you see what that means?'

They did. Ruddy young faces broke into smiles everywhere.

Raeder's weary, sick old face cracked into the semblance of a smile. 'I see you do. It means that a large convoy of, say, some twenty-five to thirty fat, juicy merchantmen, heavily laden with supplies for the Ivans, would be at the mercy of any surface ship,' he lowered his voice significantly, 'such as the *Deutschland*.'

The ship's crew could stay silent no longer. After two years of inactivity since their last action in Norwegian waters in the Spring of 1940, the *Deutschland* was going into battle again. Spontaneous cheering broke out everywhere. *Kapitänleutnant* Krueger, in charge of the parade, frowned, but no one paid any attention to him now.

A bearded old *Obermaat*, whose burly chest bore the medals and decorations of the Old War, stepped out of the ranks, raised his cap and bellowed hoarsely, 'Three cheers for the Admiral! Three cheers for Admiral Raeder, boys. This is the best news we've heard in many a day. *Hip-hip* . . .'

Without turning his head, a grinning Brandt called, 'Well, go on, you bunch of flat-footed base stallions – don't be scared of me. Cheer with them!'

Next instant the great shed exploded with cheer after cheer after cheer . . .

Captain Barthels, the skipper of the *Deutschland*, scanned the excited, drink-flushed faces of his officers, who had all crowded into the ward-room to hear the plan. He nodded and smiled faintly to Brandt, who was at the far end of the ward-room, as befitted a non-fighting officer, leaving the front space to the gunnery officers and the like. Brandt returned the smile and waited.

Barthels nodded to the CPO guarding the door, and he withdrew immediately, locking the door as he went out and posting himself on sentry-go outside. The officers looked at each other significantly. Barthels was taking no chances.

The captain put down his mug of steaming black tea and rum and said, in that quiet, undramatic fashion of his, so unlike the bold, aggressive utterances of his rivals, the U-boat skippers. 'You're wondering no doubt why I'm emphasizing security, when by now our mission will be known in every whorehouse, bar and waterfront dive in Bergen? I'll tell you. I'm hoping that the Norwegian underground will relay that information back to the Tommies!'

If he had expected a reaction to his statement, he got it – and then some. Several officers made angry protests. A couple whistled like football fans irritated by some foul tactic. One sprang to his feet and raised his fist.

Barthels remained unmoved, his healthy, ruddy face still smiling. 'Did I shock you, gentlemen?' he asked softly. 'Good. Then I hope I shall be able to spring a similar surprise on the Tommies. I'll put my cards on the table, gentlemen. This proposed mission of ours has a twofold purpose: a military one,' he hesitated momentarily, 'and one connected not only with Admiral Raeder's future, but with all our futures. Let me explain,' he added hastily, seeing their bewildered looks.

Pox raised his hand like a timid schoolboy. 'Yes, please do, sir. And could I have one with pictures, because I'm very simple.'

Barthels smiled, but Pox's sally didn't raise a laugh from the others; they were far too bewildered by the sudden strange turn in the briefing.

'I'll try, young fellow. Now, our military function is quite clear. We are to sink as many Tommy merchantmen as possible without endangering ourselves, then trot off back to Bergen before the Tommies can send in their air. Our other mission is somewhat less clear, gentlemen.' He drew a deep breath. 'The Führer in his infinite wisdom, has no faith in our big ships. For two years, so he reasons, we've sat on our fat bottoms in harbours all over Northern Europe, contributing virtually nothing to the war effort. Why? Well, the Führer reasons that Raeder is afraid to lose a capital ship in any one-sided action with the Tommies – as happened to our sister ship, the poor old *Graf Spee* in '39. The apple of the Führer's eye is Doenitz, the Big Lion, and his precious Lords. They're *always* in action. And hasn't Doenitz sworn to bring the Tommies down to their skinny knees?'

The officers muttered their agreement. 'A bunch of damned parvenus!' someone grumbled, and Hairless commented grumpily, 'Most of those U-boat skippers couldn't navigate themselves round a large pisspot. Terrible losses they're having, the cocky young shits!'

Barthels held up his big hand for silence. '*Einverstanden, Kameraden – einverstanden*. But let's not waste time grumbling. So what is the situation now? I shall tell you. If Admiral Raeder cannot convince the Führer that the big ships have some value, then the lot of them will be moth-balled. Admiral Raeder will be relieved of his command in favour of the Big Lion, and you, gentlemen' – a mischievous grin played around his humorous lips – 'you could well be learning to navigate yourself around a large pisspot in very short order. In other words, the lot of us would be transferred lock, stock and barrel to Doenitz's U-boat service.'

'But surely, sir,' Brandt objected, 'knocking off a few Tommy merchantmen won't convince the Führer of the need to retain the big ships. One of Doenitz's wolf packs could do the same job, perhaps even more efficiently than the *Deutschland*, and certainly at far less cost – and risk. There are forty men on a sub – nearly a thousand on the *Deutschland*.'

'Exactly, exactly, my dear Brandt,' Barthels agreed, with a wink. 'Obviously you paymaster fellers are not all calculating machines and pay stoppages.'

For the first time since he was thirteen and the French maid at his father's castle had caught him peering up her skirts as she had cleaned the window on the grand-staircase, Brandt blushed.

'No, gentlemen,' the Captain continued, 'the Führer and the Big Lion believe that Raeder wants this action so that we can knock off a few freighters and prove that the big ships have some value after all. His eyes narrowed slightly. 'But the *Grossadmiral* is after bigger fish. An Ami cruiser!'

There was a gasp from the assembled company.

Once again Barthels savoured the surprise he had sprung on them. 'Yes, Raeder might look old and weary, but he isn't altogether lacking up top.' He touched his temple significantly. 'The Allies will have the usual shadow covering force behind this new convoy. They've always done it before and they'll do the same thing this time. According to information from our people in Boston and New York and decodes from the B-Service,[1] the USS *Augusta* has just joined the British Home Fleet at Scapa Flow. Now gentlcmen, how would our reputation look – and that of Admral Raeder, too – if we succeeded in sinking the pride of the US Navy, the cruiser which has twice transported that crippled President of theirs to his meetings with the old sot Churchill? *Eh?*'

[1] German decoding-service.

'God in heaven!' Pox cried, 'it would be tremendous. There'll be tin in it for us all. My manly breast feels positively naked without any decoration except the Military Sports Badge, Third Class.'

The others laughed briefly, but Brandt could see from the excited gleam in their eyes that Pox's remark had struck a chord. Most of the U-boat skippers and officers were heavy with decorations, while the officers of the *Deutschland* were singularly lacking in medals.

'I take your point, sir,' Brandt said, as the laughter died down. 'It would be a tremendous achievement. But how are we going to do it. What's the Admiral's plan?'

'This. The Tommies won't expect us to attack the merchantmen until they're beyond Bear Island. That's the information our brave blue-jackets will undoubtedly be passing on to the local whores for immediate transmission to London at this present moment. But what, gentlemen—' Barthels' eyes narrowed again '—if we are waiting for them *before* they reach Bear Island? You can imagine the shock we could give them. With a bit of luck we could sink the *Augusta*, blow up a few merchantmen on the side, and be heading hell-for-leather for the protection of the Norwegian coast before the Tommies and Amis knew what hit them. The Allies would never anticipate such audacity on our part.'

'What if air reconnaissance discovered us, sir?' Guns objected. 'Believe me, sir, I'm not trying to throw cold water on the scheme. I'm all for it. I'm just trying to play devil's advocate.'

'We're expecting a permanent low for the next week or two.' Barthels nodded at the porthole. 'Look at it – it's already Spring and it's still damn well snowing. No, if we've got luck on our side, their air will never discover us. We'll already be in position by the time they attempt air recce.'

'What about Russian coastal radar, sir?' someone else asked.

'To be taken care of. Tomorrow the Fifth Air Fleet will

start systematically bombing the few stations they have up there.'

'Subs, sir?' Brandt asked quietly.

Barthels' happy smile vanished. He frowned and looked almost annoyed. 'You mean enemy submarines, Brandt?'

'Yessir,' Brandt answered calmly. Some of the other officers looked at the tall, one-handed lieutenant-commander as if he had just farted.

'Naturally we've given some thought to that danger, Brandt. But the British have never operated submarines in that area before. Why should they now? They're no use against our own submarines – and apart from torpedo boats, those are the only German vessels up in the Barents Sea. Who ever heard of attempting to protect a convoy with submarines?'

There was a mumble of agreement from the others. Brandt knew his objection hadn't been welcome; the rest of them wanted to sail, regardless of the danger. Still he persisted; at the back of his mind was the memory of just how purposelessly the old *Graf Spee* had been thrown away back in '39. 'But if, as you say, the Norwegian Underground will inform London that we've sailed, sir, what's to stop the Tommies from sending submarines into the area?'

'By the time we're in position, it'll be too late, Brandt, that's why.' A note of irritation had crept into Barthels' voice; Barthels obviously was irritated by Brandt's persistence. 'They could never sail a submarine flotilla across the Atlantic in time – not even if they risked our bombs and sailed on the surface the whole way.'

Brandt opened his mouth as if to ask another question, but then, slowly, he closed it again and gave a faint shrug. Why should he ask about the possibility that the British might *already* have subs operating in the area, just waiting for the *Deutschland* to come out? As events later proved, it was a fatal omission.

FIVE

The convoy beat forward at a snail's pace, fighting an icy headwind that came racing down straight from the Arctic Circle. Daylight had come later than was normal for this time of the year. A pale yellow sun had peered over the heaving grey horizon, lay there as if exhausted for a while, then disappeared in the first of the day's snow flurries.

The men of the Murmansk Run didn't object to the bad weather this particular day. It was their last before they reached the shelter of Iceland, and with luck the snow and the grey, overcast weather would keep away the German bombers from Norway; it might even discourage the submarines, too.

On the bridge, Rogers and Savage surveyed the scene, sweeping the horizon with their binoculars. All was quiet, but in common with all the other escort skippers, they were taking no chances. Behind them on the bridge wing which housed the gunners, they could hear the bored, frozen ratings discussing the pros and cons of the tankers which made up half the convoy, and generally enjoying their first real rest since leaving Hull.

'Yer can stick all them fried eggs and ice-cream the Yanks give their crews on them things,' a cockney named Harris was saying. 'Them poor buggers are sitting on a sodding volcano.'

'But they've even got pictures on the bigger ones,' someone else objected, 'and sheets on their bunks.'

'So what?' Harris sneered. 'And yer've gotta crawl around the sods in slippers so yer don't cause no sparks. Yer can't even have a fly spit-and-a-draw on deck in case she goes up in flames. No thanks, mate. Mrs Harris's handsome son can do without them there tankers, thank yer very kindly.'

Rogers lowered his binoculars and pinched the bridge of his nose wearily; his eyes were sore from staring at the horizon, and now that the wind-screen had been shot away, the flying particles of snow struck his face like razor-sharp knives.

Savage did the same, and wiped his heavily mittened hand across his streaming, red-raw face. 'Getting you down, Number One?' he asked, breaking a long, brooding silence.

'Well, I'm not exactly enjoying it, sir,' Rogers replied, and started cleaning the damp lenses of his binoculars. 'God, I never knew it could be this cold!' He shivered violently.

Savage thought back to the first winter in the camp before the Red Cross food parcels had started to arrive, when the floors of the huts had been solid sheets of ice at night. They had even burnt the roof joists in a vain attempt to keep warm. He refrained from telling Rogers that. Instead, he reverted to the subject which had been troubling him ever since they had been ordered back from the attack on the U-boat.

'Have you noticed anything strange about those tankers, Number One?' he asked.

'Well, I've noticed most of the deck crew of the Russian one seem to be women – as far as one can judge their sex with all that gear on them.'

Savage had long lost his appetite for small talk. He ignored the younger man's comment. 'No. I meant the American tankers.'

Rogers shook his head. 'No sir, I haven't.'

'Well, let me enlighten you. You've noticed how high they're riding in the water – that is, if they're fully laden, which I presume they're supposed to be.'

Rogers looked puzzled. 'Of course, sir. Why should their Lordships put lives at risk for half a cargo of oil to Murmansk . . .' He stopped short, his mouth dropping open a little stupidly. 'Oh, I see what you're getting at, sir. It's like the *American Minuteman*. She wasn't fully laden either.'

'Yes,' Savage said grimly, tugging at the hood of his dufflecoat so that the wind couldn't get at his ears, which were already white with cold in spite of his blue woollen balaclava. And why weren't we allowed to continue our attack on that damned U-boat? It looked almost as if Commodore Jenkins *wanted* her to get away.'

Rogers nodded. 'Well, what do you make of it, sir?'

Savage shrugged. 'I wish I knew, Rogers. There's something strange going on. This convoy isn't what it's supposed to be.' Savage gave a baffled sigh. 'Ah well, take over, Number One. Everything seems quiet enough. I'm going to have a look at the men's quarters with the CPO. I promised him I would.'

'Ay ay, sir,' Rogers touched his gloved hand to his cap.

'Home sweet home, sir,' CPO Johnson said, as Savage ducked and entered the long, narrow room, lined with bunks and lit by a single naked electric bulb. The place stank of diesel oil, damp metal and human sweat. Hammocks hung the length of both sides, while the middle of the room was dominated by a metal table, a wasteland of dirty tin mugs and plates, with a big opened tin of plum jam holding pride of place, from which protruded a dirty carving knife.

'I've seen worse,' Savage commented quietly. He knew that the CPO, a severe-looking man with grey hair who had served as a boy at the Battle of Jutland in '16, would expect him to look shocked. He indicated the loaf of white bread, smeared with oily fingerprints, half of it soggy with spilled tea. 'Very wasteful, Chiefie. Where I've just been for the last two years, a fellow could get into serious trouble for wasting bread like that.'

'Yes sir,' said the CPO, eyeing the Captain narrowly. Obviously he was wondering where he could have been for the last two years and what kind of squalor he must have lived in to beat the terrible crew accommodation on this beaten-up old Yank Destroyer. 'May I show you the heads, sir?'

'I suppose so,' Savage answered without enthusiasm. He knew that the purpose of this conducted tour was to arouse his sympathy for the miserable conditions under which the crew lived – as did most Royal Navy crews at this stage of the war. But he wasn't really interested. He had lived under worse.

'The ablutions, sir.' The CPO indicated the line of galvanized iron basins fixed into holes on a wooden table, all thick with soap scum. 'And there's the heads.'

Savage surveyed the crude drawings of naked women and men scratched on the dirty metal walls and the usual warning, '*It's no use standing on the seat, the crabs in here jump six feet.*'

'We try to stop them freezing up by pouring hot water down regularly,' the CPO continued, pointing out the blackened kettle steaming on the little stove at the end of the ablutions. 'When the lads come off watch, they're supposed to pour hot water down the sods – pardon my French, sir – but most of 'em make themselves a cup o' char, or—'

'*Sir!*' A frightened, excited voice cut into the CPO's explanation.

Startled, Savage swung round. An ashen-faced rating in deck gear stood at the companionway, gasping for breath.

'What is it?' Savage snapped. 'Out with it, man!'

'Mines, sir . . . scores of the buggers . . . they're everywhere in—'

Savage was no longer listening. Pushing by the scared rating and leaving the CPO staring after him, open-mouthed, he doubled up the metal stairs two at a time.

On the deck, the master-at-arms was hurriedly passing out rifles to the look-outs, while others craned their necks to stare down at the heaving green sea below. Savage flashed a look at the bridge. Rogers was at his post and he had already reacted; the *Ypres* was slowing down even more. He nodded his approval and dashed to the port side.

'There, sir,' a look-out cried, stretching out his gloved hand. 'Can you see, sir – a couple of the sods!'

Savage swallowed hard. He could see them all right. Two dark, horned objects bobbing up and down in the trough, some fifty feet away. Beyond, there were another three. The frightened first look-out had been right; there were scores of them. Probably some cunning German pilot had sneaked in after the minesweepers which led the convoy had passed and dropped them right in the path of the advancing merchantmen. Now, with the ships bunching together as they prepared to enter Icelandic waters and the port, the mines were bound to strike some of them.

Savage turned and called to the master-at-arms. 'Rawlings, get some of your marksmen over this side. I can see at least five of them!'

'Ay, ay, sir,' a sweating, harassed Rawlings called back. 'But there's at least a dozen of them to starboard too, sir!'

Savage made way for the marksmen and hurried over to the other side. Between the *Ypres* and the Russian tanker some two hundred yards away, the green sea was dotted with the evil black balls of high explosive, any one of them capable of breaking the Destroyer's back. He bit his bottom lip as the marksmen took up their positions and began to try to explode the mines before they came too close.

Savage shot a glance at the Russian tanker. The women deckhands seemed to be paralysed by the sight of the mines; they simply stood there, staring at them wordlessly, while the unwieldy tanker ploughed on at ten knots, its wash floating the mines ever closer to the *Ypres*.

Savage ducked as the first marksman struck lucky and a mine exploded with a great thunderous roar, showering the deck with icy water.

'That's the stuff to give the troops,' he cried. 'Keep up

the good work, chaps!' Then he raced up to the bridge, where Rogers, his face white with fear, was watching the sweating helmsman as if his life depended upon it.

He flung a quick glance to his front. There the sea seemed empty of mines. Offering up a quick prayer, he made his decision.

'Give her full ahead, Number One!' he barked.

Rogers swung round on him, his eyes wide with shock. 'Full ahead, sir?'

'You heard, Number One! Full ahead!' He nodded out to sea ahead of them. 'I'm taking a calculated risk that there are no more of the devils to our front. And the marksmen are—' he paused momentarily as yet another mine exploded, to the cheers of the ratings watching the marksmen '—taking care of those too close to our own port and starboard side.'

'I know, sir. But if we start up engines like that, our wash could well push them in the direction of the tanker.'

'It's a chance they'll have to take, Number One,' Savage rasped. 'They're not particularly worried about our safety, are they?' He indicated the tanker, which was now beginning to draw ahead of the almost motionless Destroyer. 'My main concern is the *Ypres*. Get on with it, man.'

'Ay, ay, sir,' Rogers said, but his lips were white with pent-up fury. He rang the bridge telegraph and gave the fatal order, as yet another mine exploded to the rear of them.

The *Ypres* quivered. Her deck tilted slightly. Here and there a marksman grabbed hurriedly for support. At her stern, the water rippled, turning rapidly from a dark green to a bright, gleaming white. Now the tanker started to fall behind. Savage clenched his fists. Everything depended now on the *Ypres* not running into an unsuspected mine to her front. Already the screws were doing the trick, thrusting away the mines to her sides and carrying them directly into the path of the tanker.

Rogers stared to starboard, full of anger and apprehension. The Russian skipper was making absolutely no attempt to steer his ship away from the approaching danger. Still the fat, dumpy women on board did nothing, just kept on staring at the mines with an almost fatalistic calm, as if they had already accepted their inevitable fate.

Another mine thundered, sending a spout of white water racing madly for the sky. Now the *Ypres* was almost out of danger, those mines that were left rocking violently, driven by their wake directly into the path of the Russian tanker.

'Come on! *Come on!*' Rogers privately urged the Russian captain, hands clasped into painful, sweating fists. '*Do* something, you idiot. *Do something!*'

But the Russian did nothing. Then it happened. The tanker came to an abrupt stop, as if she had run into an invisible wall. Almost instantly her bow reared up, as the mine exploded. A woman was flung over the side, her skirt flaring out like a parachute to reveal knee-length woollen knickers beneath. Next instant, the rest of the group to which she had belonged vanished as a great searching blow-torch of scarlet flame shot the whole length of the long deck, burning everything in its path.

'*Oh, my God!*' Rogers exclaimed in horror, as a man already aflame sprang from the bridge, hit the deck below like a sack of wet cement and began crawling to the side, weakening by the second until finally he collapsed, his head lying in a pool of burning oil.

'The mine hit the oil tanks, too,' Savage said coldly. 'She hasn't got a chance now. Look – she's already beginning to sink.'

He was right. The Russian tanker was settling down rapidly in the water, burning oil flooding the sea in a bright scarlet circle around her.

Now, more and more panic-stricken Russians were starting to run the length of the burning deck, zig-zagging violently to avoid the flames, trying to find a flame-free spot in the water. Here and there they succeeded, plunging into the icy sea, drenched with oil, choking and gasping frantically as the waves caught them, waving their arms and begging for help.

Rogers took his horrified gaze off the sinking tanker and flashed an inquiring look at Savage.

The Captain shook his head. 'No, Number One,' he said calmly, but firmly. 'We can't run the risk of the mines. We'll have to leave them to the tail-end Charlies—' meaning the three small craft which brought up the rear of the convoy and whose job it was to pick up survivors of sunken ships.

'But sir, it'll be too late by then. Look at the poor devils. The sea's already beginning to kill them. It's worse than the flames.' He pointed to a corpse tossed back and forth by the waves; nearby, a group of frantically struggling Russians held up their hands piteously for assistance. 'That water is way below freezing, sir. I think—'

The words froze on his lips. Savage's eyes had narrowed to vicious, crazy slits, his sunken cheeks aflame with rage. 'You think nothing, Number One! *I* do the thinking on this ship, do you hear?' he hissed, spitting each word out in burning fury. 'I'm not risking the *Ypres* – not for *anybody*. This isn't the damned *King Alfred*, you know,[1] with its naval history and noble deeds and gallant sailors. This is total war. Dog eat dog, no quarter given or expected.' He swallowed hard, gasping for breath, chest heaving with the vehemence of his outburst, as Rogers backed away from him. 'We're fighting to survive – survive and kill, that's all. The rest is simply ballast, Number One. Remember that.'

Rogers turned away, trying to shut out the white, desperate faces of the Russians vanishing into the green, heaving waste of the ocean. For minutes their piteous cries were still audible: '*Pashalsta . . . Pashalsta . . . Please . . . Please . . .*'

Then they were gone and there was no other sound save the steady throbbing of the engines and the mournful howl of the wind.

[1] Wartime naval training ship.

SIX

Slowly the ships entered the icy, deep-blue waters of Hvalfiord below the snow-capped hills, watched by the silent, hard-faced Icelanders. The presence of these foreigners was still resented, in spite of the fact that they had brought unbelievable prosperity to the remote island. From the decks of the Cruiser squadron, already lying there at anchor, cheer after cheer came floating across the placid water, returned by the excited blast of the merchantmen's sirens and the *whoop-whoop* of the escorting Destroyers.

Already local Icelandic launches were putting out for the new arrivals, eager to barter or buy rum or whisky from the sailors at highly inflated prices – for Icelanders loved their drink. On Commodore Jenkins' ship the Aldis lamp began to flicker, sending out the message '*No booze for the locals. They don't deserve it. Shore leave for the merchant service . . . RN captains will report to me at fourteen hundred hours.*'

'They're welcome to it, sir,' the helmsman grunted to Rogers as they came closer and closer to the little town of Hvalfiord. 'Hvalfiord, I mean. Fancy whores in taxis at five quid a go; one ruddy canteen serving Canadian beer and a free fight at the drop of a hat. I never thought I'd find a place worse than ruddy Scapa, but Hvalfiord beats it hands down!'

Rogers grinned and watched as the rising sun tinged the peaks of the snow-tipped mountains a delicate pink, sending the shadows sliding down their rugged bare slopes to the grey giants anchored below. 'It does look anything but inviting, I must admit.'

They were now approaching the one cargo vessel anchored among the Anglo-American Cruiser squadron, dwarfed by the Royal Navy flagship HMS *London*, in which Rear-Admiral Hamilton, commander of the combined force, flew his flag. Like the rest of the approaching convoy, her deck was cluttered with stores, but these were peculiarly shaped, long and metallic, with their centres covered by tarpaulin.

'What do you make of that deck stowage, Corrigan?' Rogers asked the helmsman, an old three-striper who had been at sea when Rogers had still been at his prep school.

The helmsman took his eyes off his instruments for a moment and flashed the strange cargo a quick glance, before returning to his wheel duties. 'She's a navy boat, an auxiliary, carrying naval cargo, sir. But what them things are is beyond me. Look like giant torpedoes, or something like that.'

Rogers nodded and focused his glasses on the strange objects for a moment longer, before the cargo ship disappeared again behind the light grey bulk of the US *Augusta*, her decks scrubbed white, her brasswork gleaming in the thin rays of the new sun, as if she were expecting to receive the President aboard at any moment.

Ten minutes later they had anchored, and the *Ypres*' ratings were watching the first Liberty boat being lowered from the leading merchantman, packed with eager, newly washed and shaven sailors, out to sample the limited sexual pleasures of Hvalfiord and its taxi-cruising whores.

'*Give her a poke for me, mate!*' yelled a deck-hand from the *Ypres*.

'*You watch, matey – it'll come right off in her hand afterwards!*' jeered another, before being chased back to his duties. For soon the Destroyer escort would be leaving to rendezvous with the convoy again, north-east of Iceland. First, however, fresh supplies would have to be taken aboard, ammunition used on the voyage to Iceland replenished, new medical stores stocked, the maximum possible amount of oil taken on board for the long cruise to Murmansk, for there would be no more refuelling at sea from now on. In the waters they would soon be entering, that would be tantamount to suicide.

Now all was hustle and bustle as supply launches chugged back and forth, and red-faced, harassed pursers checked off the supplies, at the same time trying to keep an eye on would-be pilferers; theft was rife in the fiord. The Icelanders, the naval seamen and their mates of the Merchant Service were always on the lookout for something to steal, especially if it was liquid and alcoholic.

At one-thirty, Savage and Rogers set off in the *Ypres*'s launch to join the other launches heading for the freighter flying the flag of Commodore Jenkins, the convoy commander. There the young captains, hardly one of them over thirty, were handed large pink gins and pork pies, which had been specially made for the occasion by Commodore Jenkins' cook.

'Ptomaine poisoning, here we come!' quipped one of the naval captains, and the room rocked with laughter, for today, after the strain of the convoy to Iceland, the young skippers laughed easily and a lot.

At two o'clock precisely, Jenkins, a large, bluff man with a red drinker's nose, but hard blue eyes, who had spent a lifetime at sea in both the Royal Navy and in the Merchant Service, indicated that the stewards should leave the ward-room. The briefing could commence.

'Well, gentlemen,' he said, as silence settled over the smoke-filled room, 'I'd like to thank you for your help so far. Two vessels lost on the first leg isn't bad. I've seen worse, at least. Now you know the drill for the second leg. The rendezvous will be delivered to you just before you sail in a sealed envelope – just a routine security measure. We can't trust the Icelanders an inch, though I doubt if any of you gentlemen will have much time to enjoy the favours of Hvalfiord's ladies-of-the-night, for what they're worth.

'Now, your job will be to act as a screen, with the shadowing force under Rear Admiral Hamilton in the

London bringing up the rear. That's just in case one of the enemy surface raiders cuts loose between here and Bear Island – a very unlikely possibility. After Bear Island, as you know, we're on our own. The Cruisers turn back. Winnie won't risk his precious big ships in that area. However . . .' Jenkins paused for a moment, and the bluff look disappeared from his face, to be replaced by one of hesitancy and uncertainty. He rubbed his heavy chin, but still didn't continue.

An uneasy silence fell on the roof. Still Jenkins didn't speak.

The old leather armchairs creaked as the Destroyer officers shifted their weight from one buttock to the other. Someone knocked over a glass of pink gin. Officers looked at each other in bewilderment. Whatever was wrong with old Jenkins?

The Commodore drained the last of his gin and made another attempt.

'Gentlemen, I really don't know how to tell you this – but please understand, you couldn't be told in advance. One of you might have given the game away . . .' Again his voice trailed away awkwardly.

Someone at the back of the crowded ward-room said, 'Well, come on, pee or get off the pot! Spill the beans – for Gawd's sake!'

The Commodore now looked very unhappy. He cleared his throat and tried yet again. 'All right, gentlemen. Let me put it like this. I, you, the lot of us – we've all been part of a deception, a trick that their Lordships in London have played on the Germans.'

Savage frowned. Suddenly the noisy ward-room was very quiet. People craned their heads forward, cocking them to one side so that they could hear better.

'You see, we're not taking anything very important to Murmansk – just half cargoes or deck-cargo in most cases, and obsolete weapons that'll be precious little use to the Russians.'

Rogers flashed Savage a meaningful look. So that was

why the *American Minuteman* had empty holds and the Russian tanker was so high in the water . . .

'But why, sir?' someone asked – and there was anger in his voice. 'Why risk our lives and those of the merchant skippers, just to take half-cargoes or useless military equipment to the Russians?'

'Yessir. *Why?*' half a dozen other angry voices joined in.

Jenkins held up his hands for peace, his ruddy face now purple with embarrassment. 'Please, gentlemen, please . . . Hear me out. After all, it wasn't *my* plan after all, you know!' The angry noises died down, Jenkins continued. 'You see, we have been and are the bait their Lordships needed to lure out the *Deutschland*.' He flashed a look at Savage. 'That's why I had to stop you going in for the kill with that Jerry U-boat, Savage. Believe me, it hurt me as much as I am sure it did you.' He smiled briefly, but Savage didn't respond. His eyes remained as hard and as dangerous as ever. 'We wanted to make quite sure that that sub radioed back to Berlin that we were on the way. We now know that our ruse worked. Information from Bergen tells us that the *Deutschland*, one of their ten-thousand-ton pocket battleships, has sailed on a northerly course. Your guess is as good as mine where she's heading. But I'd bet my wage packet for this month that she's coming in our direction! What's she after? Naturally us, once the heavy Cruiser squadron has departed. This time, instead of the dive-bombers and the U-boats, the Jerries are going to employ a battleship against us.'

Savage's eyes flamed with crazy ambition. It was the chance of a lifetime! The dream of every young captain! One last, bold attack by a lean racing Destroyer against the slow grey colossus of a battleship: David versus Goliath!

Next instant, however, his hopes of glory were dashed. Jenkins continued:

'Our hope is that the *Deutschland* will walk into a trap

set by us immediately the heavy squadron turns about and apparently leaves the convoy defenceless save for you escort chaps. Now, what *is* the trap?' He answered his own question. 'Submarines. Mini-submarines!'

'*Mini-submarines?* What the hell are they?' someone asked in bewilderment. Savage, meanwhile, stared at the deck in sudden gloom. It wasn't going to be a fight between Destroyer and battleship after all. There was nothing of the 'Nelson Touch' about this one.

Jenkins went on. 'A new kind of a very small sub. The Japs and Eyeties developed them first, but we got onto them fast enough. Ours are fifty-three feet long and weigh thirty tons. They can dive to three hundred feet and make eight knots underwater. They're crewed by four men, including the skipper. They're code-named X-craft, and I don't suppose I need to tell you that they're still an official secret.' He paused and looked significantly at the young officers, who were obviously impressed; until now none of them had believed that it was possible to invent a submarine of such small dimensions, capable of standing depths of up to three hundred feet.

'Now, these X-craft are armed with external explosive charges and limpet mines, so they have to get right up close to their target before they can do any serious damage. That's where the two-man human torpedo comes into action. You've all heard of them. It's an idea we stole from the Eyeties after they sank the *Valiant* and the *Queen Elizabeth* in the Med with the damned things. They've got a range of twenty miles and an endurance of seven hours. At three-and-a-half knots per hour, they can deliver a warhead of seven hundred pounds of high explosive – enough to stop the *Deutschland* long enough for the X-craft to finish her off.'

'But how are these . . . er . . . X-craft and two-man human torpedoes going to get here in time, sir?' asked one of the young skippers.

Jenkins chuckled. 'They're already here, my lad. Didn't you see that naval transport behind HMS *London*? Well, those objects covered by tarpaulin are the X-craft and the other things. For once, their Lordships seem to have thought of everything.'

'Yes,' Savage said with sudden bitterness, 'they certainly have! They've made fools of us – *and* your merchant skippers – letting us risk our lives, while these wonderboys in their funny craft gain all the glory.'

'Hear Hear! . . . You tell him, Savage!' Cries of approval came from all sides. Obviously the deception plan had touched a raw nerve in these young skippers, who had done their utmost to ensure that the convoy had got so far only to find that the whole business was an elaborate trick. 'What about our chaps who bought it? What did they die for, eh, Commodore?'

'I know, I know, gentlemen! I assure you, I feel as bad about it as you do. *I* lost two merchantmen, and in the case of the Russian, almost an entire crew as well. But I suppose their Lordships, in all their undoubted wisdom—' the cynicism was apparent in his voice now '—thought it was all worthwhile. You know, you can't make an omelette without cracking eggs. All the same, gentlemen, you have a great role to play in this deception. You see, the basic problem is to get the X-craft and human torpedoes into position when the *Deutschland* makes its appearance east of Bear Island. At the speed they sail, they've got to be right up there on the day. So, what better way of doing that than by your own ships?' He beamed at them.

'You mean the Destroyers will take them up to meet the *Deutschland*?' Savage asked.

'Exactly.'

Savage looked at the older man with undisguised disgust. 'So, we've really been relegated to the role of bearers to the great white hunter,' he snorted. 'We take them up; *they* get all the glory. And you call that a worthwhile role, sir!'

Hastily Rogers dug his skipper in the ribs and stopped his impassioned outburst. Not a moment too soon, either, for Jenkins had flushed angrily at the young skipper's words, glad to find some outlet for his temper after a very frustrating thirty minutes.

'Now that's quite enough, Savage. We know all about you and your disobedience of orders back in '40. Whether or not there's glory in it for *you*, Lieutenant-Commander, you'll damn well obey orders! The main thing is that we sink the *Deutschland*,' he added with a sneer, 'not that Lieutenant-Commander Rodney Savage gets another gong or promotion.' He took his gaze off a suddenly red-faced Savage, and turned his attention to the other Destroyer skippers. 'And that applies to the rest of you, too. You'll obey orders. I'm not going to have any of this Nelson turning the blind eye business from you. From now onwards, you obey without discussion or dissent. Their Lordships want the *Deutschland* sunk, and I'm here to ensure that their orders are carried out to the letter. Be quite clear about this,' Jenkins added, lowering his voice menacingly and looking momentarily at a bent-headed Savage once more, 'I shall break anyone who doesn't live up to that precept.' He opened his mouth as if he were about to say something else, then changed his mind and dismissed them with a brisk, 'That's all, gentlemen. You may go.'

Miserably and in silence, the Destroyer skippers trailed back to the waiting launches, their shoulders bowed against the icy wind. Again the cruel, cynical, bitter war of the Atlantic had overtaken them. Here nothing was sacred. Their own comrades had to be sacrificed as bait. All that counted was the defeat of the enemy; the cost was not important.

Rogers held out an arm to assist a smouldering-eyed Savage into the launch and said miserably as the rating cast off, 'It's a rotten business, sir, isn't it? You'd think there would be some other way of doing it . . .'

But Savage seemed not to be listening. He simply hunched there, his lean, worn face sunk deep into the collar of his greatcoat, not seeing, not hearing anything, save the crazy words that those inner voices kept repeating to him. Over and over again they hammered their crazed message home.

'Savage, you must sink the *Deutschland* . . . Cost what it may, Savage, you must sink the *Deutschland* . . . *You must!*'

THREE: BATTLE OFF BEAR ISLAND

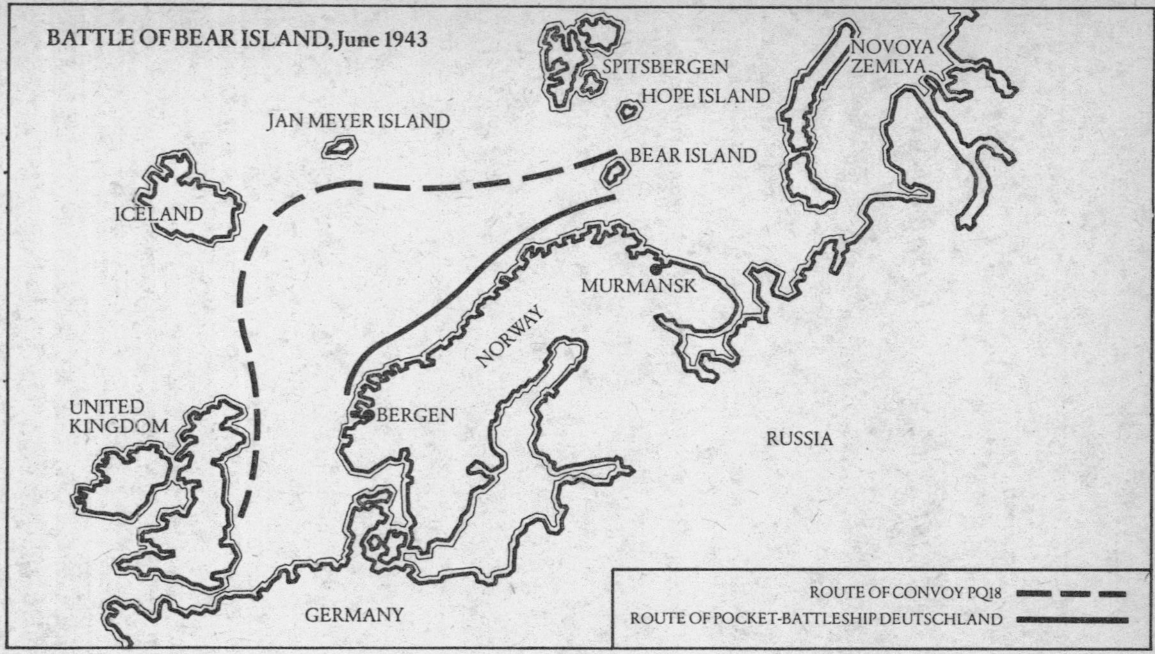
BATTLE OF BEAR ISLAND, June 1943
SPITSBERGEN
HOPE ISLAND
NOVOYA ZEMLYA
JAN MEYER ISLAND
BEAR ISLAND
ICELAND
MURMANSK
NORWAY
UNITED KINGDOM
BERGEN
RUSSIA
GERMANY
ROUTE OF CONVOY PQ18
ROUTE OF POCKET-BATTLESHIP DEUTSCHLAND

ONE

The dive-bombers came in at sea-level – fifty of them, little black dots skimming across the smooth, green water. This time the German pilots were making no attempt at evasion. They were coming in for the kill, relying on their superior numbers to swamp the convoy's defences.

The young *Luftwaffe* pilots were supremely confident, eyes gleaming with excitement, nerves jingling with the drug preludin. This morning was a max effort. For every pilot who sunk an escort the Knight's Cross would be awarded; for every merchantman, the 'fried egg', the German Cross in Gold. Boldly they swept into the attack from port and starboard.

For a moment there was silence below. The ships plodded on at a steady ten knots, dragging trails of bright white behind them in the green sea, black smoke curling from their funnels into the thin grey of the morning sky. Suddenly the guns erupted everywhere and battle commenced.

The first flight came zooming in from the rear. Pom-poms opened up everywhere. A wall of white tracer hit the sky. It seemed to the watchers that nothing would be able to get through it. But one did. A Junkers came racing in. It seemed to be touching the sea, trailing smoke after it, its perspex shattered. It dipped. The gunners prepared to cheer. No – it recovered again. It shuddered. A torpedo hit the water in a flash of white. Next instant the Junkers disintegrated. But the dying pilot's suicidal courage paid off. The torpedo struck a merchantman. She reeled frighteningly under the shock, smoke instantly pouring from her midships.

But now the dive-bombers were everywhere. Another Junkers was hit and blew up in mid-air. The pilot was the sole survivor, sailing through the black-peppered sky, head tucked in, hands clasped around his knees, bowling through the convoy like a lost cricket ball. He smashed into the side of one of the Destroyers and disintegrated.

Now, despite the intense barrage, the dive-bombers were flying so close that the gunners found themselves looking *down* at the racing Junkers, the pilots' faces clearly visible. They swooped and swerved, coming in from all sides, often narrowly missing each other, their cockpits glowing an evil incandescent orange colour in the light of the explosions, dropping their chubby twin torpedoes and then streaking away high into the sky, furiously trying to avoid the deadly guns.

Inevitably, some of the scores of torpedoes now cutting the sea everywhere found their mark. An American Liberty ship made a hard left rudder to avoid twin torpedoes heading her way, and ran straight into another one on her starboard side. It penetrated deep into the engine room before exploding devastatingly. The ship's engines died immediately. She started to flood. The crew panicked. Men ran screaming for the boats, but the captain was quicker. He grabbed the tommy-gun hanging on the hook at the rear of the bridge and, dropping down onto the sloping deck, fired a burst over the heads of the panic-stricken sailors.

'Get back, you rats!' he snarled, rolling an unlit black cheroot from one side of his mouth to the other like a Hollywood gangster. 'Get back from them boats, or I'll drop the lot o' ya!'

A Russian tanker was torpedoed, her women gunners fighting back to the very last, while a fountain of black oil came gushing up from her as if from a hose, showering down in a sticky rain on the dead and the dying. Next instant her bow rose high in the sky and there she towered for what seemed an age, standing on end, until finally she slid under in an ever-widening pool of burning oil, taking all her crew with her.

Now the Junkers were taking severe casualties. More and more of them, wings shot away, engines knocked out or burning, hurtled straight into the sea or attempted to limp away, sinking lower and lower until finally the waves reached up and claimed them. But some still fought on, taking suicidal risks as they pressed home their attacks, zooming in through that tremendous wall of fire to launch their deadly tin fish.

Finally it was over, and the last of the attackers set course back to Norway, leaving the burning and sinking wrecks behind them. The sky still rang with the echoes of that tremendous barrage; everywhere seamen hurried to bring in the casualties and clear the decks of the mounds of steaming yellow shell-cases.

'*Cease fire! Cease fire!*' the order went up on all sides, as harassed skippers tried to assess their casualties and damage, and Commodore Jenkins attempted to gather his scattered flock together once more.

Savage pushed away a trailing wire that had come down from the mast and clattered down the deck of *Ypres*, which was littered with fist-sized pieces of hot shrapnel and brass cartridge cases from the 'Chicago pianos'. He stumbled through the débris to where one of the life-boats lay hanging at an angle, its sides shredded by slugs. A leg hung over the side. Obviously someone had hidden out there during the raid, so as to be first in the boat if the worst came to the worst. 'Come on, damn you! Get out of that boat and back to duty!' he snapped, impatient to see the rest of the damage to the *Ypres*.

The owner of the leg didn't move. Angrily, he tugged at the leg. Next instant he found himself reeling back, the leg, severed at the thigh, in his hand. Retching with horror, he dropped it from his nerveless fingers, as the ropes parted and the shattered boat fell into the heaving waves below, bearing with it the riddled corpse of the dead rating.

'Sir.'

Bracing himself, he swung round. It was the old CPO.

'Yes?' he asked thickly, wiping the vomit from his frost-cracked lips.

'Got the wounded down in the galley, sir. Warmest place in the whole ruddy ship.' The CPO wiped away a trickle of blood from the side of his face and added, 'No important damage to the ship, sir. Except that.' He indicated the life-boat bearing its cargo of death, floating away slowly to nowhere.

Savage gave a sigh of relief. 'Thank you, Chiefie. All right, I'll have a look at the wounded.'

There were three of them sitting up and two lying silent and very pale on the dirty floor of the kitchen, among the shattered plates and mess of spoons and forks.

Ward, the effeminate medical orderly, was busy sewing on a sailor's ear, while the rating swallowed aspirin after aspirin to alleviate the pain. He looked up, and Savage nodded that he should keep on with his task.

'Old Dodds here, sir,' the CPO said, 'he's bought it bad, poor sod.' He indicated one of the two men lying on the floor.

'What's up with him?' Savage asked, staring down at Dodds, a typical old Stripy, a long service man with three good-conduct stripes. The wounded man lay on his side, a blood-soaked blanket half-covering his inert body, his breathing shallow, hectic and fast.

By way of answer, the CPO, with surprising gentleness for such a hard man, rolled back the blanket.

Like some monstrous child, the Stripy's intestines lay cradled to his stomach, a hideous grey-pinkish colour, pulsating all the time. Savage felt the hot vomit of disgust fill his throat and fought it down just in time.

'What's his chances, Sickbay Tiffy?' the CPO asked Ward over his shoulder.

'He's got no chance whatsoever, Chief, unless he's taken over to one of the Cruisers immediately,' the medical attendant replied, pausing in his task, his fingers running scarlet with blood from the rating's wounded ear. 'He's in urgent need of major surgery, sir.'

The CPO looked at Savage. Behind them, the wounded rating swallowed another handful of aspirins to dull the pain.

Savage shook his head slowly. 'Simply can't be done, Chiefie,' he said. On the deck, the dying seaman flicked open his eyes and stared up at him with a look of animal despair, as if he knew his fate was being decided at this moment.

'I've known old Doddsie there since we were on the old *Warspite* together, back in the thirties, sir,' the CPO said, his voice emotional now. 'He was a good shipmate then . . . We *can't* just let . . .' He broke off, seeing that his words were having no effect on the tall, tense skipper.

Savage turned away from the dying sailor and towards the sickbay attendant. 'When you've finished with that ear,' he said, his voice devoid of feeling, 'you can help Seaman Dodds on his way.' He made a gesture as if he were forcing home a syringe. He touched his hand to his cap and went out without another word.

The CPO looked at Ward, and the sickbay attendant looked back.

'You know me, Chiefie,' said Ward, 'I never like to speak bad of anyone, but that one . . .' He shook his head. 'He's a real bastard!'

'Ay, you're right there, you little pansy sod. You're right there . . .'

Over in the Cruiser squadron they had watched the aerial attack on PQ 18 helplessly, still obeying the Admiralty's instruction and keeping at a distance of ten thousand yards from the merchantmen, out of range of any concentrated aerial or submarine attack, while they waited for the surface situation to clarify itself.

Now, under the command of the Admiral in HMS *London*, they were entering the waters through which the convoy had just passed. The sea was covered with patches of burning fuel oil, with here and there a drifting ship's lifeboat or the wreckage of a downed plane; German fliers could be seen bobbing up and down in their rubber boats, shooting off red distress flares at periodic intervals in the hope of being picked up by their own rescue seaplanes. But they had no time either for friend or foe stranded out there in the freezing sea. If they were lucky, the tailend Charlies would pick them up; if they weren't, the sea would have them by nightfall. Although it went against all the Admiral's instincts not to stop and pick up shipwrecked sailors, he daren't stop. If he did, his ships would be an open invitation for any German sub in the vicinity.

At midday, with the sky growing increasingly overcast and a thin, grey, cold fog rolling in from the east, a worried Admiral Hamilton in the *London* took stock of the situation; although the weather could well keep away the German dive-bombers, there was a strong risk of surface raiders or subs sneaking up on the convoy to his front. He therefore ordered all available aircraft to take to the air and recce ahead of the convoy.

Immediately the catapult crews went into action and succeeded in launching six of the Walrus and Catalina seaplanes which the Cruisers carried, while Hamilton observed their wobbly starts anxiously through his glasses, sighing with relief when the last of the clumsy, slow planes was finally airborne.

Now all the Cruisers could do was to sail on, waiting for the spotter pilots to report, and hope that their reports would be negative. Hamilton did, however, take the added precaution of signalling the Destroyer screen to alert their X-craft and two-man-torpedo crews for immediate action.

Thus it was that Rogers, on the bridge of the *Ypres*, spotted the signal *Charlie–Mike*, which meant 'Follow Me', being hoisted on the lead Destroyer in the same instant that Sparks came rushing up to the bridge with the signal to put the X-craft and two-man-torpedo crews on stand-by.

Five minutes later, the Destroyers were zig-zagging forward at high speed, leaving the convoy behind. The *Ypres*, meanwhile, though going flat out on a steady course, started lagging further and further behind, with an enraged Savage stalking her bridge impatiently, as if physically willing his old ship to catch up with the others. But it was not to be. By two o'clock that afternoon, with the fog getting ever thicker and the nervous look-outs imagining ships and icebergs everywhere, the HMS *Ypres* found herself absolutely alone in the green, rolling ocean.

TWO

'*Object, port bow, sir!*'

The look-out's sharp voice broke into Brandt's reverie as he smoked moodily on the deck of the *Deutschland*, watching the fog rolling in ever more thickly.'

He looked up and stared at the look-out, a tall, blond sailor, muffled in heavy leather gear, binoculars held in gloved hands as he tried to penetrate the grey gloom.

'Where?' called the officer of the watch, raising his binoculars too. It was Pox, now sporting a week's growth of beard, which he had sworn not to shave off until they had sunk the *Augusta*.

'Green one-zero, sir,' the look-out replied smartly.

Brandt turned in the direction indicated, narrowing his eyes to slits.

And there it was. A clumsy lumbering shape, glimpsed momentarily in a break in the fog.

'Seaplane, sir,' the look-out called.

'See it, look-out,' Pox replied, hastily adjusting his binoculars.

'One of ours?' Brandt called, as the fog rolled in again and the dark, slow object off their port bow disappeared again.

'Don't think so, Jailer,' Pox replied, not lowering his binoculars. 'Just caught a glimpse of it, mind you. But I thought it was a Tommy Walrus flying boat. Can't be sure, though.'

'*Grosse Kacke am Christbaum!*' Brandt cursed, feeling a wave of excitement surge through his frozen body. 'If they spot us here, then the clock's really in the bucket!'

'You can say that again,' Pox said, still sweeping the

billowing clouds of fog with his glasses in an attempt to find the lone plane once again. Behind him, the handsome young midshipman who was seconding him this afternoon had already informed the bridge, and the alarm whistles were shrilling over the Battleship's public address system. In a moment the gunners would be pelting for their weapons, flinging on extra winter clothing as they ran. It was bitterly cold.

Now the *Deutschland* was some three hours away from the convoy, whose location had been accurately pin-pointed for them by the Junkers dive-bombers, which had raided the Tommies earlier on. Beyond lay their target, the Cruiser squadron; once again, the *Augusta*'s exact position in relation to the flagship, HMS *London*, had been reported by the *Luftwaffe* observers. Everything seemed to be going perfectly, just as planned. The weather was bad, with more fog predicted, so that they should be able to sneak up on their unsuspecting target without difficulty. Air sweeps had indicated that there were no British submarines in the area, and it was generally assumed by the *Deutschland*'s staff that after the massive dive-bombing attack of the morning, the Tommies wouldn't be expecting any further attack today. But if this lone British plane succeeded in spotting the *Deutschland*, all their carefully worked out plans could be dished.

Brandt knew all this, as did the rest of the ship's crew – even down to the most humble galley-cook. As he gripped the rail in his gloved hands, he could almost smell the tension that had now descended on the great grey ship as it slid through the rolling banks of fog. On deck the look-outs continued searching the sky for that lone plane that might well spell disaster.

The minutes passed by leadenly, the only sound the steady throb of the *Deutschland*'s engines and the splash and hiss of the green, rolling waves far below. Brandt licked his parched, cracked lips and tried to convince himself that the Tommy hadn't spotted them. Surely the mist had hidden the *Deutschland* from his prying gaze?

'What do you think, Pox?' he called upwards.

With surprising ill-humour for him, his nerves obviously very strained, Pox replied, 'How should I know, Jailer? Am I Jesus or something? Do you want me to walk—' He stopped short.

Next to Brandt, the look-out who had first spotted the enemy plane, moaned, 'Holy strawsack!'

'What is it?' Brandt gasped.

'There she is again!' the sailor replied and hurriedly swung his big hooded sea-glasses around.

Brandt cocked his head to one side. Yes – there was the faint blurred drone of an engine. *The Tommy was coming back!*

'Coffee, sir – black?' Sparks asked, balancing himself between the two pilots, holding a cup and thermos.

Sub-Lieutenant Graham-Andrews, at the controls, freed one hand to rub his weary, red-rimmed eyes, and said in the pseudo-Cockney accent he affected these days to cover his somewhat plummy public school voice, 'Not 'arf, old cock.'

Next to him, Sub-Lieutenant Ramsbotham, known behind his back as Ram's Arse, said in his surly Yorkshire voice, 'Did yer remember to put a good dash of Nelson's Blood in it, Sparks?'

'Against King's Regs, sir,' Sparks replied, and winked hugely. 'Take the back of yer tonsils off, it will, sir!' After pouring a cup for the pilot, he filled another one for the co-pilot, then peered over their shoulders at the billowing clouds of grey fog below, with here and there an open patch through which he could glimpse a square of heaving green sea. 'Not much cop is it, sir?' he said.

Graham-Andrews took a careful sip of the steaming coffee and nodded. ' 'Eaven 'elp a sailor on a night like this.'

Sparks grinned. Graham-Andrews, who was really quite a toff and whose father was supposed to own half of Hampshire, was a card.

Ramsbotham scowled. He had come up from the ranks and wasn't amused by his companion's affectations. 'We've got juice for another half hour, skipper. Don't you think we'd better turn back? It's gonna be the devil's own job finding the *London* as it is.'

Graham-Andrews smiled. ' 'Old yer 'orses, matey. We'll give it another little go, as the actress said to the bishop. We—' Suddenly the pilot nearly dropped his cup of coffee and let out a gasp in his plummiest public school voice. 'Good grief, Ramsbotham. Do you see what I see?'

Sparks craned his neck forward and stared down at the open patch directly beneath them.

There, in the centre of an area of green sea, steamed a long, powerful, grey shape fringed with white, its every detail clearly visible, from the great menacing gun-turrets right down to the myriad black figures scurrying everywhere like ants under an upturned log of rotting wood.

'Stone me, sir!' breathed Sparks. 'It's her! It's the *Deutschland*!'

'Yer right!' Ramsbotham snapped. 'There's no mistaking that funnel and those forrard gun turrets. And she's seen us, too.' He broke off abruptly, as from below a line of scarlet flashes rippled the length of the ship's port side. Almost instantly the sky in front of them filled with grey, light puffballs of smoke. The Walrus rocked alarmingly.

'Get on that radio, Sparks!' Graham-Andrews yelled above the racket of the exploding flak. 'Report her position! For Chrissake – at the double, man!'

Sparks dropped his thermos and started hurrying back down the swaying corridor towards his radio, as more and more guns opened up below.

Sweating now in spite of the cold, eyes bulging from his red, strained face, the pilot began to swing round the unwieldy Walrus – top speed just over a hundred miles an hour – while the flak came zipping up into the sky in a solid white rain of death. Two hundred yards away to port, the fog was thick and rolling once more. If he could make it that far, he reckoned he had a decent chance of escaping. Next to him, Ramsbotham sat tensed in his seat, hands on the controls, dripping with sweat and white-knuckled with fear and suspense, but ready to take over at any moment . . .

Now the Walrus had straightened out. She was flying the whole length of the battleship, and guns and machine-guns were firing from all sides. It seemed impossible that anyone could survive the deadly barrage. But somehow the lumbering old-fashioned seaplane seemed to bear a charmed life. Shells which would have blown her apart missed her by feet. Twice, vicious bursts of tracer ripped the whole length of her fuselage, tearing metallic rents in her fabric, but without hitting a vital part.

One hundred and fifty yards . . . one hundred . . . seventy . . .

They were going to do it – *they were going to do it!*

Jaw clenched, drops of sweat gleaming like pearls in his thick eyebrows beneath the leather flying helmet, Sub-Lieutenant Graham-Andrews physically willed his plane to gain the cover of the fog banks, while to the rear the radio operator at his desk, his face an eerie, unnatural, sickly hue in the green glowing light, called over and over again, 'Hello, One . . . Zero . . . Five-Five, do you read me? Over . . . Hello, One . . . Zero . . . Five-Five, do you read me? *Over!*'

Fifty yards to go now.

'I think we're going to make it!' Ramsbotham hissed. Still they flew on, with shells bursting to both sides of them; but now the bank of fog was temptingly close.

'It looks like it, matey,' the pilot grunted through clenched teeth, as he held onto the controls with all his strength.

Suddenly a shell exploded directly below them, buffeting the seaplane with a blast of violent air. The Walrus shook at every seam. A wave of hot, acrid air swept through the plane, followed by a blast of cold. With all his strength Graham-Andrews hung onto the controls as the plane's nose dipped and there was a series of frightening, violent blue-red sparks and lights to the rear.

Ramsbotham shook away the blood that was threatening to blind him and flung a glance back down the fuselage.

A great hole had been torn amidships. Débris and twisted metal lay everywhere. Sparks was slumped over his shattered instrument, his severed head still suspended by the earphones, oscillating sickeningly back and forth.

Ramsbotham swung round, the green bile flooding his throat. 'They've got Sparks,' he gasped. 'We've been hit.'

'Nice turn up for the books,' Graham-Andrews said, trying to forget the burning pain that ran the length of his shattered back, desperately holding on as the stricken Walrus dropped lower and lower. Now, the bank of fog seemed a million miles away instead of a mere twenty yards. They wouldn't make it . . . The *Deutschland* was going to escape after all.

'*Lower a boat!*' someone yelled above the hectic chatter of the 20mm flak that was now pouring one thousand shells a minute in the direction of the Walrus. The stricken plane was now almost down to sea-level, trailing black, oily smoke from its crippled, silent port engine as it crawled towards the cover of the fog.

'*Knock the Tommy bastard out of the sky!*' a harsher voice cried. '*No time for the niceties of sea warfare now. Kill the swine before he gets away!*'

Brandt clenched his fists, while just behind him, multiple machine-guns opened up with a hellish chatter, empty yellow cartridges raining down onto the deck in their hundreds. White tracer zipped after the dying seaplane, its entire left side now ripped apart and drooping almost to sea-level. Brandt caught a glimpse of a figure falling forward over the controls, shattered metal flying everywhere; then the plane was gone, swallowed up by the fog, and the bugles were sounding '*Cease fire . . . Cease fire.*'

Wearily, the sweating gunners stared at each other in the echoing silence, one unspoken question written all over their faces. *Have we downed her?*

Brandt relaxed his hold on the rails and walked slowly back to his office, a worried frown creasing his handsome face; the 'phantom pain', as the bone-menders called it, was nagging him where his hand had once been. He was remembering the tragic end of the *Deutschland*'s sister ship. If that plane *had* managed to crawl away, it could be 1939 all over again: a trapped, desperate *Deutschland*, outnumbered by a powerful enemy Cruiser force, scuttling herself ignominiously rather than fight it out with the Allies . . .

He shook his head as he opened the door to the office, where his middle-aged paymasters and clerks were busy over their files and calculating machines; to Brandt it was as if they were back in Kiel or Wilhelmshaven, not in the middle of an ocean, where every man's hand was against them and their whole silly little world of paper and figures could explode in terrible fury at any moment.

For a while he sat there staring blankly at the pile of paper in front of him, unable to work; then he could stand the strain no longer. He knew that like all the active-service officers, Guns had better things to do than to answer his queries, but all the same he called him.

'Guns, I know you think I'm a nervous Nelly, but put me out of my misery, old comrade, and I'll buy you a Korn in this mess tonight.'

'Fire away,' Guns boomed in his hearty way. 'Even Paymasters are warm-blooded and have human emotions – or so they tell me. Where's the fire?'

'That Tommy seaplane. Of course, you don't know whether she crashed or not. But one thing; did our people pick up any radio signal from her?'

Guns chuckled. 'You rear-échelon stallions worry too

much. Leave that sort of thing to us front swine. No, my dear Jailer, for your information, she didn't. Our radio detection picked her up, trying to get a signal through. But it was never acknowledged, we reckon that shortly afterwards the plane's radio was knocked out by *my* guns. You got the emphasis I hope, old friend?'

'I did indeed.' Brandt breathed out a little sigh of relief. 'So, unless that Walrus gets through, the operation can proceed as planned.'

'Exactly, old house. Not a thing to worry about – not a thing at all,' he declared.

But for once, Guns was wrong.

THREE

At first it was just the *cough-splutter-cough* of a plane in serious engine trouble. Then a glowing-red distress flare coloured the banks of rolling grey fog an eerie crimson. Another flare followed – and another. It was as if a blind man were groping his way through the night . . .

Now the *Ypres* had slowed down to ten knots. On all sides the look-outs searched the grey wall for the crippled plane. They knew that in that condition it could present no danger to them; but what was it doing out here, so far away from the convoy? And how had it got into such a mess?

The noise continued. At first it was to port; then to starboard, getting louder. Then it died away again, just when the look-outs were hoping it would emerge from the fog at last and clarify the mystery. To left and right the fog glowed red, as if on fire. Standing on the bridge next to an impatient Savage and a worried-looking Sub-Lieutenant Orde, the officer in command of the X-craft and the two-man human torpedoes, Rogers shivered suddenly, the small hairs at the nape of his neck standing erect. There was something eerie, frightening about the lost plane out there, but he didn't know quite what. Yet all the same, he knew instinctively that it meant trouble.

For over four hours now they had been locked in the fog banks, completely cut off from the Destroyer screen somewhere to their front and the convoy and its Cruiser shadowers somewhere to their rear. They were unable to make contact or even to find their exact position – for Admiral Hamilton had ordered strict radio silence. Communication was to be by visible signal only. And Rogers didn't like it. There was something unnerving about being out here alone in the middle of the ocean, a tiny vessel pitted against the might of the sea. After a while, the endless billowing clouds of fog played tricks on your eyes, so that you could imagine almost anything out there, waiting for you . . .

Savage had grown very strange, too, as the day had worn on. He was as impatient and bitter as ever, of course, hardly ever standing still, a bundle of nerves; yet at the same time his dark eyes had taken on a peculiar, inward-looking aspect. More than once Rogers had observed his lips moving, as if he were holding some strange interior dialogue with himself. The crew had noticed it, too.

Ever since word had got around that Savage had ordered the Sickbay Tiffy to finish off Dodds with an overdose of morphia, everyone recoiled from the skipper. Rogers had seen it immediately. Even the ward-room steward seemed to approach him with trepidation, placing the mug of coffee-and-rum down in front of Savage and immediately snatching his fingers away as if the skipper were some monster who might snap them off.

Rogers licked his frost-cracked lips and shuddered involuntarily. The HMS *Ypres* wasn't the most pleasant place to be, this long, fog-bound day.

Suddenly an excited cry cut into his gloomy reverie.

'*There she is! To starboard! It's one of ours!*'

'Famous last words,' muttered Sub-Lieutenant Orde as the officers swung round instantly, glasses raised.

'Walrus!' Rogers identified the plane first, as it came coughing and spluttering out of the fog, port wing tilted under the weight of the dead feathered engine, thin brown smoke trailing from its shattered fuselage, its floats almost touching the waves.

'Good grief!' Orde exclaimed, as the Walrus disappeared as if for good, then came flying out of the spray again, the pilot fighting desperately to keep her airborne. 'She's really copped a packet.'

'The *Deutschland*.' Savage broke his long, brooding

silence. 'She's run into the *Deutschland*.' Suddenly those dark, inward-looking eyes were filled with an unnatural animation. 'Number One, give her a signal. Tell her we're friendly. Order her to land . . . Go on, man – snap to it!'

'Ay, ay, sir.' Rogers was galvanized into action. Grabbing the flare pistol that hung from a nail on the bridge, he clattered down the dripping stairs and jumped the rest of the way to the deck.

The Walrus was some hundred and fifty yards away now, violent bursts of scarlet flame shooting from its one remaining engine, its whole right side splintered and rent with shrapnel and bullet fire. Through the gaping holes, Rogers could see a headless torso slumped across a shattered desk, a head hanging by wires coloured a ghastly green hue by a small desklight. Swallowing hard, he raised his flare pistol, watched by the men of the X-craft and the two burly Marines who manned the human torpedo. He pressed the trigger. The flare hissed into the sky. A soft plop. An explosion of green light – and abruptly all their faces were coloured the same sickly colour.

For a long moment Rogers thought the pilot of the Walrus hadn't seen the signal. Then the white blur of his face turned slowly in the direction of the ship below.

'He's seen us, sir!' shouted one of the Marines, clad in a thick rubber frogman's suit. 'Look, he's trying to turn the crate . . . The poor sod!'

Infinitely slowly, the pilot was beginning to edge the crippled seaplane round, the spray splashing up high and dashing against the front of the shattered cockpit.

Rogers held his breath, flare pistol clutched painfully in his gloved hand, as the pilot brought her round. The engine was coughing and spluttering alarmingly now, threatening to cut out and plunge her into the sea at any moment. Now she was just topping the waves. One false move and she would go under. But the unknown pilot was grappling gallantly with the controls of his crippled plane. Now he had straightened her out. Both floats were parallel with the sea. He was going to land!

Rogers gabbled off a quick prayer. Everything depended upon the pilot landing with both floats on the rough swell. If he didn't, the force of the waves could easily overturn the plane, which was clearly underpowered now and wouldn't be able to rise again. He swallowed hard. It was now or never. That sole engine wouldn't last much longer, he could hear that.

'Cor,' the big Marine gasped in awe, 'how's he do it, sir? I can feel the piss trickling down me right trouser leg already.'

Rogers didn't answer; he couldn't.

Now, only a matter of feet separated the floats from the surface of the sea. Still the pilot held them parallel. Obviously with the last of his strength he was waiting for the right moment and a smooth patch of sea where the swell wouldn't overturn him.

'There he goes!' the Marine cried.

Rogers yelled out loud with joy as the plane touched down on the waves. In the very same instant the sole surviving engine gave one last splutter and stopped dead, its propeller whirling round aimlessly and ever more slowly until it ceased rotating altogether. From the watchers there was a small cheer, and on the bridge someone pulled the siren and gave a couple of triumphant *whoops* on it. The engine telegraph rang, and slowly the *Ypres* began to heave to.

Rogers didn't wait for instructions. He knew that Savage would be bellowing commands in a moment. This time he would beat him to it. Speed was of the essence out in these waters. He ordered the boat lowered and waited as the men manning the life-boat rowed all out to bring back what they had found on the strange, crippled seaplane, now sinking ever lower into the water.

'The *Deutschland*!' Graham-Andrews gasped, as he lay

dying on the galley floor. His blood was now flooding the third bandage which a helpless, sweating Ward had applied in a vain attempt to stem the bleeding. A gaping wound occupied almost all of the pilot's back, so that his heaving grey-blue lungs could be glimpsed through the gleaming white of his rib-cage. 'It was the *Deutschland*.'

'Are you sure?' Savage persisted, bending low over the ashen-faced Fleet Air Arm pilot. 'Are you *sure*, man?'

Graham-Andrews nodded weakly, and with the effort, a thin trickle of black blood ran down from the side of his mouth.

Ward looked helplessly at Orde and Rogers.

Rogers shook his head. There was nothing he could do to call a halt to the skipper's cross-examination. Nothing mattered to him now but his own glory. Ward bit his bottom lip, waiting for the order to inject morphia into the pilot's arm and give him the blessed relief of death.

'Where?' Savage rapped.

There was no answer from the dying pilot. His eyes flickered weakly, as if he no longer had the strength to open them.

'*Where*, man?' Savage persisted brutally, bringing his hard face close to that of the pilot, whose breathing was now getting shallower by the moment.

Still no answer.

Rogers swallowed hard. In a minute the skipper would strike the dying man, he was sure. Orde, meanwhile, looked on in horror, his handsome young face plainly shocked by such naked brutality.

Slowly, Graham-Andrews' right hand reached out to where a pool of his own blood lay on the floor. Weakly, his forefinger rubbed into the stuff and lay there for an instant, while the others watched in awe, Savage included. Then he started to trail something on the deck with his finger, using his own blood as a kind of scarlet ink.

Ward reached out to help, but Savage grabbed his arm in time, his eyes flashing. '*Don't!*' he hissed. 'He's trying to tell us something, you fool!'

Now even Rogers and Orde forgot the pilot's terrible suffering, as they bent close and tried to make out the letters and figures he was scrawling on the deck.

'*L*,' Savage hissed. 'That must be for latitude . . . L. 41 . . . 0 4 N.'

Rogers hardly dared breathe, as the pilot's hand moved with infinite slowness, fighting a last, desperate battle with death to deliver his message.

'L . . . *Longitude* . . . 14 . . . 1 . . . 3 . . . 0 E.' Savage's face lit up maniacally. 'We've got it! Forty-one, zero-four north . . . by fourteen hundred and thirty east!' His mad eyes flashed from Rogers to Orde. 'Don't you understand, damn you? *We know the* Deutschland*'s position!*'

But no one else in the crowded, dirty galley shared their skipper's enthusiasm. Instead they stared down at the poor dead youngster, his finger already still in a pool of his own blood, now beginning to congeal . . .

'But we *must* inform the Cruiser squadron, sir!' Orde protested indignantly, as they all sat in the ward-room, nursing cups of steaming coffee-and-rum. Their faces still revealed their sense of shock at the events of the afternoon.

'Absolutely out of the question!' Savage snorted. His evil temper had vanished now, to be replaced by a kind of hectic, untypical euphoria. He even smiled as he spoke the words. Obviously, the news that the dead pilot had brought so unexpectedly had changed his whole attitude. 'Even if they couldn't break our code, those people on the *Deutschland* would soon locate us, and that would be that. They'd be off like a shot.'

'Then what are we to do, sir?' Rogers asked. Already he had a fair idea what was going on in Savage's crazed mind.

'Isn't it obvious? Tackle her ourself, Number One,' Savage replied enthusiastically. 'It's the only way!'

Orde looked at Rogers aghast, as if expecting him to

protest; but seeing that he remained silent, he cried, 'But that's impossible, sir! One over-aged Yank Destroyer against one of Germany's newest and finest ships, armed with guns that could knock us out of the water before we were within range . . . My God, sir, the *Deutschland* could blast us to Kingdom Come at a range of ten thousand yards or more! We'd have to get within two thousand even to have a chance.'

Savage wasn't impressed. 'So? We've got the fog, haven't we? And surprise!'

'But, sir,' Rogers objected, 'even if we *did* succeed in getting within range, could we really put her out of action with our guns? I mean, the torpedoes might have a chance—'

Airily Savage waved away his objections. 'We've got young Orde here and his merry men, haven't we? That was the original plan, wasn't it? So we get close enough to the *Deutschland* to employ your people, Orde, and then, when you've done your bit, we go in for the kill.' His eyes gleamed excitedly.

'You make it sound all very easy, sir,' Orde said severely.

'Where's your enthusiasm, man?' Savage retorted in high good humour. 'Don't you see, man? There's fame and glory in this – for *all* of us! Fame and receptions at the Palace. The country badly needs a victory this Summer, and I intend to give it one.'

At this point Rogers gave up. But Orde, who, with the innocence of his youth didn't realize that he was confronted by a man who no longer lived in the world of reality, persisted. 'But, sir – all this is against orders!'

'Damn orders!'

'And what if the *Deutschland* escapes?'

Savage smiled at him, but it was the smile of a madman; hard-eyed, fixed, gleaming, hypnotic. 'But my dear young fellow,' he said softly, an almost cunning look on his face, 'she *won't* escape, will she? She *can't* now . . .'

It was the logic of the insane.

FOUR

A high silver moon hung over the low, drifting banks of fog, casting its spectral light on the rolling grey sea. A wind had sprung up, but as yet it wasn't powerful enough to sweep away the last of the fog. The men on the bridge of the *Deutschland* were quite happy with the conditions; the fog was thin enough not to be dangerous, but thick enough to conceal their stealthy approach. For now, like a grey timber wolf edging out of the primeval forest, intent on its unsuspecting prey, the Battleship was sailing steadily through the dark, cold swell towards the Cruiser squadron, positively identified by the *Deutschland*'s radarmen. The only sound was the deep, throbbing note of her powerful diesel and the *whir-whir* of the rotating radar screen.

Brandt smoked silently, reflectively, on the quarter-deck, his good hand cupped over the red, glowing end of his cigar, staring out at the silver-tinged waves and wondering idly what it would be like. It was nearly three years now since he had last seen action with the ill-fated *Graf Spee*.

His mind turned back to those days back in 1939. Captain Hans Langsdorff, his skipper, had been intensely proud of his record: he had destroyed nine British ships totalling fifty thousand tons with the loss of not a single German life. At forty-two, he had commanded one of the Third Reich's most powerful ships; he was a hero, decorated by the Führer himself, his name making headlines all around the globe, boldly evading capture time and time again. That December, Langsdorff had been on top of the world, believing that nothing, no ship afloat in the Southern Atlantic, could stop him and his beloved *Graf Spee*. Yet within a matter of days, his whole proud reputation had been shattered, his ship had been trapped by the Tommies' superior tactics, and he had seen no way out but to scuttle the *Graf Spee* and commit suicide himself.

'*Wie gekommen, so zerronnen*,'[1] whispered Brandt to himself, staring out at the spectral sea, thinking of those far-off days, and realizing yet again that nothing was certain save the unexpected.

'Talking to yourself, Jailer?' asked an amused voice at his elbow. 'It must be the strain of worrying about my pay.'

Brandt turned, a little startled, and then chuckled. It was Roof-Hare, dressed in thick anti-flash gear with a soldier's helmet placed squarely in the centre of his big head. The helmet was much too small for him and was perched there like a child's toy.

'You're getting a swollen head,' he countered. 'Couldn't you find a bigger size?'

Roof-Hare ignored the comment. 'Just getting ready for the big show, old house, that's all.' He looked hard at his old crew-mate. 'Problems?'

Brandt shook his head, still keeping his cigar shielded so as not to expose the light. 'Not really. Just thinking of the old days on the *Spee* and how damned confident we were that nothing would go wrong then.'

'No comparison between then and now, Jailer,' his friend said confidently. 'You had your backs to the wall in 1939. Once Langsdorff made the mistake of entering Montevideo harbour, his number was up. He should have stayed out to sea. Once he was in harbour, he was trapped – the Tommies were just waiting for him to come out so they could blast him to eternity. It was either scuttle or fight to the finish. Our position's different. We might be heavily outnumbered. But we've got our options. Surprise

[1] Roughly, 'Easy come, easy go.'

is on our side – and we *do* have the freedom of the open sea.'

Brandt took a last draw at his cigar. 'Perhaps you're right,' he said softly. He remembered that last day, with the *Spee* settling at the bottom of the bay, as quiet as a cathedral. The bubbles had stopped gouting from her side now, and the only movement came from the mops, the odd cork jackets, the unused floats, the ship's model some seaman had been making for his boy back in the Reich, all floating on the surface. By now she would have taken on the colour of her tropical surroundings, rusting and barnacled, shoals of multicoloured fish moving in and out of her rooms, eels twisting on the shattered stanchions, crabs lumbering up and down her plates like miniature tanks. Once she had been a ship, a proud ship, powerful and frightening; now she was simply a heap of twisted, useless metal, not worth salvaging, at the bottom of the Atlantic.

'I *know* I'm right, Jailer,' Roof-Hare said, with the confidence of a man who hadn't seen it happen before and didn't yet know the pain and the feeling of loss. 'At dawn tomorrow, old house, we'll hit the *Augusta* one hell of a blow! Then we'll show the Amis, with their big mouths and terror bombers. They'll learn that this war isn't all ice-cream, Coca Cola and fat steaks.'

Roof-Hare's confidence was infectious. With an air of finality, Brandt stubbed out his cigar and tossed it into the waves far below. 'Of course you're right, Roof-Hare!' he said determinedly. 'Those Amis really deserve a damn good kick up the arse. Come on, let me buy you a drink in the ward-room before they run out of firewater altogether.'

Arm in arm, they strolled away to the mess, as they had once done in the good old days as carefree young midshipmen in Kiel, leaving the silver, glowing sea behind them.

*

Not a million miles away, as the HMS *Ypres* plodded steadily ahead to its date with destiny, Lieutenant Commander Rodney Savage was also in a reflective mood. But unlike Brandt, his thoughts were not sombre and foreboding. On the contrary, they were filled with a burning delight at the knowledge that now at last he would have a chance to wipe out the humiliations of the past. All those years in the bag since he had been captured at St Valéry, the soul-destroying monotony and frustrating boredom of the prison camp – all that would be wiped out for good. Soon it wouldn't just be his gong and the patronage of the Court which had made him acceptable to their Lordships in Whitehall; it would be the fact that he, the pariah, who had had the audacity as a young sprog to disobey an order, had sunk the pride of the German fleet: the *Deutschland*.

'*You'll do it, Rodney*,' those wild little voices chortled. '*You'll sink her, never fear*.'

In the glowing darkness of the bridge, Savage nodded his agreement. When they had first started talking to him back in Germany during the escape, he had been, admittedly, very frightened. Then, he had tried to rationalize; maybe they were something to do with the tension and lack of food; he had heard or read somewhere that men deprived of food and water hallucinated readily. But even after he had been nursed back to health at the Hasler in Portsmouth, they had still persisted. By then he had lost his fear of them – indeed, he had grown accustomed to them. He missed them when they didn't speak in that high-pitched confident way into his ears. Now they were with him most of the time, whispering to him, comforting him, urging him; and he knew they were right. *They were!*

He shivered a little in the night cold and pulled the hood of his dufflecoat tighter around his neck. The fog had almost lifted now and the soft swell was tinged a hard silver from the moon. It bathed the superstructure of the *Ypres* in its light too, giving it a shimmering, unearthly, wraith-like appearance. Around him the bridge watch glowed too, subdued into silence by the soft throb of the pulsating diesels.

'A ghost ship, Captain,' the voices whispered and chuckled, 'a ghost ship out to sink the *Deutschland*!'

Savage nodded, but didn't reply this time. Instead he stood there, staring out into the night, listening to the rhythm of the engines, drinking it all in. Absorbing the power and strength of *his* ship . . .

Below in the ward-room, Sub-Lieutenant Orde prepared for the ordeal ahead. He was being fed weak pink gin at regular intervals by a worried Rogers, while he donned his thick rubber pants and several layers of pullovers and thick cable-stitched sweaters. The X-craft were freezingly cold.

'Every time I do this, I tell myself I should dress as lightly as possible. With these ruddy things,' he indicated his heavy sea-boots, 'I haven't got a chance in hell if we're hit. But at the same time I think of the long, freezing hours in that little tin bitch. So I put 'em on.'

Rogers re-filled his glass, his face sombre in spite of Orde's attempt to lighten the atmosphere. The other young off-duty snotties had left the ward-room for their own quarters. He handed the glass to Orde, who took a sip, and busied himself putting on a kind of woollen skull-cap he intended to wear beneath his regulation cap. 'It's madness,' he said, 'absolute madness!'

'But what are you going to do about it?' countered Orde. 'He's the skipper. You're just the Number One.'

Rogers flung a frightened glance at the bulkhead. It was still closed; there was no one listening. 'But surely there must be something in Regs about getting rid of a captain who's completely off his head?'

Orde paused in his preparations and stared at the white-faced Lieutenant across the stained ward-room table. 'Do you really think it's that? You're sure it isn't just honest-to-goodness naked ambition, Number One?'

Rogers shook his head firmly. 'No, I don't. I could understand that. What I can't understand is a captain who throws his crew's lives away to absolutely no purpose. Admit it, Orde, you're not going to stop the *Deutschland* with your mad marines and your little boat. So what *are* we going to do? Why offer ourselves to the Jerry eleven-inch guns? All we'll be doing is giving them target practice so that they can get ranged in before they start slaughtering the merchantmen.'

'But we *might* have a chance, Number One. Those marines are damned good, and if we can get close enough to attach limpet mines in the region of – say – her screws, then we'll have a good chance of holding her up till the *Ypres* puts a couple of tin fish into her – from a nice discreet range, of course, and without putting the ship at risk.' He laughed – but with little conviction.

Rogers wasn't impressed. 'Listen, you know as well as I do that your two-man torpedoes and X-craft are best employed in a confined space where the enemy has little room to manoeuvre. The *Deutschland* has got the whole ruddy Arctic. Okay, suppose your gallant marines stop her for a while with the suicide attack, as the captain thinks they will; what'll her reaction be? I'll tell you. Their skipper will turn the whole sea around into a battlefield. He'll have his searchlights on and his anti-sub nets out before you can say Jack Robinson. Now, do you *really* think you'll get through that lot and be able to plant your limpets? Come on, Orde, grow up!'

'Ours is not to reason why.' Orde started putting on his heavy nailed sea-boots. 'Listen, Number One. A year ago I was still at school in deepest Devonshire. We never even had an air raid at my school. Plymouth and Pompey were another world.' He grunted and managed to get his foot into the right boot. 'Now a year later, I'm going into action for the first time to tackle a German battleship in a craft not much bigger or sturdier than the skiff I used to row at school.' He took a deep breath and started on the second boot. 'Frankly, I'm bloody well scared – not only of the enemy, but of your skipper and the fact that I might well make a balls-up of it.' With a grunt he wiggled into the second boot and looked up at Rogers, his round young face flushed and earnest, the laughing look gone from his eyes now. 'Let's call it kismet. There's nothing we can do about fate, is there?'

'Kismet, my arse!' Rogers snorted with unaccustomed vulgarity. 'Of *course* we can do something!'

Sadly Orde shook his head and then, seizing his cap, went out, leaving Rogers to stare blankly after him. His mind was racing, he was wondering just what he could do before it was too late. Instinctively he noted that the *Ypres* was beginning to slow down, his ears aware of the rattle of the winches as they prepared to lower the X-craft into the water.

'Fate?' he whispered to himself. 'Surely we don't just have to accept it like dumb animals being led to the slaughter?'

But even as he said the words, he knew they had. Somewhere, someone had already settled their fate. There was no turning back. Numbly he seized his cap and went out after Orde to face what had to be faced . . .

FIVE

'Stop . . . *Stop both!*' Savage commanded, lowering his glasses, which had been focused on the dark blob on the horizon standing out in the silvery darkness. It was the *Deutschland* all right; the *Ypres*' radar had just confirmed that.

Slowly the *Ypres* came to a stop and rode the waves, swaying a little more to port and starboard now that her engines were no longer driving her. On deck Rogers called softly, 'All right, lower away.'

'Lower away,' the CPO echoed gruffly.

All the ship's officers were extremely cautious now, speaking in low tones in spite of the fact that the *Deutschland* was over nine thousand yards away. At night in the Arctic, sounds carried a very long way, and the German ship had reduced speed considerably, due to the icebergs floating everywhere in the freezing pre-dawn cold.

The rating in charge directed a stream of boiling hot water on the winch to remove the ice – they dared not use hammers in case they were heard – and as the ice began to dissolve, the rusty cogs started to turn, lowering the torpedo and its two-man crew clad in black, goggles already over their eyes, into the still, dark water.

'All right, sir,' the corporal in charge called softly upwards, as the tiny craft, little more than a motor attached to a huge chunk of explosive steel, hit the water. He released the hook.

Now it was all down to the X-craft. Hastily the crew clambered aboard the narrow cigar of steel, with its mini conning tower. There were muffled exclamations of '*After you, Cecil, no, after you, Claud'* – catch phrases stolen from ITMA – and '*Going down now, sir . . . Don't forget the diver!*'

Rogers grinned in spite of his apprehension. It was all very British.

Meanwhile, Orde poised on the cockpit of the mini-sub, checking that his three crew members were in position. Rogers raised a gloved hand. 'Look after yourself, Orde.'

'Thank you, Number One.' He grinned in the glowing light, looking very boyish and callow, eyes unsteady with fear. 'Once more unto the breach, and all that sort of thing.'

Rogers gave a smile of farewell, knowing instinctively that he would never see the boy again. He touched his hand to his cap in a half-hearted salute, then Orde lowered the hatch and the winch began to creak as it lowered the mini-submarine into the water next to the waiting two-man torpedo. There was a soft splash, followed a moment later by the softer hum of electric motors starting up. 'All right,' Rogers commanded, 'haul her up!'

The donkey engine grunted and the winch came up the side, dripping water behind it.

Below, the marine in charge of the human torpedo had started his motor too. Now the two strange suicide-craft waited, engines running. The plan was for the *Ypres* to leave the spot before they set course for the *Deutschland*, since three moving blips on the German's radar screens would give them away. They would then disperse, the two-man torpedo taking the lead, followed at an interval of one sea mile by the X-craft, with the *Ypres* making a circular course around the *Deutschland*, sticking as close to the icebergs as was consistent with safety. When and if the two suicide crews struck lucky, the *Ypres* would come racing in at top speed for the kill.

Savage saw Rogers' hand signal and commanded 'Half ahead both!' The telegraph rang, and instantly the engines below began to throb powerfully. Beside the *Ypres*, the two small craft rocked violently; then the Destroyer was pulling away firmly, heading straight for another series of icebergs, glittering like diamonds in the silver gloom.

Rogers flung a last glance at the two tiny craft rocking in the *Ypres*' wake, and then they were gone and the *Ypres* was surging forward at fifteen knots.

The hooded divers were now firmly astride their 'chariot', as they called it, heading straight for the monstrous German ship, which seemed to fill the whole dark sky. They were travelling at a steady three and a half knots, steering for midships by means of a primitive rudder, knowing that they had to keep well away from the *Deutschland*'s screws.

As with all of the 'charioteers', they were volunteers, hardened by months of underwater swimming in the coldest of seas; both knew that there was little chance of their being picked up once they had completed their task. Nonetheless, both 'Number One', who controlled the machine and sat forward, and 'Number Two', who sat astern and became operational once the suicide device reached its target, persisted doggedly in their mission, as if unaware that within minutes the pair of them might be dead or floating in an icy ocean, a hundred miles from the nearest shore.

Now the *Deutschland* loomed ever larger. There seemed no end to her. Here and there they could make out chinks of yellow light as someone moved the blackout curtains carelessly on the upper decks. They could hear the *throb-throb* of her powerful engines growing louder by the instant. It was time to dive. Number One gave the signal by means of a raised and then down-turned thumb. Number Two nodded his understanding. With his thickly gloved hands, Number One trimmed the chariot down by flooding the main ballast tank and pumping water into the two trimming tanks. Now the two daring young marines were below the water save for their hooded heads.

Now Number One gently eased the joystick forward. The nose of the chariot took on a gentle downward slope. Down they went into the icy green water, with only their rubber suits between them and the heart-stopping cold. The pale green water became darker and darker. Number One kept his eyes glued on the glowing green needle of the depth-gauge. Ten feet . . . Fifteen feet . . . *Twenty feet!* Deep enough. Gently he pulled back the joystick, and the chariot flattened out perfectly.

Even at their present depth, the two marines could hear the powerful throbbing of the German battleship's engines and feel the increasing turbulence of the water as she approached. Number One said a quick prayer of thanks; fortunately she was moving slowly to avoid icebergs; otherwise they wouldn't have had a chance.

There she was! A red-grey steel shape, sliding through the dark water immediately ahead. There was only a minute before they would be churned to bloody pulp by her great whirling screws. Number One let out the stick, trying to ignore the terrible buzzing pain in his ears and nose due to the pressure. The chariot hissed forward. As always, he was awed by this contact with a great ship. It was almost as if the *Deutschland* were some huge steel monster asleep in its lair, and he and Higgins, his Number Two, were tiny flies crawling along its immense bulk.

Now he turned the craft, drawing it parallel with the *Deutschland*'s hull; they were falling behind rapidly because of the difference in speeds: ten knots against three and a half. Both men reached out their right hands. There was a first hollow boom . . . Then a second. In spite of terrible pains in his ears that threatened to burst his head apart at any moment, Number One grinned. The magnets were in place, and now the chariot was being carried along by their victim; it was a pleasurable thought.

Hastily they attached two more magnets, noting the phosphorescent glow of their hands, as they trailed myriad tiny specks of glowing light behind them in ghostly, eerie, slow motion.

Now Number Two went to work with his free hand while with his right he continued to grip the magnet that linked them with the hull of their unsuspecting victim. He released the torpedo. It clamped hard to the hull with another soft, hollow boom. Now it was firmly in position – nearly half a ton of high explosive, stuck somewhere halfway down the length of the *Deutschland*. He freed his throbbing right arm, red hot pincers of pain nipping it agonizingly, and tapped Number One on the shoulder. It was the signal. They were going up. They had exactly five minutes to clear the enemy ship.

Switching to 'slow ahead' and setting the planes at 'Hard to Rise', Number One carried out the actions as if they were still back in training at Pompey. The chariot responded perfectly, taking on a steep climbing angle. The two marines swallowed and swallowed, trying to fight the air pressure that was set to burst their eardrums at any moment. Next instant they had broken the surface and their little craft was floundering in the turbulence caused by the *Deutschland*'s screws, bobbing up and down like a cork in a maelstrom. Moments later she had passed by and they were alone in the ocean, two brave men who would never see Pompey again . . .

There was a sudden mind-rending shudder. It began midships and worked its way aft, rattling through each compartment, flinging men to the deck, tossing them from bulkhead to bulkhead like caroming billiard balls, showering them with a mass of gear and flinging them out of wildly swinging hammocks.

In the engine room, dials splintered. Light bulbs popped. Steel fixtures snapped as if they were made of wood. There was a sudden rush of steam. A stoker screamed as the flesh was seared from his naked upper body. A petty officer blundered down between the boilers in the sudden half-gloom, his face slipping down onto his chest like red molten wax.

A series of mighty shakes seized the *Deutschland*. On deck the look-outs hastily grabbed stanchions, which vibrated crazily in their panic-stricken grip. The mighty ten-thousand-ton pocket Battleship heaved from left to right, and in latter years, those who survived the war would swear that in those terrifying few seconds the *Deutschland*'s superstructure even touched the water.

On the bridge the warning lights were flashing red. The overhead lighting became ever dimmer. Frantically the duty men stared at their instruments, which raced crazily back and forth across the dials. Cursing and sweating, a chief petty officer, blood dripping from his forehead in great red gobs, wrestled with a jammed telegraph, while behind him in the little shack, the radar operators stared at the green lights which now shot wildly in every direction across their round glowing oscilloscopes.

'*Grosser Gott!*' Brandt cursed, picking himself up from the glass-littered, crazily tilted ward-room floor. 'We've been hit, Guns!'

Guns didn't move.

Brandt bent down and grabbed him with his one hand. 'Guns, didn't you? . . .'

The words faltered away and died on his lips. Guns' skull had been neatly split in two, as if with a butcher's cleaver, revealing quite clearly the intricate dull-yellow folds of the brain.

For one moment Brandt knelt there, the vomit running down his chin, his skinny tall frame racked with spasms and sobs, while outside heavy sea-boots clattered back and forth. Orders and counter-orders were bellowed, and the *Deutschland*'s speed decreased by the instant.

Brandt pulled himself to his knees, then to his feet. With all his strength he wrenched open the ward-room door. Men were running everywhere. Obscene great bubbles of water were exploding to port, while from below came the faint cries of men, weak like those of fretful, sickly babies. A rating rushed by. Brandt caught him by the arm hastily.

'What is it?' he cried. 'What in God's name happened?'

The rating, a blond youth with a torpedoman's badge, swallowed his fear. 'Don't know exactly, *Herr Kapitänleutnant*,' he gasped, his thin chest heaving. 'But I think we've been hit in the engine room!'

Torpedo?'

'Don't know, sir, but it could be.' The next instant he wrenched himself loose and was running after the rest.

Brandt started to run along the deck, past the officers' galley, where a cook lay slumped over a stove among rolling apples and upturned bins of flour, slowly frying on the glowing hot plates. He would take over Guns' turrets of 76mm cannon on the starboard side. If they had been torpedoed, there had to be a sub out there – and a sub could attack again. He wanted to go down fighting, not burning Navy pay forms and other 'top secret' papers of that kind.

He doubled down a companionway, zig-zagging to avoid collisions. Everywhere there were sailors running, although running was forbidden.

Ducking under a dead gunner, who hung suspended in his harness, both ankles broken in the upward blast, Brandt pushed inside the twin-gun turret. The gunners were all at their posts, peering anxiously into the darkness, the loaders already cradling the next shells ready to reload.

'Brandt,' he gasped, '*Kapitänleutnant* Brandt . . . *Oberleutnant* Hermann has been killed. I'm taking over!'

The senior petty officer, a grizzled *Obermaat* who looked as if he had been at sea since the days of the sailing ships, glanced down at Brandt's gloved artificial hand. 'But, sir—' he began.

'*No buts!*' Brandt interrupted harshly. 'Get that searchlight on – at the double now. The Tommy devils are still out there!'

The urgency in the new officer's voice had an impact.

The grizzled old petty officer sprang forward and flicked the switch which operated the searchlight on top of the turret. A knife of bright silver light slit the darkness. Searchlights came clicking on the whole length of the ship as the *Deutschland*, still limping along at an awkward angle, tried to find her assailant. Under the glare of the lights, the water to starboard and port turned as bright as day, and half a hundred guns of all calibres stood ready, waiting for the ship's unknown, unseen adversary to appear.

'That's ruddy well torn it!' Orde gasped to himself, and hurriedly withdrew the two inches of his slender periscope, blinded by the brilliant white light which now surrounded the *Deutschland*. Just as a gloomy Rogers had predicted, the captain of the German Battleship had formed a circle of searchlights while he estimated the damage. Soon he would start trailing anti-sub nets to port and starboard. The X-craft would have to close and complete its part of the mission soon, or it would be too late.

He rapped out his orders to his three crew, all of whom lay or crouched in the tremendously tight confines of the little sub – there was only one place in the whole boat where a small man could stand upright, and that was directly under the periscope. The electric batteries carried the little sub forward almost noiselessly. Orde's second-in-command, another sub-lieutenant but junior even to himself, manned the main motor and hydroplanes control; next to him crouched the diver who would place the limpets, dressed for shallow water diving, save for his face-piece.

At a steady six knots the X-craft closed with the *Deutschland*, every man tensed and nervous, though professional enough in spite of their youth. Soon the German Asdic would pick them up; it was inevitable. But by that time Orde hoped they would be too close to the ship's hull for the Germans to drop depth charges without damaging their own ship. The only catch would be if the Jerries had already succeeded in dropping anti-sub nets; that certainly would hold the X-craft up. Perhaps fatally so . . .

The minutes passed by leadenly. Next to the second-in-command, the diver prepared to go into the wet and dry compartment; from where he could leave and enter the tiny sub without disturbing the trim or allowing water to enter any of the sub's other three compartments. Orde nodded his approval. It took a brave man to enter the 'W and D'; it measured only two feet, six inches long and three feet high, and now the diver was about to enter it under active conditions. If he *did* bump into an anti-sub net down there and the Jerries noticed, there was a strong risk that they could start tossing grenades – or worse – at him.

Orde took a chance. He raised the periscope again. It was a wide-field bifocal instrument, and he didn't need to extend it more than a couple of inches above the surface of the water in order to obtain an excellent view of what was going on above him. At that level it was almost invisible, even to the keenest anti-submarine look-out.

Carefully, not to disturb the surface of the water, he swung it round, already blinking at the brilliant white light reflected down the tube. The steel wall of the *Deutschland* towered high above him like a grey, dripping mountain. He could see every rivet, every dent in the plating. He cocked the lenses slightly, and groaned. Already, German sailors, outlined stark black against the blinding glare of the searchlights, were dropping steel anti-submarine nets overboard. Again Rogers had been right. The *Deutschland*'s captain was reacting exactly as the HMS *Ypres*' Number One had predicted.

Orde swung the periscope around. Otherwise nothing unusual. Obviously the Jerries knew that a submarine of some kind was out there. Equally obviously, they knew nothing about the two-man torpedo. Presumably they thought they had been torpedoed by a conventional submarine. He smiled to himself and lowered the periscope once more, carefully. All to the good. For the time being, the diver could start working on the nets in the knowledge that the Germans wouldn't be looking for him. Their attention would be concentrated further out to sea on the assumption that their assailant was lying in wait for them *there*. Gingerly, the tiny underwater craft hardly moving, he guided her towards the nets.

Soon everything would be in the hands of the diver. Armed with his mechanical cutters, he would start cutting the net strand by strand, until he had a hole big enough for the X-craft to pass through. But his task didn't end there. He would then have to regain the wet and slippery hull of the tiny submarine and, as it moved slowly ahead towards its target, walk *with* the passing strands of the steel net to the aft of X-craft to ensure that none of them became entangled with the sub. Finally he would return for his limpets and attach them, while the X-craft lay virtually motionless beneath the enemy's hull. When – and *if* – all that was completed, the X-craft, now lightened considerably, would make a hasty departure to within one thousand metres of the victim to watch the fun.

Slowly the bold little submarine with its crew of four drew closer to the great, grey hull of the *Deutschland*. Each one of them knew that above them, one thousand men, as young, as cunning and as dedicated as they were themselves, waited and sweated, trying to outguess them – just as *they* were trying to outguess the Germans.

The battle of wits, which could end only in death, had commenced.

For the umpteenth time, Brandt looked at his watch. It was already ten minutes since the first torpedo had struck them, yet their assailant still hadn't been spotted. Nor had the Tommy sub (he guessed it *had* to be English – the Ivans, with their unskilled Red Fleet submarines, never ventured this far from their Arctic bases) made another attack on the *Deutschland*.

Why not? The battleship couldn't be making more than eight knots an hour. At this moment, while the engineering crew laboured frantically to make an emergency repair to the severed oil feed lines, she was simply a very fat sitting duck.

Admittedly, she had her anti-sub nets out, and any Tommy skipper watching at this moment through his periscope couldn't help but see them – that had been part of the captain's defensive scheme. But surely any submariner worth his salt would have a go under such circumstances? Even in the Royal Navy, which unlike the *Kriegsmarine* was not particularly generous with medals, any skipper who had a crack at the *Deutschland* would get a piece of tin for his pains – even if his attempt failed. So why hadn't the Tommy attacked?

Brandt frowned, while from below he could hear the muted commands, the hiss of the welding torches and the frantic hammering of the engineers. There was something wrong here – but *where* exactly?

An excited cry broke into his confused reverie. '*Survivors!*' Tommy survivors to port bow!'

'Survivors?' Brandt echoed in bewilderment. Survivors from what? There hadn't been any action yet, so where should *survivors* come from?

'Ready for action at any moment, *Obermaat!*' he barked at the grizzled PO. 'I'm going to have a look.'

'*Jawohl, Herr Kapitänleutnant, aber—*'

But Brandt was no longer there to listen to his query. He was out of the turret and pushing his way through the crowd of curious, gesticulating ratings, towards the railing.

There, outlined a stark black by the light of crossed searchlights, pinned down like flies on a card, two dark shapes bobbed up and down in the water. But oddly they seemed to be attempting to get *away* from the lights . . .

Brandt grabbed the glasses hanging from the breast of

the young searchlight officer next to him and in doing so dragged the protesting midshipman against his side. But he had no time to heed the man's startled protests. There was something strange about this pair of 'survivors' who were so reluctant to be rescued. Hastily he twirled the focusing wheel.

The two dark shapes sprang into view, swimming right into the centre of the gleaming, calibrated glass. He gasped. Both were wearing oxygen masks, goggles and dark rubber suits of a kind he had never seen before. Then he had it. He remembered a picture in the *Völkischer Beobachter*: two spaghetti-eaters, all gleaming white teeth and greasy black, wavy hair, sitting astride the strangest craft he had ever seen and waving in triumph. The men who had sunk the *Queen Elizabeth* in the harbour of Alexandria!

'*Human torpedoes*,' he exploded. '*They're human torpedoes!*'

'*Human torpedoes!*'

'The words flew from mouth to mouth along the line of sailors manning the searchlights and machine-guns. '*Human torpedoes . . .*'

Brandt hesitated a moment. What could they do? Perhaps at this very moment there were more of them directly below, planting deadly devices which would blow the *Deutschland* sky-high. He slammed his metal fist against the railing in frustration. He – *they* – couldn't just stand there and let it happen, as years ago they had let it happen to the *Graf Spee*. The *Deutschland* mustn't perish so easily. There *had* to be a way of stopping the Tommy swine!

Suddenly he had it. Ignoring the fact that he wasn't the senior officer present on deck, he cupped his hands to his mouth and yelled above the noise from below: 'Everyone onto the anti-submarine nets! Get grenades and submachine-guns! Come on, move those fat butts! Put some pepper in yer pants, for God's sake! *Los! Dalli dalli!*'

Driven by the urgent commands of the one-armed

officer, heavily-clad ratings armed with stick grenades and machine pistols started swarming over the side, balancing as best they could on the nets and peering down into the dark water far below.

Thrusting two stick grenades into the sides of his tall sea-boots, Brandt clambered awkwardly over the swaying side of the *Deutschland*. He knew he was being a damned fool to try it with only his one hand. One slip and he'd be done for. The captain would never heave to to pick *him* from the sea, that was for sure. But he had to show these slow-thinking ratings what had to be done, come what may.

The only sound now was the muted whine of the electric batteries, as the X-craft nosed its way forward at a snail's pace. 'E.R.A.,'[1] Orde called, 'give me a reading, please.'

The sailor crouched next to Orde's second-in-command hesitated a moment, earphones clutched to his head, manipulating his powerful Asdic transmission set. The Asdic acted like a powerful invisible underwater searchlight. It sent out a wireless signal in a straight line. When this signal hit a solid object, it sent back an echo. The frequency and strength of that echo told a skilled operator how far away the object was. '275, sir,' he answered at last.

Orde nodded his approval. It was just as he expected.

'Green 37,' he commanded, and queried, 'Now?'

'276, sir.'

'Red 25. *Now*.'

'277 – 'The rating broke off suddenly as the little sub nudged softly into something and the tense men inside the craft heard the scrape of metal against metal. They had hit the nets. They were now directly below the *Deutschland*!

'Asdic reading getting louder and louder, sir,' the rating

[1] Engine room artificer.

announced. Though his voice was professionally calm, he still couldn't quite hide the note of excitement in it.

'Where are we exactly?'

'Off the starboard bow, sir.'

'Midships?'

'Think so, sir.'

'Grand.'

'Stop engines, sir?' asked his second-in-command.

'Stop engines, Number One.'

The rush of water ceased. Now the sweating crew could hear the beat of the *Deutschland*'s propellers quite clearly – a steady *throb-throb* like the beat of a huge, metallic heart. To the front of the stationary craft there was a slight rush of air escaping. The diver was leaving the 'W and D'.

Orde slumped against the periscope and breathed out hard, his innocent young face worn and pale. They had struck the anti-submarine nets. Now everything depended on the diver.

Awkwardly, *Kapitänleutnant* Brandt clambered down the net, wet and slippery, the thick wire broken here and there and ripping painfully through his thick gloves and into his fingers. Above him, the others hesitated. It was a very dangerous business climbing down the net – like descending a swaying, moving cliff-side. The ratings didn't like it. But Brandt didn't see the danger; he was animated by a picture in his mind's eye of bold men, clad in rubber, cutting through the net under the water, toiling away doggedly until they could pass through and attack the *Deutschland*'s hull. He had to stop them. *He had to!*

Now he was some ten metres above the silver swell of the waves. He paused and surveyed the heaving water, hanging on grimly with his good hand. He could see nothing. Outwardly it seemed as if the sea below was empty. But he knew that wasn't the case. The devils were down there somewhere. The question was, where?

Suddenly he felt a tingling, a trembling of the wire at his feet.

He flashed a look upwards. None of the ratings clinging like grim death to the wire had moved. The movement had come from below.

'Direct one of those searchlights down here!' he commanded hoarsely. 'At the double . . . for God's sake!'

A hard, white beam of light shot down the side of the *Deutschland.*

'Back and forth – slowly!' Brandt yelled.

Slowly the beam roamed the surface, penetrating the water to a depth of a couple of metres, while Brandt, his eyes narrowed to slits against the icy wind, followed its progress. And then he saw it: a trembling of the net, with far below, a vague, wavering black shape!

'There he is!' he cried urgently. 'Let him have it! Keep the light still. *Los! Los!*' With his artificial hand he plucked the first stick grenade from his boot, pulled out the china pin with his teeth and flung it as best he could. It dropped over the side and exploded in a spout of whirling white water. The next instant, machine-guns opened up the length of the *Deutschland*, whipping up the surface of the water with a deadly volley of fire. Brandt flung his other grenade. The trembling in the wire ceased. But he knew the danger to the *Deutschland* wasn't yet averted. The miniature submarine was still down there somewhere.

'Keep firing!' he cried above the hectic snap and crackle of small arms fire. 'Get a satchel charge, someone – *at the double*!'

A minute later, a petty officer clambered over the side, six grenades bundled together with cord in his free hand. Brandt pointed downwards hastily. 'There!' he yelled, as the still, black shape of the dead British diver came bobbing to the surface. 'Fling it there!'

The petty officer pulled out the pin, counted two, and dropped the satchel charge directly onto the diver. The charge and the diver went down together. A muffled roar.

A flash of ugly scarlet. The water heaved and swayed. Brandt clung on desperately as a great green-and-white gout of water hurtled into the sky, drenching the men clinging onto the nets. Next instant the tiny black shape of a miniature submarine hove into view, its screw threshing the waves purposelessly, its trapped occupants desperately trying to escape their fate.

But there was no escape this day. Grenade after grenade rained down onto the sub. It reeled back and forth under each fresh impact. Its thin periscope snapped off. Chunks of metal flew from its dwarf conning tower. The screws ceased whirling. She bellied there in the waves, giving off great gouts of compressed air. Oil started to stream from a damaged diesel. And then, as suddenly as she had appeared, she went under, belching forth a wavering column of bright white exploding bubbles.

'*Sieg Heil!*' someone screeched in ecstasy.

'*Heil! Heil! Heil!*'

The cheer rose from half a hundred hoarse, triumphant throats, while Brandt clung there, gasping, as if he had just run a great race . . .

SIX

'*They've done it!*' Savage cried excitedly, as the *Ypres* dodged behind yet another iceberg, running parallel with the listing Battleship that was now only two thousand yards away. '*They've damn well done it!*'

For a moment Rogers thought of that callow-faced youth who had been too scared to back out of his suicide mission, his teenage crew and the two tough marines, and felt again the waste that was war. Would anybody be interested in the fate of the *Deutschland* in a month's time? What did it really matter, when those boys were gone for ever – dead before they had even lived?

Savage obviously wasn't troubled by such thoughts. His face glowed with almost supernatural joy and energy, his dark eyes sparkling crazily as he saw the flame and smoke belching from somewhere inside the crippled ship, which was now limping along at a snail's pace. The *Deutschland*, which he had glimpsed in what seemed another age now, was ready for the kill. The question now was, how? *How* should he attack?

Rogers seemed to read his thoughts. He didn't want to suffer the same fate as young Orde; he wanted to live. 'Sir, she's been badly hit. Why don't we let the Cruisers come in and finish her off? We can simply stay here and shadow her.'

Savage swung round upon him, but not in anger; he was too far gone for anger. 'Shadow her! Let the Cruisers finish her off!' he exclaimed excitedly. 'After we've done all the hard work? Let *them* have all the glory? *Never!*'

'But we might be throwing lives away unnecessarily, sir,' Rogers protested. 'I mean, her armament's still completely intact. We can't hope to deal with those guns of hers. That's a job for the Cruisers' eight-inchers.'

'Absurd!' Savage chortled, with a mad laugh. 'Besides, we've got our tin fish, haven't we? Once we're in torpedo range, what good will her big guns be to her then?'

'But we've got to get within range first,' Rogers persisted.

'I've got it all worked out.' He pointed to the east, where the sky was already beginning to glow a weak yellow, heralding the dawn. 'We can come right out of the sun, using the icebergs to cover us as far as possible, hit her with our tin fish and then make off hell for leather!' He beamed at the younger man as if it were all a matter of routine – as if nothing could possibly go wrong.

'But sir, their radar . . .' The protest died on Rogers' lips. He saw that the captain was no longer listening. For now those inner voices had taken over again, and he was deaf to all but their mad urgings.

The sun rose beyond the horizon ten minutes later, colouring the sea a sickly yellow, against which the stricken battleship stood out a stark black. But soon it disappeared from sight and the cold started to harden once more, closing on the waiting men with steely fingers. The wind came shrieking in from the North Pole, chopping the sea into heaving white spume, and turning the *Ypres* a pale frost-covered ghost, moving on slowly under the grey dome of the sky into a world of darkness and death.

Now they were less than a sea-mile from the *Deutschland*, confidently moving out of the cover of the icebergs, for the sudden storm of wind, mixed with flurries of hail and snow, had cut down visibility to virtually nil.

All on board were tense, waiting for the battle; freezing in spite of their heavy clothing, they peered forward, ready for the first sight of the *Deutschland*, resigned to the fact that in all probability they wouldn't survive the next hours. Yet despite that knowledge and the almost unbearable tension, they were possessed by a strange excitement. Some talked incessantly. Others told joke after joke. A few smiled a lot at nobody and nothing. Tramping around the frozen deck, among spars and stanchions heavy with glittering hoar frost, checking that everything was ready, Rogers felt that they had all been infected by Savage; that they were *all* a little crazy now.

The ritual commenced. Through the voice pipe, Savage double-checked on Rogers, making sure that nothing could go wrong once they started that wild dash for the *Deutschland*.

'Turrets,' he demanded.

'Turrets closed up, sir,' came back the sharp reply.

'Oerlikons.'

'Oerlikon crews closed up, sir . . .'

The brisk, harsh litany of battle went on, until finally Savage was satisfied that all action stations were closed up. He nodded, pleased with his ship and his men, muttering and mumbling to himself as he did all the time now, watched by the helmsman out of the corner of his eye, a little frightened by this strange skipper who seemed to live in another world from the rest of mankind.

Now they were less than five hundred yards away from the still invisible *Deutschland*, steering towards her on a radar heading. The torpedo ratings tensed at their deadly weapons; the gunners peered through their firing slits, trying to penetrate the whirling white gloom for their first sight of their enemy in this remote sea.

Savage swung round on Rogers who now stood behind him on the slightly swaying bridge. 'All right, Rogers – this is it,' he said through gritted teeth, his eyes sparkling unnaturally. 'I'm going to engage – *now!*'

With a vast, ear-splitting snarl, the Destroyer leapt forward, unleashed at last. Madly, Rogers grabbed for support, as the bow tilted upwards. Two great banks of foaming white water rose to left and right. Aft, the screws whirled mightily, leaving the foam piling up behind them like solid snow. At thirty knots the *Ypres* dashed into battle.

*

The young officer crouched over the torpedo switch panel, eyes narrowed to slits as he waited for his ratings to report. Below his feet, the whole deck shivered as the *Ypres* struck wave after wave, shooting forward at a tremendous speed, her every plate howling in protest at the almost unbearable strain. Any moment now they would break out of the cover of the snow flurries and confront the German monster.

'Close up, sir,' the tense rating whispered, as if he were afraid the Germans could hear him.

'Stand by for torpedo attack,' the young officer said, and whispered a fervent prayer that they would strike lucky; they would never get a second chance.

'Stand by tubes!' the skipper's harsh, imperious voice crackled down the voice pipe. 'Open fire as soon as you can bring to bear!'

The torpedo officer swallowed. The side of his face ticked nervously. The strain on him was almost unbearable; his nerves cried out in protest.

Around him the ratings, their faces ashen and greased with nervous sweat, also swallowed hard, their throats parched, their nerves jingling.

'*There she is!*' someone cried.

'*The Deutschland!*' the torpedo officer gasped.

As the *Ypres* came careening out of the snow flurries, the German Battleship seemed to fill the whole horizon, little black dots racing madly along her decks, red signal flares hissing into the sky in alarm.

The torpedo officer hesitated only a second, bent over the three-pronged sight, damp sweating hand on the torpedo firing button. The *Deutschland* slid dutifully right into the sight. He stabbed the button with his thumb. *Once . . . twice . . . three times . . .*

The *Ypres* shuddered violently. There was a frantic hiss of compressed air. *Whoosh . . . Whoosh . . . Whoosh . . .* One after another, in rapid succession, the two-ton torpedoes slammed into the water. Immediately their motors started up and props whirled. For a second they churned the sea a brilliant boiling white. Then they had vanished beneath the surface. At forty-five knots an hour, leaving a trail of exploding bubbles behind them, they shot towards their target.

Up on the bridge, Savage flung up his glasses. Behind him, Rogers started to count off the seconds. At the wheel the helmsman, tensed for immediate evasive action, began to pray. It was now or never!

'Torpedo starboard bow . . . *Torpedo!*' the look-out screamed, as the Destroyer which had appeared out of nowhere heeled to the right, throwing up a tremendous wall of white foam, and the first startled, wild shots from the *Deutschland* exploded.

On the bridge the captain rapped out an order. The *Deutschland* answered immediately, in spite of her list. She heeled violently, scattering instruments everywhere, as the first torpedo hissed past.

The captain didn't need the look-out's cry to tell him where the next one would come from; he could visualise the enemy pattern in his mind's eye. As guns erupted the whole length of the pocket Battleship, he brought her about again and the second torpedo missed her by a matter of metres. He beamed at his second-in-command, the beads of sweat hanging like opaque pearls in his bushy brows. '*Na, Hannes*,' he grunted, 'we dodged those . . .'

The words died on his lips as the *Deutschland* was struck a tremendous hollow blow that nearly flung him from his feet.

'*Um Himmels Willen*,' he cursed. 'What in three devils' name was that?'

'They hit us, sir,' his second-in-command replied; then he grinned. 'But they fired a dud.'

'*A dud?*'

The second-in-command extended his hands like a head waiter inviting a guest to take a special seat. 'Can't you see, sir? We sail on.'

The captain's face lit up.' *Natürlich, mein lieber Hannes . . . Natürlich, the Tommy fish had no teeth . . .*'

Triumphantly the *Deutschland* limped on.

'In!' the loaders roared in unison.

'Ready!' the gun layers yelled.

'*Fire . . . one! Fire two!*' Brandt bellowed above the chatter of the machine-guns to his right and the *thump-thump* of the Oerlikons above the turret.

The layers pressed their triggers. The firing pins hit the detonators. They exploded with an unholy roar, smashing into the great wads of gun cotton. The immense wave of gas shot the hundred-pound shells up the long rifled tubes. At four times the speed of sound, they roared from the slender muzzles. The blast raced back at the speed of a railway express. But the recoil system cushioned the tremendous shock, and the two guns moved backwards on their mounts like two elderly *Omas*[1] settling back on their cushions for afternoon coffee.

Brandt grinned. *That* should put paid to the damned impertinent little Tommy Destroyer.

Ypres's gunners, blinded, mesmerised, shocked by the tremendous hail of fire coming from the German Battleship, fought back bravely, as for a few fleeting seconds the racing Destroyer ran a parallel course with the *Deutschland*. They tried not to see the horrible things which were happening to their ship, as the tracer and shells ripped great gaping holes in the superstructure, chipping and ripping the woodwork, gouging savage tears in the thin steel plates. Everywhere could be heard cries for help from the wounded and the agonised, unbearable moans of dying men, trapped among the smoking, shattered débris on deck.

'Hard port!' Savage screamed, as yet another salvo of

[1] Grannies.

eleven-inch shells roared in like express trains. The *Ypres* reeled. A sailor, caught off guard, went overboard, screaming, and was churned to a bloody pulp by the racing screws. A shell exploded only yards away. Fist-sized chunks of red-hot shrapnel hissed through the air. Water rose a hundred feet and cascaded over the Destroyer. A gun crew vanished over the shattered rail, a mess of whirling arms and legs, to disappear in the heaving water.

Savage grinned crazily at Rogers. 'They'll have to do better than that, Number One,' he began. 'Drop smoke floats . . . Drop smoke floats at the double!'

Almost at once dense smoke started to rise on the sea behind them, somehow seeming to deaden the ear-splitting racket of the enemy guns. It was like hot, fetid breath engulfing the whole boat. Men suddenly seemed no longer afraid, grinning at each other with smoke-begrimed faces, believing suddenly in this fragile protection. They had done it! They had escaped their just retribution for having dared to tackle the great steel monster!

But it was not to be. Just as Rogers was beginning to believe that they would pull it off after all, Brandt's carefully laid salvo hit them with a great hammer-blow. The whole ship reeled and heeled under the massive impact. The last of the superstructure came tumbling down. Men screamed, trapped beneath the flying débris. Others sank to their knees, grasping at their throats, retching and choking in the acrid fumes. Some simply died where they stood, not a mark on their bodies, but with their lungs ripped apart by the awesome blast.

Slowly, very slowly indeed, as the *Deutschland* disappeared behind them into the snow and the smoke, HMS *Ypres* started to lose speed . . .

SEVEN

HMS *Ypres* was an indescribable mess. Below decks, the water was knee-deep. Everywhere was grotesquely twisted metal, mixed with the crew's possessions – uniform caps, tins of duty-free tobacco, bottles, mops and brooms and a hundred other objects. Dead men lay sprawled out extravagantly or occasionally crawled in tight balls, hands clasped firmly to their ears, as if to cut out the noise, but dead all the same. Even the ship's cat was dead, head sliced off by flying shrapnel and lying beneath the old leather settee in the ward-room.

But still the Destroyer laboured on, the stokers half-submerged in freezing water as they tried desperately to pump the flooded engine-room clear. Five minutes at a time was all they could stand before they were relieved, faces white and peaked, frozen to the very marrow of their brawny bodies, writhing in agony when sensation started to return to their tortured bodies.

Fortunately the snow flurries had thickened, giving them the cover they needed as they limped on unseen, still on a parallel course with the *Deutschland*. The radar room was undamaged and they were still able to pick up their erstwhile victim, but this was the only piece of technical apparatus still functioning. The wireless was long dead and they were unable to send or receive – and Rogers guessed that the *Deutschland* was in exactly the same position. Crippled as she was, she would hardly give her position away.

Thus, in silence, and cut off from the great world outside, David and Goliath limped on.

Savage, a towel held to his gashed head in an attempt

to staunch the flow of bright red blood, limped around his ship, ignoring the grating of the shrapnel lodged in his knee, assessing the damage. It was snowing again – soft, white, sad flakes, drifting down over the jumbled, battle-littered deck.

Rogers followed warily, wishing he could read the skipper's mind, for he knew instinctively that Savage hadn't given up in spite of the beating the *Ypres* had taken. Here and there he saw the numbed, shocked looks on the men's faces and knew they were too far gone to react. They would obey; they would do anything Savage wanted, however crazy. The spirit had been beaten out of them. They would go to their deaths without protest, like dumb animals.

'Casualties?' Savage asked finally, leaning for support against a canvas screen which had been ripped down the centre with machine-gun fire.

'Ten dead, eighteen badly wounded. Most of the rest with cuts, bruises, superficial wounds.'

'Enough then,' Savage said, staring out into the white gloom that hid the *Deutschland*.

'Enough for what, sir?' Rogers asked, though he knew what Savage meant well enough.

Savage didn't answer his question. 'Engine rooms?'

'The ER9 estimates that we'll have nearly full power within the hour, sir.'

'Excellent. Excellent,' Savage said, taking his eyes off the sea and straightening up again. He looked hard at Rogers, as if seeing him for the first time. His eyes were no longer crazy, just completely blank of emotion; stern, hard, unyielding, revealing nothing of what was going on in his mind. 'What do you think they'll do, Number One?'

'You mean the *Deutschland*?'

Savage nodded.

'Turn soon and head for Norway, keeping between Bear Island and Hope Island. They know our people – the Cruisers, I mean – won't follow them into tricky waters like that. Then they'll bear due south and head for the nearest Norwegian port, once they've whistled up air cover.'

Savage nodded. 'My guess too. On their present course that seems the most likely possibility.'

Rogers had to force himself to ask the next question. 'Why do you ask, sir?'

Savage smiled suddenly, but it wasn't the smile of a normal man; it was that secret, arrogant, all-knowing smile of a crazy man, who thought in his madness that he could outwit the whole world. 'Because I aim to stop them. They shan't get away after what they've done to *my* ship.' He dropped the towel from his head and extended his hand at the shambles of the deck, now slowly turning white under the softly drifting snow.

Even though he had been expecting the answer, Rogers recoiled. 'But with *what*, sir? How can we stop the *Deutschland* in the shape we're in? A-turret has had it. Our ammo's about gone, and what shells we still possess won't even make a dent in the *Deutschland*. We're down to two torpedoes . . . Sir, I don't see what earthly good we can do under present circumstances.' He tried to keep his voice under control, but it was an effort.

Savage smiled. 'I agree with everything you've just said, Number One,' he said mildly. 'But there's one thing that we *do* have left, isn't there?'

'Is there, sir? I wouldn't know what.'

'Why, the *Ypres* itself, Number One.'

'The *Ypres*!'

'Yes.' His smile broadened and he beamed at his second-in-command like an indulgent parent at a particularly slow child. 'Haven't we still the ultimate weapon that every RN skipper has always used when there was nothing else left to him?'

'Forgive me, sir, but I don't think I follow you,' Rogers stuttered. 'What exactly do you mean?'

'My dear chap, we can still ram her if everything else fails.'

Rogers' mouth dropped open stupidly.

'The skipper's gonna ram her!'

The words passed from mouth to mouth in an awed whisper. It had started with the sickbay attendant. He had slipped it to his particular friend, a greasy little cook from Liverpool with long sidechats. The cook had passed it on to one of the stokers, who was trying to thaw out in the galley. Slowly but surely it went round the whole awed ship.

'*The skipper's gonna ram her!*'

But as a bemused Rogers walked the littered decks, supervising the clearing-up operation, he could see that the startling news didn't affect the men quite as he had expected. They were awed by it, that was for sure; but the prospect didn't appear to frighten them. It was as if they, too, had been infected permanently by the captain's madness, and were now prepared to forget that this crazy battle could have only one outcome for them – death. As he listened to their whisperings and saw the look of awe change to one akin to delight, he felt like grabbing the nearest sailor, shaking him violently and screaming into his face, 'What the *Hell* is the matter with you? Don't you see? *The skipper's taking us all to our death!*' But he didn't. Instead, he walked the decks, gave out orders, his voice coming as if from far away. He felt like a zombie, ordered by a Fate against which there was no appeal, to go blindly to his own death.

As the snow ceased and the first hard, black shadows of night started to steal over the dark green water, dragging the unknown behind them, the first news of the long afternoon was brought to the bridge by an excited radar operator.

'She's turning, sir!' he cried. 'Turning on a north-easterly course.'

Savage flashed a sombre-faced Rogers a triumphant look. 'Just as I predicted! Just as I predicted, Number One. She's breaking off the battle with the convoy. She's had enough. She's heading for the channel between Bear Island and Hope Island. Once she's picked up air cover, she'll be scurrying for cover. We've got her on the run!'

'Got her on the run!' Rogers muttered under his breath – but Savage wasn't listening; he was hearing those inner voices again, head bent, lips moving silently, eyes glittering with excitement as he made his crazy calculations.

'The engine-room chiefie tells me we can make twenty knots now without straining the boilers,' he said after a moment. 'On that basis, I calculate that we could reach a position halfway between the two islands by dawn and well ahead of the *Deutschland*. It's unlikely that the planes of their Fifth Air Fleet will set off to meet her before visibility has improved. After all, they'll have to pick her up visually. So that gives us perhaps an hour before they arrive to have a crack at her.'

It was that phrase that finally roused Rogers from his mood of restraint.

'*Crack at her*, you say, skipper!' he exploded. 'We'll never have a *crack* at her! We risk suicide by trying to ram her. If her guns don't blow us out of the water by the time we get within ramming distance, and we do manage to hole her badly enough to sink her – which is hardly likely – then we bloody well go down with her!' Only with difficulty did Rogers restrain himself from grabbing hold of Savage by his coat and shaking the life out of him. 'Don't you realize that? For God's sake, *don't you*?'

Chest heaving, fists clenched into painful white-knuckled balls, Rogers glared at the skipper, while the radarman stared open-mouthed at the two of them, facing each other on the shattered bridge.

Savage remained unmoved. 'Don't worry, Number One. I shall have every remaining boat readied for immediate release as soon as we've rammed. With the dead, there'll be sufficient room for everyone on board.'

'And who's going to pick us up before we freeze to death?' Rogers began, and then with an angry shrug of his shoulders, muttering to himself, he gave up. It was no use. Savage was crazy; the whole damned bunch of them were crazy; he could do nothing with them.

The captain gave a thin smile and with a benevolent nod and a 'Good work, Smith' to the radarman who had brought the news, he returned to his calculations. The *Ypres* sailed on.

On the *Deutschland* that night, the mood was similarly apprehensive and sombre. The high excitement and optimism with which the ship had set sail had vanished. Now all of them, right down to the greenest Moses,[1] knew that their bold venture into the Atlantic after two years in harbour had been a complete failure. There would be no sinking of the *Augusta*; no triumphant return to Bergen with the bands playing and the land rats cheering and waving flags. It meant the end of the big ships. Admiral Raeder would have to go and the 'Big Lion', Doenitz, would take his place. There would be no holding the U-boat skippers from now on, and their own careers as big ship men would be over; they, too, would have to go into the underwater boats.

'We'll get back all right, I've no doubt of that,' Roof-Hare said, nursing his Korn, his face dark and brooding. 'The Fifth Air Fleet has been alerted to provide us with air cover in the morning. There's a double watch on duty. By now it's too dark for Tommy air to locate us, and even

[1] Nickname in the German Navy for the youngest member of the crew.

if they did, they'd never manage to get their Cruisers up here in time. You know how slow the Tommies are.' He took a sip of his Korn and pulled a face, as if he wished he hadn't touched it.

Brandt nodded. 'But there's still that Tommy Destroyer out there somewhere, Roof-Hare.'

'Yes, I know. And we also know she was steaming a parallel course with us for a while, but before I went off watch, the captain told me she'd disappeared off the screen. It's pretty obvious she's taken off – back to Iceland, I suppose. She was pretty badly knocked about when I last saw her.'

Brandt nodded. 'Well, I suppose this is the last active service voyage I shall be taking.' He looked down at his gloved artificial hand. 'Old fire-eater Doenitz will have no time for a cripple like me in his beloved U-boats.'

'Yes, I suppose you're right, Jailer. I'll volunteer for the subs, of course, I've got to think of my pension, after all. I need to make rank while the going's good.' He grinned.

Brandt grinned back, but his eyes remained dull and weary.

'But I guess it'll be a shore-based job for you, old friend. But cheer up. Fancy sitting in a nice warm office in Kiel or Wilhelmshaven for the rest of the war – a big fat rear-echelon stallion in a fancy uniform, with a good piece of tin to attract the secretaries.' Roof-Hare leaned over and punched his old friend in the shoulder. 'Heaven, arse and cloudburst, Jailer! What more could you want . . . Why, man, you'll be living like God in France!'

But *Kapitänleutnant* Brandt was fated never to become that fat rear-echelon stallion and live like God in France; and somehow, in that quiet, dark-panelled ward-room, its walls hung with the yellowing portraits of the heavy-set bearded worthies who had formed the old Imperial German Navy, Brandt knew it. With the sudden absolute clarity of a vision, he knew that this was to be his last voyage ever. He shuddered violently.

Roof-Hare looked at him in surprise. 'What's the matter with you, old house? Is the Korn that strong?'

Brandt forced a grin. 'No, Roof-Hare, not at all. I was just thinking . . . A louse must have run over my liver.'

'With hob-nailed boots, I suppose!' Roof-Hare quipped, eyeing his old friend carefully.

'Suppose so.'

They lapsed into silence, each man wrapped in a cocoon of his own thoughts and forebodings. The *Deutschland* steamed on. The actors were in place; the curtain was about to go up, and the last act commence . . .

EIGHT

Dawn broke cold, grey, and vicious.

A cruel wind tore flatly across the sea, tearing at the waves with white fingers and hurling the cold green spray at the men huddled in layer on layer of clothing on the bridge of the *Ypres*. The wind buffeted them with such force that it was difficult to breathe, and they were forced to converse in monosyllables, speaking only when necessary. The icy air stabbed their lungs like sharp knives.

But in spite of the damage she had sustained and the fierce head wind, the *Ypres* ploughed on steadily through the green, heaving waves, coming ever closer to the rendezvous; and the men were on their toes, too. Breakfast for most of them had been cold, greasy bacon sandwiches, washed down by milkless tea laced with rum. Savage had ordered that the surviving cooks would stand by for deck duty now. Every single man was needed to fill the gaps in their ranks. Despite this, there was none of the usual grumbling. Even the cooks, notorious moaners, had accepted their new task with alacrity.

In his two years in the Wavy Navy, Rogers had never seen a crew so eager and so selfless. 'My God,' he whispered more than once to himself in awe, 'you'd think they were *glad* to be going to their deaths.'

It was just after six when the look-out at the bows called, '*Smoke to port, sir! Enemy warship, bearing west!*'

Rogers didn't listen to the rest of that excited cry. He swung up his glasses, feeling his heart rise into his throat as if it were about to choke him. Time and time again he was forced to swallow with nervous tension. In an hour, he might well be dead! It was hardly possible to believe that overwhelming reality: within sixty short minutes, this apparently so solid body would exist no more.

Savage had no such thoughts as he lowered his glasses. Calmly, in an almost matter-of-fact manner, he announced, 'It's her all right. The *Deutschland*.'

'She's spotted us, sir,' Rogers said, lowering his glasses too as a series of recognition flags started to flutter on the grey ship over two miles away. 'Won't be more than a matter of minutes before they recognize us.'

'Let them!' Savage said with supreme confidence. 'By then it'll be too late.' He flicked on the switch of the loud hailer system, blew down it a couple of times, and said, 'Now hear this. Now hear this.' His voice echoed back and forth metallically. 'This is it, lads. This time there's no stopping us. We'll hit her, and then it's into the boats – at the double.' Savage paused for an instant, and Rogers at his side could almost feel his mind working as he formulated his last words to the doomed crew. He could see Savage was about to make a calculated, cunning appeal to their patriotism and loyalty. '. . . I know I haven't been with you long, and you don't know me. But I think I know *you*. I know that you're brave and loyal and won't let me, the ship, or your country down. Thank you – and God bless you!'

He flicked off the switch. Down below, the old CPO, his grey, weary face animated by a kind of emotion that Rogers had never seen before, cried, 'Three cheers for the captain! Three cheers for the old Wipers! Hip, hip, *hurrah*!'

The battered survivors burst into a wild, excited cheer, and Savage stared at Rogers for an instant almost in triumph, as if telling him that he, Savage, had won and that his sullen-faced Number One had lost. The old appeals to the old values of glory and patriotism had triumphed.

Then Rogers was forgotten and Savage was rapping out orders. The *Ypres* began to make smoke. Her nose lifted. She started to gain speed. Rogers gripped a stanchion.

Everywhere the men tensed at their posts, the wind rushing past their ears. The roar of her engines grew ever louder. The wind lashed at their faces in icy fury, the spray whipping up and over the bows. The shattered superstructure streamed water.

Rogers flung a last look at Savage. The skipper stood there, legs spread apart, lean, dark face exultant, eyes gleaming. At that moment Rogers thought he had never seen a man so carried away by excitement as the skipper. It was as if his excitement would tear him apart if the tensions weren't released soon.

Rogers blinked his bloodshot eyes against the racing wind. Directly ahead, towering high into the sky, guns blinking the length of its deck, lay the *Deutschland*. Every detail of her was utterly clear: masts, funnels, huge eleven-inch gun turrets, hole rent in her side, the running sailors . . . There was no going back now. Rogers flung a final glance at the German Battleship, then turned to the skipper again. Savage raised himself to his full height and opened his mouth to issue his last command.

The *Deutschland*'s eleven-inchers roared. The grey sky was torn apart by their elemental fury. One . . . Two . . . Three . . . Four . . . Huge spouts of whirling water flailed upwards. Brandt caught his breath. Surely nothing, absolutely nothing, could survive that tremendous salvo? The Tommy Destroyer disappeared into the smoke and flying water. But yes! There she was again, smoke pouring furiously from her funnels, reeling drunkenly from side to side as the waves lashed her back and forth, but coming on all the same, surviving as if by magic the furious white wall of tracer and flak that came flying at her.

'God in heaven!' Brandt cursed. 'How *can* she damn well survive!'

But somehow the Tommy Destroyer did. Now the *Ypres* was less than half a kilometre away. The *Deutschland*'s gunners whirled their wheels furiously, trying to depress their pieces to meet the impudent challenge of this dying craft, her bow afire, smoke billowing out of her, her superstructure and deck riddled with bullets and shrapnel.

The *Deutschland*'s eleven-inchers boomed once more, making the whole ship tremble with the blast. But their shells went zooming way over the heeling, reeling attacker, thrashing and whipping the sea into turmoil.

Brandt had had enough. With a violent curse, he elbowed the loader out of the way and thrust his eye against the rubber suction pad. Now the flying Destroyer was neatly dissected by the wire of the calibrated sight. Not taking his gaze away for a moment, and with the enemy growing ever larger in the bright gleaming circle of glass, Brandt fumbled for the firing lever. In the glass the Destroyer lurched, as she fired her last torpedo.

'*Kippers away!*' Brandt sang out, no longer afraid, carried away completely by the mad excitement of this crazy, wild battle. The *Deutschland* heaved violently as the captain took evasive action and the *Ypres*' last torpedo flashed harmlessly by her bows. For a moment the glass of the sight was empty. Hastily Brandt adjusted it. The Destroyer flashed back into view again. He could see her every detail now. He bit his bottom lip, trying to steady his breathing and the racing beat of his heart. She was sailing into his sight. *He couldn't miss!* The bridge came into view. He could see three dark figures silhouetted stark black against the dirty white of the structure: the captain, second-in-command and helmsman. Brandt felt the sweat trickling down his face in thick pearls. His shoulder muscle tightened. His fingers curled damply round the bar. They were less than two hundred metres away, miraculously surviving the hail of tracer that came hissing towards them like glowing golf balls. 'Come . . . Come, my pretty little Tommy,' Brandt hissed to himself, teeth bared in an animal grin, eyes gleaming savagely. 'Come and be killed . . .'

The foremost figure on the bridge turned for an instant.

Despite the distance and the heaving, wildly vibrating bridge, there was no mistaking that face. He had lived with it for nearly two years. '*Savage . . . Rodney Savage!*' he breathed in total disbelief. '*Here!*'

Instinctively he pulled the trigger. The gun erupted. The turret flooded with acrid yellow and Brandt opened his mouth automatically to prevent his eardrums from being burst, as the blast slammed backwards, hitting him a flabby wet blow in the face. Now Savage was gone, and all Brandt would remember until the great whirling red light vanished for good and he was dead, was a great, echoing roar that seemed to go on for ever and ever . . .

The scream rang out shrill, hysterical, piercing, penetrating even the terrible roar of gunfire.

'*Skipper!*' Rogers cried desperately as Savage reeled back, clutching his face. 'Skipper, what the devil—' He broke off and fought back the hot vomit which threatened to choke him. 'Oh, my God!'

Savage righted himself and lowered his hands, covered with hot, red, dripping gore. His eyes had gone. Where they had been were now two dark purple oozing pits.

'Captain!' Rogers called, making himself face this sightless horror. He reached out a hand to steady Savage, but the Captain thrust it away angrily.

'Leave me alone,' he snarled, swaying dangerously, the blood streaming down his ruined face. 'Don't touch me, Rogers! *Don't!*' He raised his right arm to wipe away the blood that was blinding him. But still he couldn't see. 'You're blind . . .' the little voices hissed in his ear. '*Blind, Savage!*'

'It doesn't matter!' he cried back. 'I'll still do it, do you hear!' His right hand shot out and grabbed a horrified Rogers, chilled to the marrow by the sight of this eyeless, mad monster. 'For God's sake, Rogers, point me in their direction! The *Deutschland* . . . Point me that way!' His fingers bit deep and painfully into Rogers' arm.

'But sir—'

'The *Deutschland*!' Savage shrieked, the blood pouring down his face from those empty scarlet pits once more.

'There! *There – damn you!*' Rogers cried, and pulled the skipper round till he was once again facing that great steel monster, its side now ablaze with the scarlet winking lights of its cannon, sending tracer zipping towards the stricken little Destroyer from all corners in a lethal morse.

'Steady as you go, helmsman!' Savage cried above the murderous racket. 'Full ahead together!'

Rogers tore himself free as the *Ypres* leapt forward once more. 'You're mad . . . You're all mad!' he shrieked, and staggered back from the dying captain and the helmsman, who both remained intent solely on their task. Rogers' words went unheard. Then he was gone, racing down the débris-littered steps to the boats . . .

The last burst of machine-gunfire caught Savage in the very final instant. Bone splintered. His blood splattered the deck in huge red gobs. His ears filled with his own screams, driving away those little voices which had tormented and dominated him for so long. His helpless, shattered body slammed to the heaving plates, urine and excreta streaming down his legs. For one fleeting second his dying face softened suddenly and creased into a weary smile. Next moment he died, as the *Ypres* careened into the side of the *Deutschland* with the blow of a monstrous factory hammer.

It was over at last.

The *Ypres*' bow crumpled into a mass of bent and twisted metal, dead men sprawled everywhere on her shattered decks, like broken dolls cast aside by a careless child. For a second or two the two ships, friend and foe, clung together like helpless lovers, screws churning wildly, the Germans staring down in disbelief at the dead Englishmen below, numb and aghast. Then slowly, very slowly, the *Deutschland* began to cast her aside. The

Ypres reeled away. From below came a muffled crump as ammunition magazines started to explode. Her bow began to sink, while her stern reared high into the air, her propellers spinning uselessly in the air.

Suddenly her main magazine exploded. Five hundred metres away, the awed sailors on the *Deutschland* felt a shock as if someone had just punched them in the guts. Her stern reared higher in the sky like a great steel tomb. Slowly, inexorably, she started to slide beneath the waves, which leapt up greedily to receive her, only to recoil, hissing and spluttering angrily, as they felt the searing heat.

On the bridge of the *Deutschland* the shocked, ashen-faced officers of the battleship, feeling no sense of triumph at the death of a brave ship, raised their hands in a final salute. Then with one last, wild tumult of water, the *Ypres* was gone for good.

Majestically the *Deutschland* sailed on to her own fate, leaving the ocean empty now, save for the mass of floating débris and the lone man on the rubber float, sobbing, sobbing, as if his very heart would break . . .

ENVOI

The smell of defeat was in the air this May afternoon. Even the fresh breeze coming in across the bomb-shattered town of Wilhelmshaven from the North Sea couldn't blow it away. It had settled on the port like dreary grey dust. The town now lay in ruins, peopled by grey skeletons, trundling their pathetic bits and pieces behind them in little wooden carts, while crippled veterans in the grey uniform of the beaten *Wehrmacht* begged for cigarettes at street corners. The only sign of ruddy, healthy life in this occupied city were the khaki-clad Canadians, rifles slung over their shoulders, who strode the bomb-littered streets purposefully, like creatures from another world.

Lt Commander Rogers tapped the sailor driving his jeep on the shoulder and addressed him in his peculiar stiff voice; his latest skin graft was still very tight and it pained him.

'See if that road leads to the naval harbour, Evans.'

Evans didn't look at the officer seated behind him. He had been called up in March 1945 and had missed action; as a result he wasn't used to the horror of sea warfare. Commander Rogers' salmon-pink, skull-like face was a horror he didn't care to dwell on too often. 'The Admiral's due to arrive by train at fourteen hundred hours, sir. We could well miss him.'

Rogers tried to grin, but the pain turned it into a grimace. 'Any admiral who arrives by train, Evans, *ought* to be missed. But don't worry, I'll get you there in time . . . Just want to make a little sentimental journey, that's all.'

Evans coloured, and waiting till the hard-faced redcap directing military traffic at the crossroads signalled him on, he drove down the cobbled street, lined by bomb-shattered warehouses, their surviving walls daubed with the slogans of the defeated Nazi Empire. '*Better dead than red . . . Never again 1918.*' And over and over again, the defiant, '*Victory or Siberia!*'

Rogers nodded. These days Siberia began just the other side of the River Elbe. That was why the admiral was coming. Their Lordships wanted to have a look-see at surviving German naval resources, just in case the Red Army over there got too uppity; apparently, Churchill himself had ordered the check to be carried out.

The little jeep turned a corner. Before them lay the naval harbour, filled from end to end with wrecks, some so deep in the water that only their funnels and masts were visible. Others had keeled over on their sides, their superstructure shattered. One or two were beached in the shallows like stranded, metallic whales.

'Christ,' Evans gasped, 'they really caught a packet here, sir, didn't they!'

'That they did, Evans. The Brylcreem boys clobbered them well.'

As the jeep slowed down to avoid the half-filled bomb craters and potholes that covered the jetty, Rogers' eyes scanned the grey, half-submerged wrecks, all of them flying the white flag of surrender. He was looking for the ship he had come halfway across war-torn Europe to see, this May of 1945.

Then he saw her.

Her masts were shattered, her deck pocked with shrapnel marks like the symptoms of some hideous skin disease, listing to one side, the water around her blue with escaped oil and the scum of the harbour.

'Over there, Evans,' he ordered, noting an odd electric tingling in his hands and a sudden shortness of breath. 'Get as close as you can, please.'

Evans drove on until forced to halt before a large crane

whose arm had fallen in a mass of grotesquely twisted metal, blocking any further progress.

'That do, sir?' he enquired and pulled on the brake. But he didn't turn off the engine. Evans was an imaginative youth, and there was something definitely eerie and not a little frightening about this abandoned harbour, filled with the silent, deserted grey hulks.

'Fine,' Rogers said, not taking his eyes off the wreck. He got out of the jeep and walked a little stiffly over towards it, his boots echoing hollowly in this graveyard of ships. He paused and looked up at the ship which had once been the pride of the German Navy. The only time Hitler had ever gone to sea, he had done so on this particular ship. Now she was simply a mass of twisted, rusting metal, all her former pride gone, abandoned to the rats and the seagulls which nested in her shattered superstructure.

For a long time Lt Commander Rogers stared, his ears filled with the voices and cries of another time, frightened, wild, crazed, as they had faced up to this ship for the last time. Slow, cold tears of memory and regret began trickling slowly down the taut pink skin of his new face, the artificial product of a surgeon's hands.

There was a soft clearing of a throat immediately behind him. Rogers started and hastily dabbed at his wet cheeks. It would be Evans, worried about the damned chair-borne admiral. 'All right, all right, I'm coming,' he began, turning round. Then he stopped short.

It *wasn't* Evans. It was a German . . . A former German naval officer by the look of him. An ankle-length blue overcoat, devoid of all badges of rank, concealed the man's missing leg, for he supported himself heavily on crutches.

'Yes, what is it?' he asked, knowing that Montgomery had forbidden his troops to talk to Germans; non-fraternization, they called it.

Painfully the man who had once been known as 'Roof-Hare' freed one hand from his crutches and raised it to his battered cap, as if in salute. 'Excuse me, but I saw you looking at the ship.'

Rogers' eyes narrowed and he looked curiously at the skinny ex-sailor with his sunken grey cheeks and shabby, ill-fitting coat that looked two sizes too large for him. 'You sailed in her?' he asked.

'Yessir,' Roof-Hare answered, with the new humility he had learned in this terrible year. Once. Why do you ask, sir?' He caught the glint of tears in the eyes of this strange-looking Tommy officer. 'If I may be so bold, sir?' he added hastily.

Rogers looked at the one-legged German. The war had ruined him, too. Friend and foe once, now they were joined together in common misery and ruination. 'Once, a long time ago, I fought against her.' He jerked his thumb over his shoulder at the grey wreck.

'I see, sir,' Roof-Hare answered, not daring to ask where and when; for their new conquerors were unpredictable, touchy people. And after all, he did have a request . . .

For a moment or two they stood there facing each other awkwardly, as if embarrassed by what they knew about one another now. Then Roof-Hare gave an embarrassed cough. 'You . . . er, you don't have a cigarette, sir . . . to sell me?' he added hastily, trying to salvage something of his lost pride. 'I'll gladly pay the customary black market price . . . He freed his hand again and fumbled in his pocket, as if he were looking for Mark notes – which were worthless anyway.

Rogers shook his head. He reached into his pocket and brought out a packet of Senior Service. 'Here – you can have these,' he said gruffly.

Roof-Hare's thin grey face lit up. 'All of them?' he exclaimed. 'But I'm afraid I haven't got that much money,' he stuttered, hardly able to believe his own luck. He hadn't had a smoke for twenty-four hours. Once a Canadian had threatened him with his rifle when he asked; the second time, just when he had been about to pick up a fat, juicy cigarette-end dropped by another Canadian, the man had ground it out in front of his eyes and laughed brutally.

'There's no need,' Rogers said. 'They're yours.'

'But why, sir?'

Rogers laughed, but there was no warmth in the laugh. 'You might say for old times' sake.'

Roof-Hare looked puzzled; then he said, 'Many thanks, sir. Many thanks. You're very kind.' Again he raised a hand to his battered cap in a kind of salute.

Almost unconsciously, Rogers did the same. For a moment they looked at each other, victor and vanquished; then they turned and went their separate ways, Rogers to his admiral, Roof-Hare back to the packing case which now formed his home: survivors and victims both.

Behind them, in that abandoned graveyard of ships, the *Deutschland* remained, silent and brooding, conquered at last . . .

THE SEA WOLVES 1:
SINK THE SCHARNHORST!

Leo Kessler

The first in a dramatic new series of naval action in World War II, from the author of the bestselling WOTAN series.

The time is 1937. Nazi Germany is building her strength for the war Hitler plans, when two young naval cadets meet at the Keil Regatta. One is German, the other English. But they become firm friends.

The time is 1942. The Royal Navy makes a determined onslaught to destroy the Nazi's most formidable warship, the *Scharnhorst*. And in the carnage and sudden death of a shell-torn Norwegian fjord, the two friends meet again – this time enemies in a desperate sea battle.

Futura Publications
Fiction/War
0 7088 2060 3

OTTO STAHL 1:
OTTO'S PHONEY WAR

Leo Kessler

On the night Hitler's Panzers roared into Poland, Otto was working udercover with the sergeant's wife.

Crook, conman, Casanova, blue-eyed Otto Stahl is equally at home with an eager fraulein or a batch of black market coffee. A natural coward with a genius for saving his own skin, Otto dodges the German draft – only to be catapulted into frontline action against the Dutch tank regiments.

Decorated by Hitler, stripped by Himmler, seduced by a nymphomaniac countess, and relentlessly pursued by SS headhunters, Otto bluffs his way from bedroom to battlefield and back.

The bawdy, bloody and hilarious adventures of one man's war which tells the inside story of the Third Reich as it has never been told before.

Futura Publications
Fiction/War
0 7088 2027 1